IT WAS HARDLY AN
INNOCENT DECEPTION . . .

Had he said too much? His Grace did not altogether *want* Amy to guess who he was. It was fascinating, he found, to conduct a flirtation without his blasted rank standing in the way of everything.

"Are your credentials so unimpeachable then?"

"Oh, decidedly so," he said. "They give me entrée into most drawing rooms."

"How felicitous."

"Yes, is it not? Though I am usually condemned to talk to either the companion or the potted plant."

Amy's lips twitched. "How sad, and what a terrible waste! You must have very poor hostesses!"

"Alas, the lot of *all* impoverished gentlemen!"

"Ah, so you are impoverished."

The duke bowed, a little mockingly. Well, he spoke no more than the truth. And if it misled the fair Amy a smidgen, so much the better.

He expected her to withdraw a little. He braced himself for this, in fact, for Miss Mayhew was clearly a sensible girl and encouraging impoverished gentlemen masquerading as butlers was neither sensible nor prudent.

In his wildest dreams, he did not expect what happened next. Miss Amy Mayhew, late of the emerald green traveling dress, kissed him. . . .

<u>BOOK YOUR PLACE ON OUR WEBSITE</u>
<u>AND MAKE THE</u>
<u>READING CONNECTION!</u>

We've created a customized website just for our very special readers, where you can get the inside scoop on everything that's going on with Zebra, Pinnacle and Kensington books.

When you come online, you'll have the exciting opportunity to:

- View covers of upcoming books

- Read sample chapters

- Learn about our future publishing schedule (listed by publication month *and author*)

- Find out when your favorite authors will be visiting a city near you

- Search for and order backlist books from our online catalog

- Check out author bios and background information

- Send e-mail to your favorite authors

- Meet the Kensington staff online

- Join us in weekly chats with authors, readers and other guests

- Get writing guidelines

- AND MUCH MORE!

Visit our website at
http://www.kensingtonbooks.com

A SCANDALOUS CONNECTION

Hayley Ann Solomon

ZEBRA BOOKS
Kensington Publishing Corp.
http://www.kensingtonbooks.com

ZEBRA BOOKS are published by

Kensington Publishing Corp.
850 Third Avenue
New York, NY 10022

All Kensington titles, imprints and distributed lines are available at special quantity discounts for bulk purchases for sales promotion, premiums, fund-raising, educational or institutional use.

Special book excerpts or customized printings can also be created to fit specific needs. For details, write or phone the office of the Kensington Special Sales Manager: Kensington Publishing Corp., 850 Third Avenue, New York, NY 10022. Attn. Special Sales Department. Phone: 1-800-221-2647.

Zebra and the Z logo Reg. U.S. Pat. & TM Off.

First Printing: May 2002
10 9 8 7 6 5 4 3 2 1

Printed in the United States of America

One

Lady Caroline Darris smiled cheerfully as she carefully dotted her last i. She then *very* virtuously affixed a cross to one of her untidy ts, and blew hard. The ink dried almost instantly under this exuberant treatment, but at the expense of the ink pot. This teetered for a moment at the edge of the table before spilling little streams of purple onto the floor.

"Bother!" With great presence of mind, her ladyship heroically saved the letter. She was not so fortunate with her gown, however, this being splattered a quite noxious shade of violet.

"It will stain!" Lady Caroline cried out.

"I am delighted. You have been wearing that rag for years. The hem is too short and the sash is sadly—horribly—outmoded." Lady Caroline's companion was most unsympathetic. Indeed, she actually nodded approvingly as she looked up from her pattern cards.

"Now maybe you will be coaxed into the sea-green poplin we—"

"Nonsense! It is nothing. Now listen to this, Martha . . ."

But Martha was not paying attention, for the tea was being brought in, and it was her delightful task to pour.

Lady Caro therefore took the opportunity of dabbing at the faded Aubusson carpet, smudging her fingers and rereading her missive in silence. Apart from underlining a few key words here and there, she believed she was satisfied. Consequently, she took up the noble seal of Darris and carefully franked the very lightweight letter.

It would be conveyed to London with the first post. His Grace, the duke of Darris, may have his pockets horribly to let, but his consequence remained enormous, a fact that Caroline could not help but remain aware of, for in Bath there were forever people bowing and scraping and staring after her as though she were some prize monkey rather than merely the sister of the highest ranking peer in England.

Fortunately for her, she never resided in Bath long enough to allow the matter to irk her, though she did giggle a little at its foolishness. At Darris, at least, the duke's chief seat, she was free to do as she pleased. And this she did, with a winsome air of innocence that endeared her to every one of the duke's tenants, from the blacksmith to the baker. No one seemed to mind that she invariably set out without a groom, or stopped to eat wild blackberries off the hedges, or almost never wore a bonnet, though she was several months past seventeen. Her good nature and lively spirits quite made up for any deficiencies of hauteur, and so her governesses had told her, even when they had meant to scold.

Now she was past needing a governess, and was prim enough to actually have a companion, but since this was only dear Martha, who had nursed her since she was three, she did not mind this too dreadfully.

Lady Caroline allowed an irrepressible chuckle to escape her lips. Martha—or rightfully speaking, Miss Bancroft—eyed her suspiciously.

"You are up to your tricks again, Caro!"

"Me?" Caroline contrived to look hurt, though her eyes danced quite shamelessly.

"Well, only a small trick, Martha, dearest, and I am sure we have already discussed it a dozen times or more. Now *do* be a dear and unpoker your face long enough to listen to this."

Without waiting for a reply, she buoyantly ripped open her newly sealed missive and read it aloud with relish.

"Demian," it ordered,

> *"Do not—I repeat—do* not *come home till Sunday next. Martha's gout is healing and I have hopes we might save that confounded fox. For all his stealing ways—very tiresome, I admit—he appears to be a handsome fellow. Can you try to procure some more of that liniment? Oh, and my gowns are progressing marvelously and I am now the proud possessor of three glorious feathered bonnets, thanks to Dilly, Vicar Pendergast's peacock. Remember her?*
>
> *"I am very busy with fittings for all manner of trifles—I can hardly keep track. Pelisses, muffs, gloves, bonnets with hideous names like poke and cottage and . . . oh, Martha knows. The main thing, Demi, is don't come back. You will be bored to tears. (As I am.) Oh, and dear, dear, Demian, do try to not to be too dismal! I have a perfectly clever plan up my sleeve, but you are not to pester me for particulars.*
>
> *Caro"*

Caroline folded the letter again and resealed it in a new envelope. It was a bit crumpled now, but she knew her esteemed and noble brother, for all his impeccable address, cared less about such trifles than she did. She grinned at her confused companion.

"Now *that* should keep him away for a fortnight! I've never known a man to stand by idly when a lady has nothing to discuss but her bonnets and sashes and pelisses and gowns. Demian will have no patience with it. He is lucky he is a man. Goodness, Martha, do you *really* think I need that many?"

It was the hundredth time she had asked such a foolish question, so Martha did not hurry to respond. Rather, she sipped her tea with singular enjoyment, then stirred in a little sugar. When she'd had at least five such invigorating sips, she pushed a brimming china cup under Caroline's nose and nodded her graying head firmly.

"Caroline, you have no *idea* what a season requires! As the sister to a duke you will be expected to be a veritable fashion plate! You need walking gowns, morning gowns, bombazines, brocades, silks—the list is endless. Your court gown was one thing, but now you need ball gowns, theater gowns, opera gowns, riding habits . . . and no! You *cannot* appear twice in the same outfit—it is unthinkable."

Bright eyes twinkled in response. "Stuff and nonsense! If lords and ladies of society cannot tolerate the same outfit twice then I have no wish to enter such a rake shame set. They should all be ashamed of themselves."

Miss Bancroft sighed and took up the faded jaconet she'd been pilfering for its excellent pearl studs. Caroline was a dear, but she could be *so* pigheaded at times! She simply had no notion of what was owing to her station.

Now, the elevated young peeress of the realm watched Martha for a moment, gulped down her scalding-hot tea in a *most* unladylike fashion, and nodded approvingly.

"Keep that jaconet. I am sure we can use it for something."

There was an ominous silence as Miss Bancroft searched about for a sufficiently biting retort. Then she nodded.

"Yes, like as not the chimney sweep could do with a few extra yards of sweeping cloth."

"Martha!" But Caro's lips trembled on the brink of a very sweet smile. "Oh, do not be a scold! Throw it away and be hideously extravagant for all I care! After next week, we shall be able to afford it. Only I do wish you would buy *yourself* a few yards of silk."

Her companion merely sniffed and waved her needle airily. "Tush! I have all the gowns I need. It is not *I* who is going to be the talk of London when she is presented! And, Caro, I can only say I have a funny feeling about this scheme of yours. . . ."

"Oh, *don't,* Martha, dear! It is perfectly foolproof! Some wealthy—hideously wealthy—people want to traipse through a ducal residence. What can possibly be the harm in that? They shall see all our arbors and topiaries and stone statues and gargoyles. . . . Then, when they are pleasantly tired out from this exclusive enterprise, they shall have a superb view of the galleries, the libraries—goodness, we had better remove the holland covers—the marble floors and pilasters, the Aubusson carpets, the fountains, the turrets—we had better make the north one respectable—perhaps we can move in a carpet—the gold plate, the hideous candelabrum and so forth. We shall dress up in all the Darris finery—Demian gave me the key to the jewels eons ago—and we shall look exactly the part."

"The part? This is not a pantomime, Caroline!"

"Oh, but it is, really! These widows and merchants

are not paying ten thousand pounds—ten thousand, mark you—for a sight of me in worn frocks and you in your blacks! No, they want splendor and pomp and . . . and . . . majesty! They want gilded clocks and interminable feasts, and—"

"Caroline! Even if I were to countenance this hare-brained scheme, where are we going to muster these sumptuous feasts? We have been living on jugged hare for days, now!"

"Only because we insist on it! I daresay if I speak to Williams, the game keeper, he could procure some pheasant and duck and boar and such. I believe there is even still game, though Demian stopped stocking the woods about a year ago. Still, we can cook it all in the kitchens, and if we raid our Christmas supply . . ."

Miss Bancroft looked sadly unconvinced. In particular, she was not quite partial to the "we" that her honorable charge was bandying about so liberally. Lady Caroline eyed her with an impish gleam of amusement. However much she disapproved, dear Martha could always be relied upon to fall in with her schemes. That was what she so particularly liked about her. Impulsively, she clasped her hands.

"Ouch!" A stray needle was pulled impatiently from her doeskin glove. Then that bewitching, beseeching smile of Caroline's that Miss Bancroft never could like, simply because it was too delightful to resist. . . .

"Don't look so glum! I have some simply splendid recipes jotted down from Miss Apperton's Seminary. And we can raid Demian's store of wines—the cellars are not completely contemptible yet—"

"Over my dead body! His Grace will kill you!"

"Not if we present him with the sum of ten thousand pounds, he won't! He can discharge all his mountain-ous debts, buy the best king's burgundy and still have change to spare! Then he need not nose about for some detestable wife. . . ."

Miss Bancroft was silenced for a moment. The argument was certainly the most powerful of any that Caroline had yet produced, for truly it would be a shame to see a man as splendidly handsome and spirited as the current duke marry for the sake of convenience alone. Surely Demian, whom she had known since short coats, deserved better? Caroline was right. If there was a way, they should seize it. Still, there was no need to throw caution to the winds.

"Are you *certain* they stated that much? I can hardly credit such extravagance."

"I am certain. Here, see the letter for yourself."

Her ladyship scrabbled in the folds of her seventh-best overdress to procure the much vaunted missive. She handed it over to Martha with a small smile.

"See, Mrs. Murgatroyd is most specific. Ten thousand pounds upon admission—I believe it is to be a party of no more than a half dozen young ladies—and a further bonus if all is found to be exceedingly satisfactory. She included a small retainer as a deposit. We can use it to buy teas and sugared plums and such. Also some feathered quilts, though naturally they shan't be staying overnight."

"Are you certain?"

"As the day I was born! Why, we should never be able to keep up the charade. Well, at least I don't *expect* we should!"

"Well, of course we shouldn't, you silly child. A day shall be hard enough."

Caroline smiled. No, she did more than that. She leaped from her seat and threw her slender frame around the rather more buxom one of Miss Bancroft. "Oh, I *knew* you would see reason! I shall write at once to say that Tuesday at nine will be acceptable. I shall use

Demian's stationery and seal it with the ducal signet. No doubt they shall be dazzled from the splendor."

"Well, I hope so. They will *need* to be dazzled if they are not to notice the shabbiness of this place," came the dry retort. "I remember the day when Darris Castle was the finest residence in all of England—"

"Yes, Martha, dear," Caroline hastily interjected, for Martha could certainly run on at times, especially when it came to the long gone days of ducal magnificence. If only Richard, the fourth duke of Darris, had been a little more frugal . . . but she had not the time to start on that worn out old hobbyhorse.

"I wonder what is required to make the outing exceedingly satisfactory and therefore qualify for the bonus?" Miss Bancroft mused, squinting at the letter.

Caroline flushed. "Oh, we shall disregard that part!"

"But why? If we can attain the bonus, then His Grace will be able to restore his stables—"

"Oh, I know! It irks me dreadfully how he has had to sell off the best of his broodmares, and even the riding stock is sadly depleted, though he has left me Windspur, for which I am naturally very thankful."

"It is an impossible beast! Not fit for a lady!"

"No?" Caroline grinned. Her smile was infectious.

"Oh, get on with you, you know you are a bruising rider, I shall not deny it. But you circumvent the issue. Why shall we not try for the bonus Mrs. Murgatroyd hints at?"

Caroline made a face. It was *not* ladylike, but beyond a small sigh, Miss Bancroft let it pass.

"I believe their requirement is impossible."

"Impossible? How singularly unfair! What do they want?"

Caroline sighed. "I cannot be certain, for they only delicately hint, you know."

"Hint? At what?"

"They want, dear Martha, no less than the presence of my esteemed brother, Demian, the duke, himself."

"Ah." Light dawned in Martha's old, but nonetheless shrewd-sharp eyes.

"They are spinsters, then, this party?"

Caroline grimaced. "It may be purely coincidence. They never said, after all. . . ."

"They didn't need to, did they? Ten thousand pounds is a prodigious sum. No doubt they regard it as the investment of the century."

"Crackpot gamble, more like. But if they are silly enough to think that Demian . . ."

"Perhaps they have heard he is searching for an heiress."

"Perhaps. Still, it shall not help them overmuch. We shall not see hide or hair of him for a fortnight at least." And with these fateful words, Lady Caroline waved her missive in the air, buttoned her pelisse, forgot all about her walking bonnet of sea green chip straw, and skipped out of the room.

In a decidedly unfashionable part of London—though definitely more opulent than some of the understated addresses at the revered Grosvenor Square or Cavendish Gardens—a similarly fateful conversation was taking place. This, rather a monologue, for it consisted chiefly of the words of a large lady dressed sumptuously in scalloped sleeves and skirts. These, sadly, were dwarfed almost entirely by her turban, which was emerald in color and sported enough feathers to dress an ostrich, if that contingency was ever necessary. It would be unkind to say that the woman actually *resembled* that bird, for indeed, the feathers had been dyed such an outrageous assortment of colors that no one—not unless they were demented or dreaming—could have made such a dire mistake. Still, she presented an *interesting* sight, certainly more colorful than that of the unexceptional young lady seated beside her, who was remarkable for nothing but the luster of her dark, cropped hair, and the peculiar spark of intelligence behind slate-gray eyes. Certainly, her gown would have drawn no particular comment, for though it was undoubtedly of the first stare, it was also understated in the extreme, being a gentle dove pink and bedecked with not even *one* cluster of redeeming rosettes. Even the ribbons, drawn modestly across a deliciously—had she but known it!—intriguing bodice, were silver, not the more modish shades of flamingo and crimson and gold. Now, she folded her gloved hands patiently in her lap and attended the monologue with not a little resignation.

"Now, now, Amy, dear, you must trust me. Just because you went to Miss Simpson's Academy for Young Ladies does *not* mean your dear Aunt Ermentrude does not know what is best for you. And on that subject, why in heavens do you think we procured quite the largest diamond set from Lacey's—I had it on the best authority that it is larger even than the countess of Winsham's—when you insist on wearing those trumpery pearls? If you wish to catch a gentleman, my dear, you must not allow him to think you behind hand in any manner or fashion. And you cannot gammon me into believing gentlemen don't care for such things, for your uncle saw Lord Iverley buying the hugest bracelet of sapphires, and if Lacey had not already drawn out the tray he would doubtless have procured them for you."

Mrs. Froversham Worthing—she would like to have been known as "the Honorable" Mrs. Froversham Worthing, but, *most* unfortunately, her husband, though excessively rich, was disappointingly untitled—stopped for a short breath, but only so long as was strictly necessary to fill out the full extent of her corsetted lungs.

"And so, my dear, what I was saying from the start, was that you simply must avail yourself of this opportunity! When I think of that spiteful widgeon Amelia Corey being included in the party—and she with not an ame's ace of your beauty—it fair makes me boil with rage. You *must* go, my dear, you simply must. I insist on it, indeed I do. And if the duke should just happen to be wandering in his gardens . . . oh, Amy! Wouldn't it be delightful if he should see you standing there, like a sylph. . . . Oh, yes, you must take the diamonds, they will glitter extraordinarily in the dusk light—"

Miss Amy Mayhew could not help interjecting, at this point, to mention that it would be highly unlikely that the duke would be in residence so close to the Temperton races, and further, if she *were* ever to achieve the hideous prospect her aunt had outlined, dripping in diamonds like a . . . a *sylph*—here she stopped to stifle a small shudder at the prospect—she would doubtless remind His Grace more forcibly of his notorious barques of frailty than strike him as a serious matrimonial prospect.

At this, her aunt made shocked protest and announced that even she—who was *not* schooled in the ways of the nobility, though heaven knew, she was born above her station and fancied she knew a little about such matters, and if only Mr. Worthing would make the smallest push, he could procure for them a barony—that young ladies did *not* refer to such matters, or even know of them, though gracious knew there were enough light skirts about London to very likely fill the halls of Carlton Place.

She took another breath and pinched Miss Mayhew's

cheeks till they were pink. Amy, used to this particular display of affection, managed, somehow, not to flinch.

"But dear, dear, Amy, I *implore* you not to mention them! Pray pretend, I beg you, that you have never heard of them. Indeed, I am at a loss to know where you *did* hear of such matters! Not at Miss Simpson's, I am certain."

Miss Mayhew did not correct her certainty, though her eyes lit up with sudden laughter. What she *also* refrained from mentioning—very scrupulously too— was that the sapphire bracelet Lord Iverley had bought had gone, not to his wife, who despised such vulgar ornamentation, but to his latest mistress. She held her tongue for two reasons. First, her Aunt Ermentrude was right. She should *not* know about such matters, but since Lord Iverley's scatter wit niece was also her bosom bow, it was difficult—indeed, impossible—*not* to hear of such things. But more importantly, she knew that arguing with her aunt was a lost cause. It always ended up in prolonged swoons and episodes with sal volatile. And though she could not *herself* abide such acute displays of sensibility, she did truly love her aunt and had no wish to distress her unwarrantedly.

So she meekly promised never to discuss such distressing matters—which, indeed, was not hard to do, for she had no real notion that the topic would ever present itself in company—and braved the multiplicity of feathers to kiss Mrs. Worthing's nose.

That lady was much mollified. She adored her niece, despite her disappointingly stubborn streak on certain matters of the utmost importance. Marriage, for instance. Amy steadfastly refused to make the slightest push to find herself a nobleman, a deficiency that Mrs. Worthing found a sore trial, indeed. Now, she rose to her feet, fortified by Amy's show of compliance.

"Then you *shall* join the duke's party?"

"It is not His Grace's party, Aunt! Indeed, I would be astonished to learn that he knew anything of our intentions! Mrs. Murgatroyd has been corresponding with Lady Caroline Darris, who, I understand, is his sister."

"Oh! Well, then! It is all perfectly acceptable! I'm sure Lady Caroline must be all that is proper! Now you can have no possible objection to accepting!"

Mrs. Froversham Worthing's feathers bobbed in relief. To press home her advantage, she took Amy's hands firmly in her own. "It really is my dearest wish, Amy! If your dear departed parents were alive I feel certain they would have said the same." She added, as an afterthought, "And it is your uncle's too, I daresay."

Uncle Froversham, when applied to, looked up from his account book and nodded vaguely in the direction of his wife, his niece and his two young heirs, who were both squabbling most unbecomingly on the Aubusson carpet he had imported—at terrific expense—from Paris. He wished, for a moment, for a breath of fresh air, for though the room was decorated in the most sumptuous style—all gilt and marble and fabulous red velvets—he could not help having the oddest notion of being oppressed. All nonsense, of course, for he knew to a penny how much every fitting had cost, and the sum had been quite prodigious. One did *not* pay such vast sums to be stifled in gloom.

"See, what did I tell you? Froversham agrees."

Miss Mayhew was not convinced, but she could see at a glance that Mr. Worthing was beginning one of his headaches and it would be fatal to allow her aunt to rattle on at him. So, with a sigh, she agreed, reasoning that a frightful afternoon in the dead boring company of two chaperons and five ninnies with no more sensible thought in their heads than to ensnare the most eligible bachelor in all of England was a suitable price to pay for all the kindness she had received from their hands. For though her aunt did not move in the same social circles—and she was loath to even *think* in such terms—she was nevertheless warmhearted and devoted to her only niece.

"Very well, Aunt, I shall go. I cannot, however, think it worthy of the expense."

"Tush, my dear! You need not worry your head about such paltry matters. Your principal shall not be touched, for Uncle Froversham guards it like a dragon, I can assure you. Indeed, it puts me into quite a pelter, for the other day I was short quite a guinea and a sixpence, and do you know, he pressed me to account for it, which I was at my wits end to do until I remembered those silk stockings—which, indeed, I trust you like, though I do not believe I have seen you wearing them yet, though of course the color is one you do not . . ."

Amy stemmed the flow with a slight chuckle, which was better than a shudder, for the memory of the lime-green stockings—now consigned to the upper parlor maid—was still unfortunately ripe in her mind. Instead, she steered the conversation back to Mrs. Worthing's earlier remark about her uncle's stewardship of her fortune.

"Indeed, his management has been quite remarkable! I was astonished to see the figures he presented me with the other day. Which makes me all the *more* resolved to pay for this nonsensical extravagance you have devised."

The feathers shook wildly on Mrs. Worthing's turban, and she flung back one jewel-bedecked hand in good-natured annoyance. "Oh, do not be so absurd! Now you run along and leave the details to me, for I have been told often and often that . . ."

Amy groaned inwardly and did not stay to hear what Mrs. Worthing had been told so often and often. Instead, she slipped down to the kitchens to make up a soothing tisane for poor Uncle Froversham, whose headache appeared to be worsening. It was perhaps poor-spirited of her to think it, but truly, if *she* were married to a regular gabble monger like her aunt, she might find that she, too, would be sorely in need of some soothing relief.

As she made up the brew, she spared hardly a thought for the cynical-eyed, dark-haired paragon of all virtues, known as His Noble Grace, the fifth duke of Darris. She was too sensible a young lady to pay the least heed to Aunt Ermentrude's ambitious maundering. Besides, at four and twenty she was well beyond her last prayers and she suspected strongly that were she not an heiress, she would not have received— and therefore been able to reject—the several handsome offers that had been made for her hand. No, she did not consider a chance encounter—let alone an actual meeting—to be in the least likely.

Two

Dark eyes flashed. "The paragon," as Amy ironically regarded him, was at that moment trying very hard not to flinch. Though he was able to keep his noble composure, he would *not* have been a man had his eyes not sparked with a sudden anger, nor his jaw tightened, imperceptibly, with the effort of remaining silent. This he did, though not without singular effort.

It was not often that His Grace was at such a point nonplus, and frankly, he did not like it. Nor did he like the way in which he was being flogged, for no particular fault that he knew of. Not with a whip, of course—he was long out of short coats—but with cool words and an appraising glance that seemed blind to all the most promising of his attributes.

For an instant, his tormentor quivered. He was alert, quick to gain the advantage. She did not drop her lashes coyly, as one might have expected. Rather, she simpered and shook out her ringlets. There must have been ten, at the least. Her eyes remained dampeningly cold.

Darris sighed inwardly. The interview was not proving promising, but there was that within him which persisted. Perhaps it was the lady's beauty. *That,* he thought dispassionately, must count for something.

He therefore held himself splendidly aloof, as always, his bearing as rigid as his rank demanded, and if he gripped his gold-topped cane a little too tightly, no one—least of all the lady before him—was any the wiser.

It was fortunate, for Lady Raquel Fortesque-Benton had not finished speaking. Her exquisite lips—shaped becomingly in a delicate pink bow—were still moving. He tried hard to concentrate, but all he could see were her icy blue eyes and the magnificent arch of dark eyebrows as she moved on to her next point.

It must have been the eleventh point, at least, in the long *litany* of points she had been bedeviling the duke with all morning.

In any other circumstance, His Grace would have felt himself well justified in cutting her short with a haughty glare. He was well used to depressing pretension, despite his generally open manner. Now, however, he felt compelled to listen, albeit in a growing silence that his peers would immediately have recognized as ominous, indeed.

Not so the Lady Raquel Fortesque-Benton. She, of course, attributed his silence to the rapt attention she deserved—no, insisted upon. With a fleeting pause for breath, she adjusted one of her tiny ringlets. No man, she knew, could resist those little curls of burnished gold that peeped becomingly from the brim of her high poke bonnet. Small wonder, too, for the effect took an hour at least to achieve. Artlessly, she clicked open a fan and proceeded on to her next point.

"Now, Demian—I shall call you that, for we are practically betrothed, are we not?" For the first time, she shot him a coy look from beneath those high arches. Demian, or properly speaking, Lord Demian Charles Julius Radcliffe, duke of Darris, marquis of Hartford and eighth Earl Shrewsbury, bowed. The salutation held no warmth whatsoever, but then, Lady Raquel was not perspicacious enough to discern such niceties. She continued through to point twelve.

"I shall naturally secure the line for you. The Fortesque-Bentons are excellent breeders, as I am sure you are aware."

His Grace's dark, dulcet eyes flickered with detached interest. It was unusual for ladies to speak so plainly upon such matters, but then, the maiden in the exquisitely stitched morning gown of deep russet merino was not usual in *any* sense. It was not common for beauty— and Lord Darris was not blind, Lady Raquel was quite extraordinarily beautiful—to be allied so handsomely with a fortune. And such a vast fortune, too! It quite made one's head swim.

The lips were open again, and Lord Darris contemplated kissing them. This course, of course, would hold two felicitous outcomes. The first would be in tandem with her words, which were now slyly referring to the marital bliss which he could rightfully expect from her chamber two nights a week for precisely one hour, the length of time, she had been told, that was strictly necessary for the outcome of any future dukes of Darris and marquises of Hartford. The duke arrogantly discounted this, for he had a sufficiently high regard for his own expertise to imagine that the lovely Lady Raquel would soon be waiving any nonsensical time limits. No, the primary reason for kissing her would, of course, be to shut her up. Not very elegantly phrased, perhaps, but an adequate reflection of Demian's rather grim thoughts.

He moved toward her and cast the gold-topped cane across the desk that lay between them. Then, rather seductively, he tilted her chin so that her lips were but inches from his own. Good! She had stopped her prattling. He concentrated on her lips, for, indeed, they were quite delightfully perfect, if one could ignore the icy eyes with their cold, speculative flecks of gold just above. He drew her forward, so that her bodice was straining from the exertion. Demian took fleeting note of the fact that Lady Raquel's lips were not the *only* curves he could bring himself, with time, to admire.

He bent his dark head toward her and offered her one of his rather practiced, lazy smiles. The type of smile that had ladies customarily swooning at his feet. He permitted his eyes to linger a little on the top buttons of her morning gown, trimmed, of course, with pearls and the gentle glitter of diamonds. Such glances were known to have other ladies—of quite a different type—on their deliciously brazen backs in the twinkling of an eye. His Grace was not entirely known for leading the life of a monk.

Lady Raquel Fortesque-Benton did not blink. Rather, she puckered up her lips dutifully and permitted a chaste kiss to alight on her cheek. Then, as His Grace was rather foolishly regaining his balance across the table, she carried on speaking.

"After I have produced your first two sons, Darris, I shall naturally then be free to pursue my own interests."

"Interests?" The duke could only mimic her words in confusion. His sister, had she been present, would have chuckled. Normally urbane to a quite acute degree, His Grace's current discomfort would have been a marvel to those who knew him well. Of course, Caroline would probably, by now, have planted Lady Raquel a rather indelicate facer, for there could be no doubt she doted on her brother and consequently expected every person on earth to treat him with a similar level of devotion. Clearly, the season's most feted heiress did not.

With mild reproof in her exquisite aqua eyes, she rephrased her twelfth point.

"Lovers, Your Grace. I shall naturally take lovers

once the Darris line is secured. I perceive you can have no possible objection?"

She picked up a piece of embroidery and carefully selected a shade of yellow silk streaked with the faintest hint of gold. Lord Darris despised samplers, but he was less concerned with this further evidence of their obvious incompatibility than with the content of her last remark.

"Lovers?"

"Yes . . . you know, cicisbei."

Lord Darris did *not* know, but he gritted his teeth, retrieved his cane and inclined his head. Lady Raquel could have all the cicisbei she wanted, for all he cared. God knew, he could even find it within himself to be *sorry* for the poor misguided lechers. For a fraction of a second he wondered whether he should tell Lady Raquel that she was mistaken in her terms. A *half* hour in her chamber once a month would be more than sufficient to his needs.

He decided *not* to, though, for there were people other than himself depending on this alliance. Indeed, if it was left to him the huge edifice of Darris Castle could crumble to the ground for all he cared. As for his earthly titles, well, they were well enough, but certainly not sufficient to feed and roof the hungry tenants and crofters he'd inherited along with all the pomp. No, marriage was not so much a pleasure as a necessity. He was just lucky that he outranked the decrepit marquis of Somerford. He was certain that had he not, Lady Raquel would not now be fixing her cool blue eyes in his direction. God! If he were not second in rank to a prince, he might even now be escaping the satin coils of her gloved hand. He tried not to think of this as he took it lightly in his and placed a kiss in the requisite place.

* * *

"Are you mad?" Mr. Thomas Endicott breathed heavily as he deftly avoided being floored to the ground by a powerful fist. He did not wait for a reply before smashing his left hook into the stomach of his bosom bow. Sadly, the excellent gentleman did not tumble to the ground or at least concede defeat as he'd fully expected. Rather, he shook out his distinctive black curls and matched the blow with a stunning one of his own. Mr. Endicott teetered slightly.

"Not mad, Tom, merely perfectly sane. I am not accepting a penny in rents—the estates are all too ruinous to expect a brass farthing—so despite a great deal of scrimping and saving, I have literally *mountains* of debts! I am rethatching all the roofs in Hartford—they are rat ridden and I cannot have my dependents living in such squalor. Most of the residents of Darris need fuel for the winter and there is precious little firewood left after the recent fires. . . ."

He ducked as Mr. Endicott nearly—very nearly—planted him a facer. He seemed to take no particular offense at this outrage, for he continued on mildly. "I've vastly reduced the stables, but I still require several serviceable traveling chaises and *they* all need teams. Then there are the dratted corn laws . . ."

"Not to mention Caroline's debut. . . ."

"Yes, but the dear child refuses to allow me to outfit her! She has taken some cockeyed notion into her head that she and Martha can refurbish some of Lady Tryon's old gowns and nothing I say seems to *reverse* that opinion!"

He followed up this pronouncement with a swift blow to poor Mr. Endicott's chest.

"Have her come up to London, then! One turn in a dowdy bonnet should quickly change her mind." Thomas sidestepped the next punch, and even went so far as to land quite a notable one of his own. The duke grimaced.

"Quite! Which is precisely why I need funds when she *does* finally step out." His right hand maneuvered itself below Mr. Endicott's skillful defenses.

The thud that ensued caused the honorable Thomas to stop his rather stylish footwork and glare up at the curls, and the familiar aquiline nose, and the wide brow that dripped with perspiration yet nevertheless remained classical and aloof.

"I give up, Demian! I will not fight you in this mood! You are liable to murder me!"

Demian grinned and removed his gloves. "Murder you? Impossible! But I tell you one thing, it will be a blessing if I don't murder *her.*"

"Who?"

His Grace tried very hard to be patient with his numskulled friend.

"Lady Raquel Fortesque-Benton, very soon to become Lady Raquel Radcliffe, duchess of Darris."

". . . and marchioness of Hartford and countess of Shrewsbury—"

"Cut line, Thomas!"

But Thomas hadn't finished. "—and your wife."

There was a small silence between them.

"I *told* you you were mad!"

"And *I* told you I was sane. If there was another way, Tom, I would gladly seize it. The lady is as cold as a fish."

Now Thomas *was* shocked.

"Surely not when she is contending with the most skilled lover in all of London—saving myself, of course." He could not help being flippant, but his eyes lost their twinkle swiftly when he saw the gloom engulfing his noble grace.

"Oh, come, Demian, it can't be that bad! It is not

as if she is an antidote, after all! Why, her hair gleams with pure gold and her lips . . ."

". . . are like toffee. Clammed shut."

"You are merely miffed. Come, when she is your wedded wife things will be different."

"Indeed they will! *Then* her lips will be perpetually open. Driving me to distraction, no doubt, with her various edicts and points."

"At least they will be *open.*" Tom refused to be drawn into the melancholy. His words were laden with just the type of innuendo to lift His Grace from the doldrums. He handed him over a towel and waited for the inevitable chuckle. Finally, grudgingly, it came.

"Oh, you are impossible, Thomas Endicott!"

"Not as impossible as *you!*" came the ready retort. "And I *still* think you are mad! If you are as cross as crabs at the very thought of this alliance, cry off! There is nothing settled, after all!"

"Only a mere matter of a hundred thousand pounds to whistle to the wind. Besides, the deed is done. I proposed this morning."

"Hence your punishing form in the ring. I begin to understand."

"Do you? The lady requires cicisbei. It was number eleven—or, no, was it twelve?—on her wretched list."

"Beg pardon?"

"You heard me right. Cicisbei, and, for your ill-informed mind, that means lovers."

"I *do* retain a smattering of Italian, Demian."

"Good! Then there is no need to translate."

"Does she have anyone . . . eh . . . current in mind?"

"I assume not. She informs me that she will bide her time until her duty to the line is done." The duke's answer was crisp, but the bitterness of tone was unmistakable. Mr. Endicott conceived a sudden dislike to the wench.

"Does she, by God!" His eyes became speculative. "I believe she deserves a lesson in manners."

"Shall you be her teacher?" The duke's question was mildly rhetorical. By now, he had clad himself in a shirt of the finest white lawn—though it had been skillfully darned once or twice—and had only the last intricate knot to achieve in his cravat before stepping out from Gentleman Jackson's into the mild sunshine outside.

"Do you know, Demian, I believe I *shall!*" There was mischief in Thomas's words as he eyed the duke.

The knot remained untied.

"What devilry do you mean, Thomas Tyrone Endicott?"

"Now that would be telling, but I do wager you, Demian, that when you come to wed her you will find her entirely more biddable."

The duke's eyes narrowed. "My wife has to be above reproach, Thomas."

"And she *shall* be."

"I find that hard to believe if she is going to spend any length of time in *your* rakish presence!"

Mr. Endicott scowled and contrived to look hurt. Too bad his blue eyes twinkled outrageously as he leaned forward and completed Demian's elusive knot.

"True, true, I am sadly irresistible. Nevertheless, my lord, Your *Grace*"—he stressed this last, for he only ever used Demian's titles when he was mocking—"she shall remain as pure as snow. You have my word on it."

Demian nodded. "Then I shall be entirely in your debt, for though it is no doubt churlish of me to admit it, I am hard pressed to continue on with my suit. If Lady Raquel were softer hearted . . ."

"She would bore you to tears in a minute."

Demian allowed a languid smile to play at his lips. "Very likely! I would also, I suppose, find it hard to be as calculating. The role of fortune hunter sits uneasily upon my shoulders."

"Lucky they are so broad, then! But it is a fair exchange, and one as old as ages. An illustrious title for an illustrious fortune. Doubtless Lady Raquel has cast the die very carefully. You are really no different from thousands of esteemed peers before you."

"How salutary! And here I was, imagining, for a whisper of a moment, that I might be something very different indeed."

"And now you grow whimsical! I suppose, you beast, you want me to outline all your virtues extraordinaire! Well, I shan't do it. You may drive to an inch and have the very devil's own graces, but you shan't put me to the trouble extolling them!"

"Thank God for that!" Lord Darris regained some of his usual composure and grinned. By the time they had greeted several well-heeled gentlemen and walked the length of the long, well-polished floor, he was feeling decidedly more cheerful.

"Shall I expect an announcement in the *Gazette*?"

"Good heavens, no! I haven't approached the father yet."

Thomas raised his brows a fraction. "Whyever not?"

"He is with Lord Sefton's men at Versailles. I shall approach him directly on his return." His tone became a little wry. "I *don't* anticipate opposition."

"Lord, I should say not!"

"In the meanwhile, Lady Raquel desires to review Darris Castle."

"How appalling!"

"Quite. The place is like a mausoleum and as drafty as hell."

"Can it not be made a trifle cheerier?"

"Caro does her best. We live very cozily in the west wing, but I doubt that 'coziness' is exactly in Lady Raquel's style."

"Lady Raquel needs a hearty awakening, by the sound of things."

"Quite possibly. Are you volunteering that, too?"

Of a sudden, Thomas grinned.

"I can but try, my dear Demian! I am in your debt for ten gold guineas, I believe."

"Are you?"

"Indeed I am, for I forgot to tell you that that hamstrung bony beast out at Winsham came first in all his races. You were right, of course, though how you should be has me in a puzzle. You wagered me ten to one that the animal would show his paces."

"Did I? Lucky thing he won, then, for I have no recollection of it and certainly not a sovereign to spare!" His Grace's tone was dry.

"Well, now you have ten, though that is purely hypothetical, my good man, for I shall keep them."

"Shall you?" Amusement crept into the shadows of Demian's dark eyes.

"Yes, you wretch, it shall be my payment for escorting Lady Raquel out to Darris. Included in the charge will be that lady's hearty awakening. Mark my words, she will be as meek as milk when she arrives."

"Ha! You have not yet had an audience with the lady. You had rather give me my ten sovereigns immediately, for undoubtedly you shall fail."

"Fail? Me? Is that a challenge, Demian?"

"Oh, God rot you, I suppose it is!"

Mr. Thomas Endicott grinned.

Three

It was, unfortunately, several days later that a certain cream-colored wafer was brought to Demian's attention. It was unusual for the duke's secretary to make so careless an error, but truly the wafer was so crumpled the seal was hardly visible. His Grace had borne such an air of distraction the last few days that poor Mr. Monteforte had decided to hold back on all but the most urgent of his correspondence.

Upon reading the letter, however, the duke's unusual lethargy seemed to be shaken. Without berating his excellent secretary in the least, he nevertheless murmured that anything, in the future, from Lady Caroline, should receive the most immediate of attention. Then, with an engaging apology to Mr. Monteforte—who would be required to cancel all the most pressing of his engagements—he alerted what staff remained in his service to the fact that he would be returning to his principal seat at Darris. Such an action may have seemed extraordinary in light of the fact that he had only just arrived in London some few days earlier, but the duke's servants were all quite used to his "queer starts" and cheerfully began packing an array of valises that would require at least three of His Grace's lesser barouches to convey.

Fortunately, His Grace did not trouble himself about such matters, for he had learned that it was useless to protest to his valet, who had the very severest notions regarding what was wanting to his dignity and consequence. Instead, he permitted his household to subject themselves to a veritable frenzy of activity—for which he could see no just cause in the least—and saddled up Season's Glory, his latest—and rather extravagant—purchase from Tattersall's. Still, he had sold off most of the stables—much to the glaring disapproval of the head groom—and thus felt reasonably conscience easy with regard to the great black beast who stood, coat gleaming, on the cobbled flag way.

"My lord cannot be thinking of *riding* to Darris?" The groom, newer than the rest of the staff, and therefore not acquainted with the duke's headstrong ways, sounded a trifle incredulous.

Demian smiled perfunctorily, for he was always punctiliously charming to his staff, and nodded. "Indeed, I am, so I beg you to fasten the girth a little more tightly, and take heed of the stallion's head. I believe he is a little frisky this morning."

This, of course, was an understatement, for Season's Glory was straining at the bit for a good gallop and sensed, in his master, a similar sentiment. The air was crisp and deliciously fresh, a matter of some relief to Demian, who had no wish to be caught in incipient snows. Though he had not the slightest notion what the meaning behind his sister's garbled message to him might be, all warning bells had been alerted at the very first phrase. As for *"Do not—I repeat—do not come home till Sunday next,"* the very sentence filled him with such foreboding that he considered it a matter of first importance that he return immediately. This conviction was even stronger when read together with *"I have a perfectly clever plan up my sleeve,"* and caused him to be thankful that he had, indeed, succumbed to temptation and bought Season's Glory, undoubtedly the only horse in his current mangy stable capable of undertaking such a journey. Even so, what with resting the animal at various stages along the way, he doubted whether he would reach his destination in time for dinner, much less in time to avert any impending catastrophe Caro's words might be portending. He could but try, however, and with his own state of affairs in anything but a blissful state, the ride, at least, would do him a world of good.

It did not take very long before he was trotting steadily down the countryside, frowning a little at instances of bad husbandry or cottages in evident disrepair. His frown cleared, however, when he reached the southernmost borders of Darris, for there, the lands seemed greener—due, he believed, to a radical new irrigation scheme that only this year seemed to be showing its rewards, as well as another the practice he insisted upon using—leaving one meadow in four fallow throughout the year. All the corn had been reaped for the period, but he noted with satisfaction that the lands had been sowed and that smoke was billowing steadily from the mill, where corn and wheat were being crushed to powder even in these winter months. Several dozen sheep grazed on the higher pastures like little, round cumulus clouds overlooking Darris and its southwestern border with Monmouth. These had been introduced by way of experiment, and appeared, at a glance, to be one of his more inspired ideas. Certainly, they were looking gratifyingly fat, and if only Caro hadn't been secretly feeding them from his grain stores, he would be satisfied. There was not much else to be done with such hilly land, for pulling a plow had proven an impossible task.

The duke sighed as Season's Glory responded to his bit and turned toward home. He would see no profit from all the year's hard toil, though indeed he *could* insist upon the receipts if he so desired—but the income would insure that in the future Darris would be self supporting enough not to present any further drain on his limited resources. For if the duke had one fault, it was that of kindheartedness. He would spend his own fortune recklessly if his tenants required it. And in the last four years they had, for the fourth duke of Darris had been sadly improvident. This year, however, His Grace's dwindling cash resources need not be drawn upon. Darris, the marquisate of Hartford and the earldom of Shrewsbury were all in satisfactory repair, save for the roofs that needed rethatching and the woodpiles that needed stocking across the breadth of his lands.

It was dusk when he detected the huge stone gates of Darris Castle. He murmured politely to the sentry, who had been posted at the entrance for upward of fifty years, by the third duke of Darris, and who was now pensioned off. Nevertheless, despite all remonstrations to the contrary, he preferred to spend his days guarding the portals of the ancient—and decidedly drafty—principal seat. His toothless grin and creaking bow were a comical mixture of the cheeky, the cheerful and the respectful. Demian could never decide in which proportion.

"Evenin' Yer Grace! 'E be a hearty beast, I'm as-ure!"

"Season's Glory? A splendid animal, Carlew! And how are the chilblains?"

"Ah, Yer Grace, sure an' I 'aven't cockled up me toes yet, I 'aven't, though like as not with all this openin' and closin' of them gates wot I don't hold with, pleasin' yer 'onor, the gout will strike me yet."

Even as the duke tut-tutted sympathetically, his sharp wits focused on the ominous portent of the man's words.

"Opening and closing? There should not be much carriage traffic with just Lady Caro in residence."

There came a sharp snort in response, followed by a rubbing of hands and an eager spark to the old man's crusty dark eyes. " 'Ad 'alf of Lunnin in 'ere today, I did, must 'ave been five coaches or more rollin' up, and none of them no gentry folk neither, that's wot I say! All merchants and milliners and wot have yew."

The duke's eyes twinkled. He did not consider five carriage loads half of London, no matter what his esteemed sentry regarded it. And if Caroline had finally come to her senses regarding what was required for her upcoming season, he supposed he should only be grateful. Perhaps his haste in returning to Darris had been unfounded. All seemed perfectly normal, though his eagle eyes detected that the manse had undergone a certain degree of sprucing, for the topiary gardens had been restored and the flagstones were all gleaming. Even the huge statues of Venus and Androcles at the entrance seemed whiter than he remembered. Still, he supposed, *that* was no cause for alarm.

His complacency would have been shattered, however, had he but seen the flurry of activity within, for apart from seizing several bottles of champagne and burgundy from his cellars, the ladies of the house had gone so far as to turn the kitchens upside down by marching belowstairs personally to oversee the cooking of wild geese, several turkeys and the delicate brewing of mussel and oyster sauce. Caroline was covered in flour from head to toe, for she had been kneading dough and tammying broth when the scullery maid had come hurtling past with a great bag of newly milled flour. As she turned, the bag had collided with her hooped skirts, causing great quantities of white powder to waft about her in clouds. Fortunately, her ladyship seemed to find the matter rather humorous, for rather than scolding, she had sent the scullery maid out for her brother, and urged the two most earnestly to fish in the duke's ponds for the largest trout they could manage.

"And *that*," said Caro triumphantly, "should get rid of dear Betty for a few hours at least!" Betty was one of the neighboring crofter's daughters, newly in service, and a notorious butterfingers. It was considered a decided advantage to have her out of the house, rather than within, especially as the Sevres china was even now lying in great sinks of steaming water, ready to be dried. Demian would not be pleased if the valuable Darris tableware was shattered, no matter how excellent the cause.

Now he peered past Carlew and was startled to catch a glimpse of two liveried house servants settled neatly with fishing rods at the rim of his seventeenth-century ornamental pond. He raised his brows quizzically.

"Aye, stare wot yer will, Yer Grace, I told you there be strange goin' ons! And if that addle wit Betty don't swear it was on 'er ladyship's orders, then you may coddle me liver!" Carlew's words were dark with disapproval. Demian did not linger to hear more of the mutterings, but merely uttered a small pleasantry and rode on, stopping only to unhook a large trout dangling from a tangled line.

"There! I believe you were sitting too close. The lines were bound to get tangled. Planning on a good dinner?"

Two pairs of eyes nearly popped out of their heads.

"Pleasin' Yer Grace, it ain't for *our* dinner! Da would 'ave our hides if we stole out of yer pond!"

"Ah, uh, excellent. Who, then, is going to be the recipient of this fine specimen?"

Two pairs of lips quirked into awed giggles. "Beggars us, Yer Grace! But whoever it is goin' to be fair an' fine stuffed, for there be ten quails, too, and Wil-

liams caught a grouse, and them Christmas turkeys . . ."

"Yes?"

"Well, reckon as wot they won't see no hide or hair
of no Christmas!" Despite their awe at the duke's noble
rank, the pair could not help chortling. Demian felt an
answering smile twitch at the edges of his lips, but
controlled himself. No need to encourage the little
blighters in their high spirits! He nodded shortly, and
murmured something encouraging in the stallion's ear.
Moments later, quite unregarded by what skeleton
household he now retained, he stabled Season's Glory,
rubbed him down energetically, then entered his ducal
domain through a side entrance.

Lady Raquel Fortesque-Benton's voice tinkled with
airy laughter. She raised her crystal goblet to her lips
and silently acknowledged the worshipful gaze of Mr.
Thomas Endicott. After all, it was no more than her
due, though she *did* wish her heart would not flutter
so when his penetrating gaze rested upon her. *Really,*
she thought crossly, *it almost borders on rudeness.*

As a consequence, therefore, she turned her ivory-
white shoulders deliberately in his direction and gave
Lady Sophria Godlington her full attention. That lady
was engaged in whispering all manner of confidences
into any eager ear that might care to listen. Lady
Raquel did not approve of gossip, but nevertheless, the
eyes upon her were disturbing, so she endeavored to
smile and answer something suitable in kind. But when
the gossip turned to playful little hints that she might
herself have interesting news, she excused herself
coldly and looked about her for a seat in the stifling
crush of people. She was neither so bold nor so stupid

as to announce her betrothal with Darris until her father's permission had been obtained in form.

True, the whole matter was a mere formality, but Lady Raquel was ever a high stickler for such things. Pride—in large quantities—was one of the talismen of the Fortesque-Bentons. It had stood her in good stead in the past, and it stood her in good stead now. Doubtless, as duchess, it would be indispensable in the future.

Now, Lady Sophria was baulked of her prey, and Lady Raquel, much to her annoyance, was baulked of her seat. That dratted man Endicott had just taken the last one. If she knew no better, she would guess he had done so deliberately to provoke her. Not content with a view of her shoulders, he had glided forward with the grace of a panther, pushed his way ingratiatingly amid several dowagers and was now viewing her with unashamed appreciation from the comfort of the last seat in the whole confounded ballroom. He looked like the cat which had got the cream, for the seats were all upon slightly raised platforms, so his gaze now rested upon her elegant neckline, which was accented becomingly with a sheath of pearls and precious little else, for prevailing fashion called for the remarkably stark and low-cut.

Lady Raquel had to school herself not to allow her slender wrists to float upward to block his view. She was not a callow miss from the schoolroom! And if Mr. Endicott had the impertinence to ogle, he would soon get his comeuppance when they finally got a chance to be introduced. For introduced they surely would be, what with His Grace such bosom bows with the rogue. And he, Lady Raquel noted with faint distaste, not even a peer! Certainly, when she and the duke were wed, it would be her duty to discourage so strange a friendship. Even as she thought this, her body tingled in the most recalcitrant of ways, and she felt the most peculiar urge to set her tongue around her beautiful pink lips, for they were dry. She did not, of course, for she was perfectly certain Mr. Endicott's penetratingly blue eyes were still upon her. Her own, *equally* blue eyes, ignored him completely.

This did not seem, unfortunately, to be a suitable deterrent. She could swear he was still staring, for the tips of her . . . oh, it was unthinkable—she blushed at the very thought . . . suffice it to say she felt decidedly hot and the heat had little to do with the ballroom, for despite the candelabrum and the great throngs of people, it was winter and therefore chilly enough.

For an instant, Lady Raquel nearly rescinded her haughty edict not to dance. She had declined in consideration of Darris, who had unexpectedly been called back to his estates. It would be unseemly, she thought, for the next duchess of Darris to be dancing the night away without a suitable escort in attendance. She had therefore declined all dances except the supper dance, this being kept vacant, of course, of necessity. Now she regretted her swift decision, for whilst ladies of rank far inferior to hers drifted across the shining, polished marble floors, she was condemned to stand, watching, sipping vile champagne and concentrating on keeping her back straight. All these privations would have been bad enough, but they were rendered quite intolerable when some untitled upstart of a person insisted on searing one's décolletage with smoldering, impertinent eyes.

Lady Raquel would not admit—even to herself— that those self same stares were wreaking havoc with her normally quite sane senses. Such a suggestion— even a timid one in her own head—would have been met with a brimful of scorn. Further, she would definitely not concede that it caused her to remain rooted to the spot even when she spied Lord Wrathbone vacate his own seat on the east side. No, Lady Raquel Fortesque-Benton had many fine virtues, but strict truthfulness—even with herself—was not one of them.

As the clock struck the hour, she chided herself for declining a dance card. There had been so many protests from her bevy of suitors, one would think that at least *one* would be chivalrous enough to notice that she was now wilting like a wallflower and beg her to change her mind. Then, after some small argument, she might graciously incline her head and afford him the honor.

But no! Not one among them was so considerate. Lady Raquel did not stop to think that even the most ardent of her suitors would not dare to press her for fear of having a glacial stare cast upon his person, or that as news of Darris's suit swept across the room—for such matters were impossible to keep secret—her bevy of gazetted fortune hunters were looking about for greener pastures than *she* could now provide. So, she was stuck holding her glass and listening for the quarter hour chime of the great hall clock. She had never been more mortified in her life, especially as she had a most *particular* desire to appear comme il faut before the man seated so infelicitously in front of her.

She cursed him for a mannerless beast, for any feeling gentleman of the smallest civility would have ceded his seat upon the instant. But not him, oh, no! And what the blazes did he mean, wearing ruffles when everyone else was in high points and elegantly starched cravats? True, he did have a certain inspiring air about him, but it was piratical rather than proper, and the proper, as Lady Raquel Fortesque-Benton knew only too well, was to be revered. Why, then, could she not help stealing a sideways glance at the fellow? She would like to have said, "ridiculous fellow," but somehow, the stupid man was too imposing for that. She would have to be content with irksome, and annoying, and downright smug—not to mention impudent—impertinent, and, oh, if only he were not so damnably attractive!

Satin gloves of the first stare clenched tightly in her hands before a strange, benighted faintness overcame her. Someone was tapping her, teasingly, on the very shoulder she had offered earlier in the night for his appraisal. Lady Raquel swallowed hard and looked up. Her eyes were blazing, and there was no sign of her normal stinging calm. If she could have slapped him she would have, but Mr. Thomas Endicott was awake to such tricks. His hands moved down to her arms, pinning them, lightly, to the modish overdress of blonde lace.

"I wouldn't if I were you, madame! I might feel compelled to answer in kind." His tone was pleasant, conversational, admiring, even, but Lady Raquel could feel the force rippling from his arms and she could see the determined set of his jaw as, very sure of himself, he released her and rather whimsically offered her his seat. Lady Raquel was pleased to decline, though her feet ached terribly in their delicately ribboned bonds. If she hoped to annoy the man, though, she was doomed to disappointment. A decided gleam of appreciation appeared in his sapphire-blue eyes.

He regarded her, for a moment, as if he was rather inclined to do something perfectly outrageous—something that would undoubtedly have tested Lady Fortesque-Benton's resolve *not* to slap him fully on his audaciously handsome left cheek—then, as suddenly, he seemed to lose interest.

The young lady before him hardly knew whether to feel relieved, furious, or strangely disappointed. She settled on fury since relief would only have tacitly acknowledged he'd had the upper hand in the small skirmish between them. As for disappointment . . . well, whatever could she have been thinking? It was a non-sensical notion . . . she'd never harbored the *faintest* wish to be kissed by such an unmitigated scoundrel.

"You begin to annoy me, sir. I should not wish to have to call for a manservant."

He deliberately misunderstood her. "A footman? So that you might leave?"

She hissed at him, "No, sir, so that *you* may do so! I doubt our hostess would be pleased to find I had been unduly harassed by . . . by . . ."

She stopped in confusion. He was regarding her with such obviously piquant amusement that anger overcame her habitual coolness. Instead of saying what she had intended, which was "my fiancé's dearest friend," she ended up saying "scaff and raff!" in an utterly venomous tone. The amusement vanished from Mr. Endicott's face.

"Would you care to repeat that?" His tone was dangerously quiet, but Lady Raquel was not deceived. Half of her was exhilarated at scoring an obvious point, the other half was feverishly fearful. That was not the sum though, of what she was feeling. It was almost as though time had stood still and a curious force was compelling her to look up and stare into those magnificent eyes. They were no longer indulgent, or lazily amused, or any *other* of the singularly annoying expressions she'd had to endure over the evening. No, now they were hard and the deep blue was colder than the wintry seas. Lady Raquel wished more than anything for a wrap to drape over her shoulders, for she was suddenly chilly and her striking gown was far too revealing for comfort. Since *that* wish was not likely to come true—Madame Florentine did not, whilst designing the most exquisite of evening wear, approve of wraps—Lady Raquel contented herself with turning her back, once more, and walking away.

She was arrested by the whisper of a touch upon her person. It was not so obvious as to draw attention to itself, but it was firm enough, nonetheless. She turned around with a sigh.

"Am I never to be rid of you?"

Her tone was plaintive, like a child's. Nothing *like* the haughty Lady Raquel Fortesque-Benton the ton had come to know. Perhaps it was *that* which brought the mocking curve back to Mr. Thomas Endicott's otherwise grim lips.

"Apparently not. You might as well resign yourself, my dear. We are booked for the supper dance."

"What absurdity is this? I do not dance."

"No, but Lady Elversham is not to be held to account for your childish vaporings. If you do not wish to overset her numbers, and I am sure that you, a lady who is well bred, if not well mannered, do not, then you shall take my hand like an excellent child and allow me to escort you in."

"I will take Dallow, instead."

"Too late. I believe he is escorting Lady Sophria in. You are the only lady currently unpartnered, and I believe I am the only gentleman so placed." His tone indicated that if there were any other lady to whom he could offer escort, he might very much wish to do so. Lady Fortesque-Benton felt herself flush. The amusement deepened on Mr. Endicott's countenance.

"Yes, very annoying, is it not?" His voice sounded bewitchingly sympathetic. Lady Raquel cast him a look of vile suspicion, but he continued on blithely.

"I am afraid we shall have to accustom ourselves. And no, Lady Raquel, this is not a suitable moment for hysterics. Whilst I am not *myself* averse to high drama, I believe such behavior on your part might draw interested comment."

He smiled at her so politely that any interested on-looker might be mistaken in thinking them a handsome pair. Lady Raquel's fine, dark brows drew together in a fleeting scowl. Then she corrected herself, smiled elegantly and murmured, "Not hysterics, perhaps, but the headache. I believe I shall have to make my excuses to dear Lady Elversham at once."

"What, a coward? I could credit you with many vices, I believe, but not cowardice. You always look so peculiarly forthright."

"Dear Mr. Endicott, I believe I could spit in your eye. As for cowardice, there is not a cowardly bone in my body. I will remain."

A faint thawing appeared in the blue eyes regarding her. Mr. Endicott, despite his initial appraisal of the chit—not particularly favorable, though this was colored, to some degree, by His Grace's account of her—found himself admiring the courageous tilt of her chin, and the cool eyes that nevertheless flashed fire from their depths. And it was true what Demian had said—the creature *was* undoubtedly lovely. He regarded her smooth lines and elegant curves for just a fraction longer than was strictly necessary. No, she may not have a cowardly bone in her body, but certainly she had several rather *appealing* ones. He set aside the thought harshly. He was here to teach "Madam Uppity" a small lesson, not to filch her from Darris.

"Then shall we proceed? I promise to entertain you with decorum."

Lady Raquel nodded, not trusting herself to speak. For if she did, she would undoubtedly have shocked all who heard her with the unladylike epithets ringing in her head.

Thomas Tyrone Endicott, rightly guessing at what

lay beneath the curt nod, chuckled out loud. "Quite right, my dear. No need to set my ears aquiver, even if I *am* merely the raff and scaff."

And with *that* delightful pleasantry, he offered her his exquisitely masculine arm.

Four

"You did *what?*"

"I discharged the butler. He was as drunk as a sot, waving about my crystal decanter as though it were *not* a priceless heirloom, let alone practically the only thing I have left from Father."

"But Demian . . ."

Caroline's voice was a wail of despair. She shot a guilty look across the room at Miss Bancroft, who rose from her sturdy Queen Anne chair and composedly greeted the duke.

"Good evening, Your Grace. This is an unexpected surprise."

Demian smiled at Martha, of whom he was extremely fond, and was disturbed to intercept an equally guilty glance from her. His eyes narrowed. He was a doting brother, but years of experience put him on his guard.

"What mischief is brewing here? Come, come, Martha, spill the beans."

But for once, Martha was silent. She did not even take leave to scold Demian for his undignified use of cant. The duke's eyebrows rose at once.

"So silent? Then it is as I feared. You are in the coils of one of Caro's hideously well-meaning plots. I am glad I returned with such haste."

"Demian! You are the outside of enough! When I

most *specifically* requested you to keep away! And now you have spoiled everything by turning out poor old Hedgewig, who I am *sure* was merely sampling your port—and who can blame him when his gout aches so, and when there is a whole bottle, newly opened, for him to try?"

"Interesting, that. I distinctly remember laying the bottles down. Who has been meddling in my cellars, and why?"

Now Caroline's piquant face looked *decidedly* guilty. Still, she thrust her head up proudly, tossed away some stray curls, and adjured Demian to stop fussing over a few bottles of prime Madeira.

He groaned. "The Madeira, too?"

"Yes, and I may as well make a clean breast of it and mention the claret. There were only a few bottles left, so I thought . . ."

"Yes?" The duke's tone was rather more ominous than was his custom. Miss Bancroft's heart quailed within her, but Caroline was made of sterner stuff.

"I thought Cook could use them in the kitchens."

There was an indrawn breath where His Noble Grace, the duke of Darris, marquis of Hartford and earl of Shrewsbury counted to a full ten before diving indecorously upon his sister and half pummeling her to death. Of course, being a gentleman, he softened his punches, but Caroline emerged breathless nonetheless and could not help squawking like a plucked pigeon before diving behind a convenient pianoforte and waving her hands about wildly for a truce.

Demian, brought to his senses by the shocked look on poor Miss Bancroft's face, sighed, tidied himself a little, retrieved his fashionable beaver, which had somehow got itself crumpled underfoot, squashed it out—to the later unspeakable wrath of his valet—and seated himself upon the sole remaining Chippendale.

"Come, enlighten me. I must admit myself to be quite *breathless* with anticipation to hear what scheme you have devised for my delight." His sarcasm could not have been more obvious. Brushing down her skirts, Lady Caroline emerged from behind the burnished chestnut instrument and regarded him thoughtfully.

"There *is* that bonus . . ."

"Caroline, if you so much as *mention* that bonus, I take leave to inform you of my resignation." Miss Bancroft's lips set into a firm line. Her tone was so final that both siblings looked at her in surprise.

"My, my, you *must* be brewing something nasty to have dear old Martha turn on you so!"

"Not nasty, Demian."

Caroline could not keep the hurt from her voice. Demian's tone softened. "What, then? I am not a monster, I shall not *eat* you!"

"No, but you may have me soundly whipped."

"Good God, is it as bad as that? Reveal all, Caroline, before I shake you!"

And so, helped a little by Miss Bancroft, at certain intervals where the discourse became entirely unintelligible, Lady Caroline unveiled to the duke the full extent of all her meddling.

There was a stunned silence. Caroline coughed, for now, gazing upon Lord Darris's immaculate shirt points, she felt more than a trifle foolish. Demian was man enough by anyone's standards to do whatever required to be done. He had no need to be led by his foolish sister's apron strings. Much less, she realized, when the plan was flawed with a million knots, and ten thousand pounds, though admirable, was hardly enough to restore Darris to its ducal glory.

She choked back a tear and watched Martha sniff loudly, then reach in her great, hideously unfashionable reticule for a large—an extra large—handkerchief, decorated with French lace. Martha buried her face in it, but Caroline was not so fortunate. The tears stung at the back of her eyes so much that eventually they spilled down her elfin face. She rubbed at them crossly.

"Add handkerchiefs to your season's order with Madame Verlow, Caro. I'll warrant you've forgotten them again. And, here, use mine."

Demian indulgently wiped his sister's face dry, then shook her till her teeth rattled. Strange to say, his sister appeared to *like* this treatment, for she giggled a little and the last trace of her tears vanished beneath a sparkling smile.

"Oh, Demian, I thought you would be as cross as . . . as hogs."

"Crabs, Caro dear, and I am."

"Yes, but"—she peeked at him cheekily—"not *unforgivably* so?"

The duke sighed. The glimmer of a twinkle, however, appeared in his dark, thoroughly rakish eyes.

"Not unforgivably, no. But, Caro, you might have saved yourself a good deal of conniving. I am . . ."

But *what* he was was lost to everyone, for at that moment there came a rumble of carriages across the long stone flagway leading up to the castle.

Miss Bancroft fluttered to the window, then emitted a sharp gasp of horror. Not only were the guests arriving early, but the first snowflakes were beginning to fall. If past seasons were anything to go by, they would be snowbound by evening.

"Oh, gracious, my lord . . ."

Demian stepped up to the window. His gaze fixed on an enormous plumed bonnet that was emerging from the first carriage. He closed his eyes.

Caroline set down the handkerchief that she was still clinging to and peered out from behind Demian's shoulder. Tom, the hostler, was looking decidedly flustered at the unexpected arrivals. A few imperious commands wafted up to the balcony. None of them was very auspicious.

"I shall send Hedgewig down at once to inform them we are not at home to visitors. Perhaps they will just go away."

"And perhaps they will not. There is the small matter of the ten thousand pounds, after all." Miss Bancroft coughed apologetically as she drew the drapes.

"Then we shall return it. Caro, you shall pen a quick apology to that effect, and Hedgewig shall deliver it upon the instant."

"Demian, you forget you dismissed Hedgewig an hour ago!"

"Then go and recommission him."

"Was the decanter half empty or *entirely* empty?"

"What odds?" His Grace was growing impatient as the sound of several more traveling chaises ground to a halt. Thank goodness the party had all obviously decided to wait for each other. There had been no bold knocks, as yet, upon the ducal door.

"Well, if it was empty, Hedgewig will be rolling in some meadow by now, singing to the cows."

"Oh! Yes! How stupid of me. The fellow's inebriated. Where is Parsons?"

Caroline lifted helpless hands. "We are down to a skeleton staff, now, remember?"

Demian did. The thought engulfed him with gloom. At least that was *one* good thing to come out of his betrothal. Parsons and Dawcett and all the upper chambermaids could return en force.

"Have you the note, yet?"

"Just a minute, I am blotting it. Perhaps Martha . . . Martha, dear, *do* you think you can pretend to be a housekeeper? Only to give them the note, you understand."

Miss Bancroft blushed, though she was well past her first youth. "I shall have to change . . ."

Caroline didn't like to say that her dull, starched mourning black looked exactly like a housekeeper's anyway. She may have been flighty, but there wasn't a mean bone in her body, so she agreed, adjuring Martha only to "Hurry up!"

The duke shook his head, suppressing the whisper of a grin, for Miss Bancroft looked utterly *stricken* with panic. He winked at Caroline, who was so relieved that he was not completely furious, she threw her arms about him.

"Now, now, Caro, there is no need to cast my valet into agonies. If you continue on in this reprehensible manner my *very* elegant shirt points shall be quite ruined. Now"—he put her from him gently and resumed a sterner tone—"it is high time for all this foolishness to be put to a halt."

Miss Bancroft looked at him hopefully.

"Sit down, Martha. Caroline is merely being ridiculous. You are eons away from a housekeeper; nobody will be fooled for a moment. Come. I will put a quick end to this most dismal of all episodes by going down myself. I may be an impoverished duke, but I am, nevertheless, a nobleman. I believe that *that* satisfies the most elementary of their requirements! I shall give them a draft off Addleburies for their wretched ten thousand pounds—my credit, I believe, can stand that particular blow—direct them to the Red Hart Inn, and brook no further nonsense. I am tired of all these charades."

Caroline, *quite* reconciled to her brother taking charge and destroying all her plans, looked up at this. "*Not* the full ten thousand! That is ridiculous! Return, if you have to, the retainer. I have it in my drawer upstairs . . . oh, no! I paid for the confectionery . . ."

Demian sighed. "How much, exactly, were you given?"

"Two hundred pounds."

"Very well. I shall refund them four hundred immediately, to cover the expense of their travel—"

"Oh, Demian! I am so sorry. Is there no other way?"

"None that I can think of. Hush, now! I believe that is the knocker."

Indeed, it was, and that quite loudly. From below the stone balcony came the muffled trills of laughter and the odd shriek as flounces were patted down and downy fur pelisses were tucked becomingly over shoulders. Despite her mortification, Caroline could not help parting the saffron-colored curtains and gazing upon the scene in the courtyard.

The last of the carriages—a ponderous landau—was wending its way toward the stables. What the poor groom must be thinking, Caroline could only speculate. At least they had kept Potter on, and old Farley, too, though by the looks of the cattle they were all prime beasts. Still, doubtless Mrs. Murgatroyd's entourage of servants would be able to muck in and help.

Six young ladies were assembled upon the doorstep. Five of them, Caroline noted, were looking determinedly at the handle of the castle door. Though it was brass, and very fine, it did not warrant such fixed glances as it now received. Caroline nearly giggled at such obvious determination to enter the hallowed portals of Darris. There were two matrons accompanying them, obviously quite swimming in riches, for both were wearing tiaras crusted with gems, but whilst the one was slender and rather bony looking, the other was plump and sported two rather enlivening double chins. She turned, now, to the assembled group, and pointed out several of the gargoyles that graced the turrets. "See, my dear, generations old. Gothic, positively

Gothic, or so I am told. Or is that Grecian? Oh, one or the other, possibly both. I daresay Darris is particular to *all* the styles. Amelia, dear, you *must* ask him, when you converse."

"Tut, tut, Hyacinth!" The bony one assumed a cold, rather knowing air. "You know perfectly well Amelia cannot tell a pilaster ceiling from a Doric column! Now Daphne, here . . ."

But Daphne's talents were lost to the eavesdropping Caroline, for the few snowflakes were now dropping down like veritable snowballs and one of the young ladies actually screamed.

"My muff! Mrs. Murgatroyd, I am not used to being kept out in such hideously inclement weather! Knock again!"

"Patience, my dear Miss Anderson! Doubtless the servants are even now preparing for our arrival. We are early, remember!"

"Only because you insisted we leave whilst it was still dark!"

"Well, had I not, the roads would have been impassable. Besides, it will now be most uncivil of the duke to turn us back. I am persuaded, my dear ladies, that our sojourn at Darris will be longer than we had anticipated."

Was there a smirk of satisfaction about her thin lips? Caroline was too high up to tell, but by the smugness of the woman's tone she would have wagered a groat on this being the case.

Her slender frame heaved in indignation. "Of all the conniving, despicable turns! That old shrew never *intended* it to be a day party!"

"Well, Caroline, I *did* fear that—"

"I know, I know, and there is nothing worse than being told I told you so! But I can't help being thankful, now, that Demian has returned. He will make mince-meat of them, I fancy."

"Yes, just think how shocking it would have been if they were forced on us for a week!"

"They would just have had to eat jugged hare." Caroline sounded unusually grim. She was just with-drawing from the window when her gaze was arrested by the sixth lady of the party. The only one, she real-ized, who had *not* been avidly staring at the door knocker. Unlike her contemporaries, she was wearing a traveling dress of the deepest green merino, and though it was undoubtedly costly, it was also rather more sensible than the flimsy morning dresses of her companions, who shivered a great deal upon the steps.

She was regarding Mrs. Murgatroyd with such an open expression of contempt that even from the relative height of her balcony, Caroline could see the quiet curl of her lips and the hard expression in her slate-gray eyes. Lady Darris could not *immediately* perceive the color, but she had the fleeting impression of flint. Sur-prised to see such an expression on the countenance of the tall, willowy young lady, she moved closer to the arch of the window. Definitely intriguing.

"Caroline! Come away from there! You will be seen!"

"Who cares? They are going, anyway!"

To no avail did Miss Bancroft mutter little phrases peppered with words like "decorum" and "death of me." Caroline was too busy watching the elegant young lady turn her back on the assembly and wordlessly walk down the marble steps.

"*Miss* Mayhew!" The bony one seemed to shriek the words out, and there was a moment's pause as the young lady hesitated on the stair.

"Where do you think you are going? You will wait with the rest of us."

The lady turned. She was very lovely, though a trifle tall. Caroline admired the way her dark hair shone with luster and her lips curved ever so slightly. She adjusted the merino skirt, and Caroline was afforded a glimpse of a very well turned ankle beneath all those swathes of petticoats.

"I think not, Mrs. Murgatroyd. You may keep your two hundred pounds. I believe I have changed my mind about the day's excursion."

Lady Caroline Darris had to strain to hear the words, for in truth, she spoke rather too low for any eavesdropper's comfort. Miss Bancroft had to forget her strictures on decorum and stretch forward to prevent Caro falling from the window.

"And *why,* pray?"

The voice was shrill, accompanied by a fussy tut-tutting from the round lady, who for once found herself in agreement with her arch rival, Mrs. Honoria Murgatroyd.

"Why?" The voice was heavy with scorn. "If you have to ask, madam, it makes matters all the worse."

Both ladies looked mystified but no less venomous. The young lady in the emerald gown turned her back, once again. She was stopped only by the snow that was now covering the ancient flagway in a frosty carpet of white. The matrons laughed, which seemed to break the tension, as five other ladies did the same.

"Well! Changed your mind, did you, dear? Now, I warn you, I will not tolerate missish spasms."

"Is it a missish spasm to object to *foisting* myself upon an unwilling host? Even if his lordship were in residence, which I take leave to inform you he is *not*, it would be the height of presumption—not to say encroachment—to expect him to house us in these snows. Can you honestly say, Honoria, that that is your intention?"

Miss Amelia Corey giggled. *Now* that whey-faced Miss Mayhew was in the suds! Mrs. Murgatroyd did not take kindly to being called by her Christian name. She shifted her position, agog to hear what would develop next. Oh, how she had *begged* Mama to exclude Miss Hoighty-Toity from the party! But no, Mrs. Corey had the liveliest dislike of paying a penny more than she needed to. Amy's share of the costs had proved vital.

"Is, was, and always has been. Why, you stupid girl, do you think I chose this time of year? If I am going to pay ten thousand pounds, then I will dashed well get my money's worth! Besides, Daphne looks charmingly in the winter. *So* much less prone to freckles." She cast a satisfied eye upon a young lady dressed in primrose jaconet. "It is as well we packed the fur tippet, my love."

Miss Amy Mayhew's lips compressed. She had never before been so furious in all her life. She drew herself up to her full height.

"You disgust me, all of you. Honoria! I wish to leave for that watering post we passed some miles back. We won't make London, but I shall not batten on the duke's sister, whatever *you* may all wish to do."

"Don't be ridiculous!" Mrs. Corey bristled with indignation and silenced the chatter behind her with a tilt of her plump hand. "You have no chaperon, and no equipage to convey you anywhere. I am certainly not having the horses reharnessed for such a foolish excursion. Why, it is freezing already! If you wish to leave the party, then you must do so at a time more convenient to us all. Indeed, I am certain Mr. Froversham Worthing would have *much* to say if you disappointed him in this matter."

Amy bit back the urge to retort that dear Uncle Froversham would probably smile at her weakly and bestow a mild pat upon her shoulder before ringing for some chocolate and forgetting about the episode entirely. But her *aunt* was another matter. Aunt Ermentrude would suffer agonies of disappointment! Still, the whole thing was a matter of principle. She did not think, after being so strictly reared at Miss Simpson's Academy, that she could ever bring herself to be as unprincipled as Mrs. Honoria Murgatroyd, Mrs. Hyacinth Corey and, indeed, five pairs of youthful eyes apparently required. They were all glaring at her now, so that they had not noticed that the great castle door was standing open. His Grace, for all his frugality, kept the hinges well oiled.

Five

How much of the conversation taking place between the ladies had been overheard could not be known, but it must have been Miss Oliver, or possibly Miss Farrow, who first noticed the stark outline of the gentleman at the entrance. Both spluttered, then giggled, for in truth, neither had *ever* clapped eyes on anyone quite so wondrously proportioned or eminently endowed with classical features in all their lives. And he the butler! How much more could they expect of the master! Miss Oliver murmured something of the kind to Miss Amelia Corey, and both regarded the figure rather brazenly before chuckling into their handkerchiefs.

As one, Mrs. Murgatroyd and Mrs. Corey stepped forward. It was fortunate that the top stair was as wide as it was, for undoubtedly neither would give way to the other. Mrs. Murgatroyd assumed the most ingratiating of smiles and looked past the butler into the wide and hallowed halls. The ceilings were satisfyingly high and the sparkling ebony- and rose-colored marble all that she could have wished. She sighed in satisfaction, her swift eyes darting shrewdly to the stairs. Perhaps she might be the first to catch a glimpse of their host.

Mrs. Corey's air was less obvious. Unlike Mrs. Murgatroyd, who was prepared to be gracious to anything that smelled ducal, Mrs. Corey was more discerning. Her graciousness did not extend to butlers, however lofty. Consequently, she berated the man for leaving them all standing in the entirely infelicitous weather and handed him her card regally. "Be so good as to convey this to the duke . . . or to Lady Caroline. I believe we are expected."

Her eyes snapped at the impertinent amusement she detected in the man's dark, ridiculously handsome eyes. Then she clutched at her ebony fan as she noted his expression harden. Well! Of all the insolent upstarts! She opened her mouth to reprove him heartily, when his gaze drifted past her, past five young maidens, all shivering with cold yet nonetheless contriving to regard him coyly, to the sixth and most promising of the group, who regarded him with melting eyes that shimmered silver with defiant tears.

She opened her mouth to speak, but the intensity of his gaze hushed her, as did the slight warning motion he made with the crook of his signet finger. No one saw it, for all were staring at her with varying degrees of dislike, their backs to the castle door. *Amy* noticed it, though, and the deeply intimate nature of both gesture and expression startled her. Well, it did more than that. It intrigued her beyond measure. *More* disconcerting was that the man's glance, brief as it had been, had left her feeling quite unutterably breathless. It was as if a sudden, decidedly unexpected assault upon her senses had taken place in this, the most inauspicious of places.

Contrary to Miss Corey's belief, Amy was *not* missish. Indeed, she had been privy, in her four and twenty years, to a number of discreet kisses—all upon the hand, of course—from several rather expert libertines. Many had been motivated by her enormous fortune, but some few had also been driven by passion. And never *once,* Amy mused, had she been as moved by a single caress as she'd been by this slight lifting of the

butler's finger. Or was it, she wondered, because the
action was coupled by the smooth tilt of infernally dark
brows? She tried not to think of the approving expression in his black—no, not black, merely molten—eyes.
The thought would have unhinged her. Even so, she
felt herself color and caught the glimmer of answering
amusement from the top stair.

Now the expression was teasing, she was sure of
it, though her lashes had dropped and she would not
allow herself a peek. Oh, only the smallest, tiniest,
most ladylike one . . . yes, she was right. Definitely
teasing, though there was something more. . . .

"My good man, are your wits wandering? Call a
manservant if you haven't the capability to usher us
in!" This was Mrs. Corey at her most imperious. Even
Mrs. Murgatroyd shot her an admiring glance, though
Amy's eyes closed in sudden distress. Good Lord, they
were behaving like a parcel of washwomen. It was a
mark of the man's extreme good breeding that he didn't
send them all packing via the servants' entrance. Is it
no wonder he hesitated to invite them in at all? What
with Mrs. Corey and Mrs. Murgatroyd dripping with
diamonds . . . oh, the vulgarity of it quite sank Miss
Mayhew. Indeed, she had never wanted to cringe so
much in her life.

She stepped forward, past Miss Oliver and Miss
Kirby, Miss Corey and the two chaperons. She stepped
forward until her eyes were level with the intricate folds
of a pearl-white cravat. The style of it confounded her.
It was the mathematique, not something a common butler would effect. For an instant, she stood poised on
the truth, then her perceptive eye alighted on a very
cleverly wrought darn in the man's excellent cream
shirt. She breathed a little easier, though her heart was
still strangely hammering.

"I believe there is some error, Mr. . . ." She waited

for the butler to supply her with a name. Strange, how there was just the smallest pause before he answered, and how her cheeks burned from the appraising glance he cast her! Yet she could not detach herself from the notion that it was patently approving, so she did *not* depress his pretension. Rather, she allowed her sultry lips to curve into a good-natured smile that lit her eyes in a manner that caused the butler to somehow draw in his breath, before, very properly, supplying her with a name.

"Pemberton, miss. And may I be the first to welcome you to Darris Castle?"

Seven ladies behind her accepted this as their due and marched in, chattering, of a sudden, now that they were out of the immediate cold. None seemed to notice, for the moment, that the great hall offered little additional warmth, so intrigued were they with its obvious splendors. The marble busts in the Roman style, and the elegant crystal chandeliers all seemed to please exceedingly. The duke, it must be said, appeared unheeding to the hive of busy activity behind him. He was staring, now, quite directly, at Miss Amy Mayhew.

Equally, she was staring back, with honest, forthright eyes that seemed in perfect keeping with her willowy figure. Straight and true as an arrow. Then the spell was broken.

"How many make up the party, miss?"

The subservient tone seemed at odds with the imperious stance. Try as she could, Amy could not help the impression that here was a man used, at all times, to being obeyed. He had an air of authority about him that he wore lightly, but which was nonetheless evident to the discerning eye. It puzzled her extremely, put her quite out of countenance, in fact, so that she cocked her head to one side and smiled engagingly. This was not, properly speaking, correct etiquette to employ when dealing with a butler, but Amy always worked on instinct, a fact that had caused her many a stern lecture at Miss Simpson's Academy.

"I believe eight; fifteen with the house servants. And then there are several others employed for the stables. I hope we do not inconvenience the household too much? It is my dearest wish that we repair at once to the posting inn—"

"Miss Mayhew! Surely you cannot be prattling with the servants? We will speak to Lady Caroline about the arrangements."

The butler cleared his throat. "Ah, yes. Lady Caroline. I beg leave to inform you, madam, that Lady Caroline is . . . indisposed. I shall speak directly with her lady's maid and see if she is able to receive you. In the meanwhile, I shall take the liberty of ordering a hot collation to be prepared. If you will follow me . . . ?"

Obviously, Mrs. Honoria Murgatroyd and Mrs. Hyacinth Corey thought that they could. With eyes widening in satisfaction at the thought of a noble repast, they suppressed their annoyance at their cold reception, murmured that they hoped *dear* Lady Caroline would recover, then followed Pemberton into the dark corridor leading, after several long minutes of sapphire carpeting, to the breakfast room. His Grace deposited them there, for it was the only room he knew for certain was currently habitable. It had a fire lit—for Hedgewig had had sense enough to order that, at least—and the chestnut table was covered in a respectable ice-white damask cloth that extended over its full length, fortunately obscuring some of the ravages of time. His Grace had no funds to order in a cabinetmaker, so the damask sufficed. With a faint tilt to his lips, he noted how all the silver was gleaming, and how the brass plate had somehow crept down from storage and now adorned several of the walls and empty mantels. Well! Caroline *had* been busy! With a slight frown, he noticed his Sevres china laid out at each of the nine settings. Damn Caroline's impudence! He wouldn't trust the Murgatroyd woman with his silver spoons, never mind his Sevres china! Still, two hands were trembling in their sensible kid gloves, and short of kissing them insensible, there was nothing for it, he knew, but to let the charade continue.

What mad impulse had driven him to this crazy start, he could not attest to. Unless . . . yes. He could not fool himself. Damn Caroline, damn Lady Raquel Fortesque-Benton, fiends seize it, damn himself, and most of all, damn, damn, damn that excellent creature in her soft, warm merino. If it were not for her, he would even now be partaking of some of his very fine madeira and consigning the lot of them to the devil.

Instead, he bowed elegantly from the waist, and excused himself coldly.

He did not wait to hear Mrs. Murgatroyd simper and comment, what "a very superior sort of servant," he appeared to be, or Mrs. Corey commenting waspishly that "superior is as superior does, but it would be well if he remembered his manners," for he had stopped suddenly at a side entrance, closed the crested oak door silently behind him, then run like the wind up several flights of stairs.

He arrived breathless, moments later, in the west wing.

"Caro!"

"I know, I witnessed it all from the window! This is famous sport!"

"Infamous, you mean. God, Caro, I don't know what possessed me!"

"Don't you, now?" Caroline's eyes twinkled mischievously.

"What can you mean by that, baggage?"

"Oh, climb off your high ropes, Demian! If it was not the lady in the green merino that swayed you, I will eat my finest overdress of Venetian satin."

"And good riddance, too. It is hardly up to snuff. I wish you would pay more attention to your wardrobe, Caro." His Grace then toyed with the idea of throttling his beloved sibling, but settled on a mere smile, somewhat more foolish than was his custom.

Lady Caroline Darris could *not* restrain herself from chuckling. "Perhaps this plan was more masterful than I thought!"

There was a moment of pregnant silence before the duke advanced upon her menacingly. She bobbed in the very nick of time.

"No, *don't* injure me, you will need me conscious if we are to pull this thing off. Now, you will excuse me. If I am going to enter regally via the east wing, I'd better don some finery first."

"You look . . ."

". . . like I have just been baking sweet biscuits in the kitchen. Which, in point of fact, I have. Now, do be a good boy and tell Cook to hurry up. What are you, by the way? First footman?"

His Grace's lips twitched. "Don't be so absurd, Caroline! My consequence deserves more than that! I am the butler."

Lady Darris stifled a giggle as Miss Bancroft reached for her smelling salts. Demian strode over to her at once.

"Do forgive me, Martha, for embroiling you in all of this." He said it with such charm, and such a contrite smile that Miss Bancroft felt compelled to sit a little straighter on her chair and return the sal volatile to her ubiquitous reticule.

"Not at all, my lord! I am sure it is always my pleasure to do as you desire. What would you have me be? The dowager duchess?"

This sent both young Darrises into hoops, for dear Martha, though she took leave, at times, to scold and cluck severely, was, for all that, a timid, rather retiring person. Not at *all* like a dowager duchess.

"You shall be my dragon of a lady's maid. I shall send you on ahead of me to entertain the motley crew. And Martha, dear, when in doubt, take out your lorgnette and survey them all in regal silence. *That* should make them squirm!"

At this, Martha busied herself in her reticule until she finally found her ancient lorgnette upon a chain of burnished gold. She used it only when she felt compelled to, for she loathed to admit that she was nearsighted and had any need of the instrument. Still, she felt Caroline had a point. A lorgnette cast coldly in any direction had a certain unsettling effect. She clutched it triumphantly, as if it were a weapon as deadly as a dagger. Seeing her, His Grace groaned inwardly. If the parcel of chits below stairs did not immediately smell a rat, he would count himself fortunate, indeed.

"Ratafia?" Mr. Endicott asked politely, his elbows resting negligently on the table, his hands cupped appealingly beneath his chin. Lady Raquel Fortesque-Benton detected the whisper of a shadow where his manservant had not shaved him closely. She wondered what it would feel like, to remove her gloves and slowly trail her fingers across his arrogant jaw.

"Beg pardon?"

"Ratafia. You refused the lemonade."

"Oh!" She lifted her eyes and found them focused directly upon Mr. Endicott's. She hoped he was not a mind reader, for he had an arrogant, rather raffish expression that indicated, quite possibly, that he was. She refused to blush and chided herself for being ridiculous. Of *course* the man could not know that she had memorized every smooth muscle that proclaimed itself beneath his tight-fitting shirt, or that her pulses raced *most* irksomely whenever his gloved fingers innocently brushed against hers whilst serving. Now, he was talking some nonsense about ratafia and she was obliged to give some answer. She pushed her goblet forward.

"Thank you."

The mocking gaze softened. "Not at all, Lady Raquel." He gestured to the liveried manservant, who set down a decanter. Mr. Endicott took it up at once, and poured. His arm was just a hairbreadth from her reach. Lady Raquel averted her gaze. She had no need to see the muscles of his forearm, clearly outlined against his stark evening coat. It was cut, of course, by Weston. She knew, for it could not have more perfectly molded his form if it tried.

She sipped in silence, hoping it was just imagination that made her feel he was mocking her and enjoying the evening thoroughly as a consequence. But how foolish! He was everything that was solicitous, passing her quail, and little smidgens of Salisbury sauce and melon fritters.

"Mr. Endicott . . ."

"Yes, Lady Raquel?"

"Nothing." A small silence prevailed, where Lady Raquel tapped at her plate with her fork, and tasted none of the delicious brandy and cherry crepe that had been set on a side dish for her particular delight.

"Nothing? How edifying."

"Oh, *must* you be so beastly? It was bad enough I had to dance with you. How fortunate that it was merely a quadrille."

"Yes, you wouldn't wish to be waltzing with the lower orders."

"How perfectly ridiculous! Though we have only just been introduced, I am informed by certain very good sources you are on terms with the regent himself."

"Prinny? Well, so I am. What of it?"

"Then you are not of the lower orders, sir."

"I thought you consigned me there earlier. What was your term? Raff and scaff, if I recall."

"I see you shall hold that against me whatever I say. Very well, sir, you may go your length."

Blue eyes glittered. "Be careful what you promise, Lady Raquel. I may just be foolish enough to obey."

Lady Raquel did not understand the meaning behind the words, but they sounded, to her, like a scantily veiled threat. Then why did she shiver with such intoxicating abandon? There was simply no accounting for the matter.

"Mr. Endicott . . ." Sapphire eyes fluttered up to meet brilliant ones of an equal shade.

A dimple played above Mr. Endicott's mouth.

"Yes, my lady?"

"Why are you taking such pains to annoy me? You have been staring at me all evening, you inveigled the supper dance—and, no, I don't believe it was purely mischance—and now you tease me."

"Do I? How perfectly novel. *Do* have a strawberry." He proffered her the dish, but she turned her head away in disdain. "I believe I have had my fill, Mr. Endicott."

"You disappoint me. However, since you are now replete, I feel able to solicit your hand for the waltz. See, they are striking up even as we speak."

"I thought we were agreed that it was a very good thing we did *not* engage in so fast an activity."

"Why, Lady Raquel? Do you not trust yourself in

my arms? I, you know, shall be the very soul of decorum."

"Not trust myself? Mr. Endicott, you are as vain as a coxcomb!"

"Very true, alas! And still, you steer from the topic."

"I am not afraid of your arms, Mr. Endicott!"

"Good! Then you will stop your willful chattering and take my hand."

Willful chattering! Lady Raquel positively seethed. Still, his eye was upon her, and locked in such a steely glance that she dared not deny him lest she caused the very scene she so abhorred. So, with a measure of great disdain—which she took no pains to hide—she rose and extended her fingertips to a mere "Mr." This was a first for Lady Raquel Fortesque-Benton.

Sadly, Mr. Endicott appeared not to notice the high honor that was being accorded him. Instead, he took those delicate fingertips and slid his roguish fingers all the way down to her palm, where his hand finally clamped firmly over the full length of her glove. She could feel the strength emanating from him. Also, the firmness of purpose. She eyed him with annoyance. Then, the rush of sensation as firm arms encircled her ribboned bodice was too hard to bear. She bit her lip and hoped that the ridiculous man did not notice her trembling.

Six

Of course, he did notice. That might have accounted for the faint relaxing of his jaw and the secretive smile which he expertly hid behind an air of bored amusement.

Throughout the next few minutes, there was a silence between the pair as each took the other's measure. More and more dancers took their places, but neither noticed. Mr. Thomas Tyrone Endicott spent a peculiarly large proportion of his time fighting the urge to lessen the very correct distance between his thigh and her waist. He counted to ten; he even counted the steps of the damnable waltz, which he had danced with admirable ease dozens of times before. Being a man of strong will, he would have succeeded in keeping his distance were it not for a beautiful, swanlike neck that practically presented itself to his notice. Lady Raquel, of course, was feverishly looking the other way.

"Damn it, woman, it is the custom to engage your partner in light chatter whilst performing the steps of this foolish dance."

"Is it? Then engage me." The imperious tone was back, but there was just a hint of warmth behind the cool eyes. No, he was wrong. There was *more* than warmth; there was a hot fire burning beyond the ice. He had better tread easily or he would be burned.

So, he laughed. The sound was low, and warm, and

peculiarly intimate. Lady Raquel felt herself responding in kind, her pink bow-shaped lips opening slightly in a smile.

"A hit, a palpable hit. Lady Raquel, I concede you the point. I shall offer you a veritable fount of witticisms and in return, I expect to see more of your dewy eyes than your singularly snowy neck."

The Honorable Lady Fortesque-Benton nearly missed her step. If she didn't know any better, she would suspect Mr. Endicott of setting up a flirtation. But she *did* know better. If anyone was more likely to know of her impending betrothal, it was he. For an instant—the whisper of an instant—she wondered whether Demian had divulged the terms. She bit her lip. Mr. Endicott caught a fleeting glance of glittering teeth before they disappeared back behind those perfect bow-shaped lips.

Maybe she *had* been wildly over the top, specifying lovers, but she liked straight dealing. Marriage, to her, *was* that—a deal, where the parties mutually acquired either rank, wealth or status. It was what she had been reared to know as a child. Papa would be very pleased with His Grace, the duke of Darris. Indeed, she could not have managed better. If she were to have married a prince—as her noble birth and fortune did not rule out—she would have had to leave England. But she did not hold much with foreign titles. Neither did her father, Lord Frances Fortesque-Benton. No, becoming a duchess would be perfect.

But here was this . . . this *nobody* eyeing her with mocking eyes and a graceless manner that caused her breath to catch in her very throat. He seemed to be reading her mind, for arrogance played with amusement in those piercing, know-it-all eyes of his. His fingers clasped tighter about her waist, closing the acceptable distance subtly, so that none but she would be any the wiser.

"You play a deep game, Mr. Endicott. I just hope you do not get burned."

"Do you? I would have thought you would hope the very reverse." He murmured so softly she had to incline her head upward to catch his words.

"Oh! You *are* an incorrigible beast, then. You confirm all my suspicions of you."

"And you confirm all mine of you." His lips drew together in a tight line, so Lady Raquel did not quite like to ask him what he meant. No doubt the odious man was being hideously uncomplimentary.

She would have been surprised to learn that Thomas was amusing himself with a double entendre. From the moment he had set eyes on Lady Raquel Fortesque-Benton, he had looked beyond her obvious beauty and detected, beneath the proud stature, a very lonely and vulnerable woman. It was *that* quality which had first sparked a mild interest. Demian had said that her lips were like toffee, perpetually clammed shut. Thomas, more versed in such things, thought differently. He wondered how he could prove his theory without having to break his word to Demian. The lady would arrive at Darris Castle pure, if it was the last thing he achieved.

Lady Caroline Darris checked the diamonds at her throat. Yes, they sparkled superbly, as did the ruby ring, the hairpin of emeralds and the crescent of sapphire cabochons that hemmed together Lady Tryon's old court dress of gold filament on rose satin. She would not be seen *dead* in such a dreadfully coming ensemble in the ordinary scheme of things, but it seemed the merchant wives and their daughters were after vulgar-

ity, and vulgarity was something she could contrive to
see that they got. She almost giggled at her reflection,
especially as the servants' doors swung open, and His
Most Noble Grace, the fifth duke of Darris, afforded
her a glaring look of disbelief.

"I should have spanked you. Remind me to do so
when this is over."

"Very good, my lord." Caroline curtsied saucily—
for she was not in the *least* afraid of any threats from
Demian—then raised her hand in a languishing manner
and bade him announce her, forthwith.

At which her brother's brows drew together rather
ominously.

"Go, Demian! I'll warrant they are in a *fever* of anticipation!"

When His Grace threw open the doors of the breakfast room—as he had seen his footmen do several *hundreds* of times over—all eyes focused expectantly on
his countenance.

"Ladies, may I announce my mistress, the Honorable
Lady Caroline Darris. Proceed with your dinners."

Then Lady Caroline wafted in, all scent and silk, her
hands flowing languishingly in the air. She nodded a
brief dismissal to Pemberton, who eyed her closely,
then bowed himself out. If he had wished to linger,
perhaps, on a certain young lady in soft emerald green,
he was not given the chance. Besides, that lady, he'd
noted, with one swift, comprehensive sweep of the
room, was no longer seated. She was pacing about like
a caged animal and seemed to have no thought for any
of the delicacies that Caroline had managed to purloin
from his kitchens. Well, not *only* his kitchens. Also, he
mused, rather ruefully, his game forests, his lakes and
his cellars. Just as well he was betrothed to the lovely
Lady Raquel, else he would never recover the blow.
The thought cast him into such dire agonies of gloom

that he did not notice Miss Bancroft trailing down the stairs, a vision in a corsetted gown of stiff, ocher-striped cord. She had removed her traditional delicate, lace cap and was now wearing a starched white tippet in its place.

"A fine lady's maid I shall be," she grumbled, "if Caroline does not so much as let me brush her hair! Did you see what a tangle it was in when she made her grand entrance? I declare it was a disgrace!"

The duke's lips twitched. "Never mind, Martha, dear. I believe it was all obscured under a coronet of sorts."

Miss Bancroft, though delightful, was unfortunately of too serious a nature to know when the duke was jesting. Consequently, she replied rather earnestly that Caroline was wearing the famed Darris emeralds, a hairpin that, though not inconsequential, could not possibly be mistaken for a coronet.

The duke gravely allowed himself to be corrected and directed Miss Bancroft neatly from the breakfast room, from whence a great deal of chatter was emanating toward the kitchens.

"Oh, no! Caro will be needing my assistance."

"I think not! My little minx of a sister seems to be managing perfectly fine without either of us."

"But . . ."

"No buts about it, Miss Bancroft. The guests would certainly stare if the lady's maid entered for a meal."

This argument held a certain force, causing dear old Martha to chuckle a little at the notion.

"Oh, very well! But it is *very* ill managed! I should have masqueraded as the companion, rather."

Since she *was* the companion, the duke found himself in perfect agreement. Thus grumbling in mutual harmony, the unlikely pair found their way down to the kitchens, where Betsy had resumed her duties and the scullery maid dropped two of the duke's crystal goblets at this strange invasion. His Grace was swift enough to save one, but the second, unfortunately, sustained a severe chip to its rim, a fact that set the scullery maid wailing in his ear and the cook rushing over to alternately scold and curtsy.

"No, *don't* box her ears!" Demian broke in. "It was entirely my fault for scaring her."

The scullery maid seemed to brighten under such soothing words. She sent the cook a defiant glare. The cook, fortunately, did not notice. She was too busy gazing at her lord and master in his shirtsleeves. He was smiling at her in the most *endearing* of manners, so that it was no wonder her heart melted as quickly as the butter set aside for the lobster Périgord. For, though she had told Lady Caroline time and time again that *she did not approve of such havey cavey goings on,* the duke was impossible to resist—especially when he looked at you so, and took the hot kettle off the fire and mixed up some chocolate in a large jug, then set it upon the table invitingly, making it clear he meant *everyone* to sample it, not just his most revered self.

This they did, the groom, the scullery maid, the one remaining footman—though this was a rather grandiose title for the work he was now doing—several assorted housemaids, Betsy, Cook and Miss Bancroft. The rest of the stable hands and the remainder of the merchant ladies' maids were still to come in out of the snow.

His Grace signaled to his staff and apprised them, in a low voice, of the situation. He was not so vulgar as to mention the money involved, but indicated the matter was one of a wager. At that, the loyal skeleton of Darris retainers nodded wisely and muttered they would be "as mum as the grave"—a promise the duke had to be content with, for the Murgatroyd contingent of staff were all now entering en masse.

His grace felt very much like he was fighting a battle on two fronts, with suspicious eyes cast upon him from all sides. So he stood up, waved regally to the incoming crowd that they might take their seats, and beat a hasty retreat. Cook, he was sure, would be able to deal with impertinence from the lower orders. He was very sure that *he,* at this point, could not.

The cursed matter of the snow still bothered him, for though he was inclined to call Mrs. Murgatroyd's bluff and *not* offer succor for the night, it was increasingly obvious his options were limited. So, coming to a swift decision, he knocked upon the breakfast room door and entered.

The smell of roast duck was the first thing that assailed his senses. It was being served, in quantities, onto Mrs. Corey's plate, together with Cook's famous cherry sauce. Something told him he knew, at least, where the remainder of his Madeira had been sacrificed. Quelling the sudden urge to sit down and dine—he had ridden all day on an empty stomach, and had partaken of nothing since his light repast at Gentleman Jacks—he bowed stiffly and awaited Lady Caroline's notice.

She, capricious creature, seemed content to stuff herself languidly with fresh peaches from his hothouse and chatter to Mrs. Murgatroyd, seated on her right, about her desire for "complete lack of ceremony" in the household.

"Of course, when His Grace is in residence, all is quite different. I grow quite fatigued with the number of footmen who hover about us at every meal. Impossible to converse, of course."

Mrs. Murgatroyd looked about her. "Oh, I *wondered* why we served ourselves! Such a novelty, you know! In my house, dear Mr. Murgatroyd insists on a lackey at every setting!" She tittered. Mrs. Corey looked across at her, disapprovingly.

"My dear Honoria, *surely* you know that the most *genteel* of houses consider such displays vulgar? That is so, is it not, my dear, *dear* Lady Caroline?"

Lady Caroline steadfastly avoided catching her butler's eye. Instead, she smiled graciously, sipped a little wine—Demian thought she'd had *quite* enough—and avoided his eye. "Oh, quite so, quite so. Of course, there *are* occasions where one simply cannot have too much help. Entertaining the prince regent, for example, requires *both* His Grace's households to be in residence. Not Shrewsbury, of course—that is too far—but certainly all the *London* staff are necessary. Even several under butlers are hardly sufficient for an occasion such as that. We usually engage our housekeepers to take on whatever further staff they need. But then, of course, there are the liveries to be made up . . . oh, it is all so *drearily* fatiguing!"

Even Mrs. Corey appeared impressed.

"Do you entertain His Royal Highness often?"

"Oh, whenever he happens by Darris. He and the duke are such *particular* friends, you know."

His Grace, at that point, choked. A Corinthian of the first stare did not take kindly to being classed in the same category as the Prince of Wales. For His Royal Highness, despite being England's future king, was a rather frippery fellow, his finances in as poor a shape as his figure.

Lady Caroline frowned across the table. "Pemberton! Do you have some problem?"

"No, my lady. Begging your pardon, my throat was merely dry."

"Ah. Well. Perfectly understandable, I am sure." She then turned toward her dinner companions as if he were a mere fly on the wall.

"You were saying . . . eh . . . Mrs. . . . ?"

"Murgatroyd. Of Murgatroyd, Murgatroyd and Parsons, Inc." Mrs. Honoria Murgatroyd leaned forward across the damask. She was eager to impress her superior standing on the hapless Lady Caroline. It did not occur to her limited intelligence that Lady Caroline might not ever have *heard* of Murgatroyd, Murgatroyd and Parsons, Inc. She hadn't, but had the good sense not to say so. Instead, she managed a haughty, but vaguely interested, "indeed?" that seemed to satisfy Honoria, for she shot a smug glance at Miss Daphne Murgatroyd, as if to say, "there, *that* will make Lady Caroline take note!"

Amelia Corey seemed annoyed, for she tittered in rather a high voice and managed to mention, in passing, that although her family might not be as *famous*, perhaps, they at least had the distinction of being bankers.

Mrs. Corey laughed a little self-consciously. "Now, now, Amelia, my love, we must not put the Murgatroyds in a pelter, you know. It is not their fault, after all, that they smell so distressingly of the shop." She lifted her finger delicately in the air as she sampled some of Demian's prize champagne. "Ah, an excellent vintage, I believe."

But Mrs. Murgatroyd did not seem concerned with the vintage. She was engaged in glaring at Mrs. Corey, as though she were a viper.

Caroline, noticing that a skirmish might be about to take place, drew some of the other young ladies into the conversation, begging Miss Anderson to take another slice of game pie and answering Miss Fletcherson's carefully rehearsed questions with some rather obscure and imaginative answers. They would have had Demian in fits had he not been otherwise preoccupied.

"No, Miss Fletcherson, high poke bonnets are not in vogue at all, unless, of course, one was inclined for a picnic on the Thames, which the weather, these days, quite definitely precludes. . . . I personally favor an ensemble of capote and cottage bonnets, though of course, nothing can really rival the feathered turban." Demian did not wait to hear her strictures on the psyche knot versus the à la Titus mode, for his eyes were wandering, again, to the lady who had now stopped her pacing and seated herself rigidly across from the potted plant. She did not, he noted with approval, contribute *one* syllable to the nonsense that was patently being uttered around her.

In profile, she seemed almost more beautiful than Demian recalled. He wondered if she was aware of his staring at her, for though her back remained utterly straight, her fingers now fiddled with the silver dessert spoons. He walked over to her and leaned across her shoulder.

"May I be of assistance, madam?"

"No, I thank you. I am not hungry."

"You look pale. Would you like to withdraw to an antechamber?"

Her eyes startled. Demian thought rather ruefully that he had probably overstepped the mark a little. Butlers never made personal observations. It was fundamental to their creed.

"No." She hesitated, then looked up. He was still hovering over her solicitously. He filled her glass and their gazes locked for an instant.

Amy was shocked. The eyes that met hers had not been those of a butler. She did not know how she knew, only that she was certain of it. He was moving, now, from her setting, and edging quietly toward Miss Simmons in the crimson gown. Amy could not help feeling a sudden, disquieting sense of loss. There was no accounting for such foolishness. She took a sip of the champagne. It was sweet and fresh. Lemonade. How perceptive of him to make the switch! *And* how presumptuous! It was true, though. Another glass of the champagne would have brought on an almighty headache. Already, the room was feeling close and stuffy, and she rather wished that the fire had not been stoked so hot, inclement weather or not. If *only* she had not permitted herself to be persuaded into this excursion! Already it was hellish, and they had not yet *begun* to traipse through the galleries. And if Mrs. Murgatroyd was right, and they *did* manage to insinuate themselves into the castle overnight . . . oh! The thought was appalling!

She stood up, all of a sudden, a deep flush in her rosy cheeks. For an instant, she felt the room sway and she had the most galling sensation she might faint away. But then, she was being steadied by firm arms, and she did not have to look up to know that they belonged to that of the impeccably attired gentleman who was somehow passing himself off as the help.

Seven

"Allow me." The voice was quiet but firm. She nodded, hardly knowing what she was acquiescing to.

Lady Caroline, seated some several places down, looked up sharply. "Good Lord, the lady is as white as a sheet! Is she unwell? Shall I get her some—"

"Oh, no! *Dear* Lady Caroline, do not put yourself out on Miss Mayhew's account! I assure you, it is a nervous spasm of sorts. She is sadly prone to the megrims." Mrs. Corey tittered and Amelia shot Amy a *particularly* spiteful glance.

"Sit down, Amy. It is useless to put on die-away airs, you know. It is not as if His *Grace* is at table."

"No, to be sure, it is a great pity he is not, but indeed, my dear, even if he *were,* I am sure there is nothing more calculated to give a man a disgust of one than such coming airs! I am right, am I not, Lady Caroline?" Mrs. Corey preened and looked to Lady Darris, whom she obviously considered the ultimate voice of authority on such matters.

But Caroline, for once, was not even amused by the situation that made her the sole arbiter of fashion and decorum. Lord, up to this afternoon, she could not even remember to don a common bonnet, never mind employ a groom when riding about on the estate. Hardly etiquette the ton would approve of, but then, Mrs.

Corey knew nothing of the ton, not being privileged, as Lady Darris was, to move in the inner circles.

She therefore ignored Mrs. Corey's comment on gentlemen's preferences, and cast a meaningful look at Demian through her jewel-studded fringe. He nodded, ever so slightly, so she took up her cue and rather imperiously demanded that he lead Miss Mayhew out. A small imp of mischief beset her, however, so that instead of recommending him to one of the smaller drawing rooms, she rather improperly suggested a bedchamber. She ignored her brother's fulminating glance quite superbly before taking yet another sip of Darris Castle's finest.

"Take her up to the rose chamber, Pemberton. I am certain you can find some reviving sal volatile of sorts for the young lady. Oh! And you may take this envelope up to His Grace's apartments when you return." She handed him an envelope quite obviously *thick* with banknotes. The balance, he supposed, of the treacherous sum owing. He would avoid her eyes, otherwise he might laugh. Little minx!

Lady Caroline then dismissed them both with a regal waft of her hand that paid no attention at all to the faint protests from Miss Mayhew.

Making matters even *more* difficult for Amy, Lady Caroline rose from the table and invited her remaining guests, with a cordial but languid smile, to enter the first of several portrait galleries she hoped "might prove of invaluable interest."

There was nothing for it but for Miss Mayhew to allow herself to be led out of the breakfast room. She was fortunately spared many poisonous glares, for the ladies of her party were engaged in retrieving their reticules and fans and fur-lined tippets and smiling graciously upon their hostess. If she gave the matter any thought at all, she would have known that her own predicament was instantly forgotten in the general quest to begin the ducal exploration.

The duke said nothing as he led Miss Mayhew down several very thick-piled carpets, a glass herbarium and a marble gallery before arriving, finally, at the foot of a wide, spiral staircase. All the while, his arm just— only just—touched her elbow, so she drew strength from his presence without actually feeling the need to draw away. He moved quickly and confidently, slightly ahead of her, so Amy had an excellent view of his noble stature and entirely edifying physique without appearing either base, rude or overly curious. Nevertheless, she sensed a curve of amusement on his lips when they finally halted at the foot of the stairs and their eyes, unavoidably perhaps, collided.

"Sir, you shall think me a fraud! I feel perfectly fine, now, I assure you."

"Madam, I beg to differ, but you appear, to me, to be breathless."

There was a moment's pause where Amy felt *more* than just breathless. She felt positively *delirious,* and the sensation had nothing, whatsoever to do with the weather, cold or otherwise.

The butler smiled. "Might I not tempt you to a little peace and quiet? The rose chamber is situated with an excellent view onto my . . . uh . . . onto the forests. It is very restful, I assure you."

Amy thought she would feel anything but rested if she followed her inclination and allowed herself to be guided into the chamber. The wicked notion brought a sudden glow to her cheeks that the duke found interesting. Well, truth to tell, he found *everything* about the delicious Miss Amy Mayhew interesting, but he was wise enough—and cautious enough—to maintain a strictly subservient distance.

Her eyelashes fluttered, ever so slightly. His Grace

drew in his breath. Miss Mayhew was not being flirtatious, merely hesitant, and he realized that upon the instant, though his pulses still quickened annoyingly, just as if he were a green boy rather than a man of the world with a wealth of experience at his fingertips.

"I should get back to my party. This is a terrible imposition. I—"

"Might I speak for Lady Caroline when I say it is no imposition at all?"

Amy did not stop to wonder at the butler's presumption. She had long since dismissed his claim to be a mere butler, though quite *what* he was she failed to guess.

"Then I shall say yes, most thankfully. The ride and its"—she just stopped herself from saying "annoyances" and skillfully slipped in the word "excitements"—"has fatigued me, I fear."

"Then I shall ring for some hot water to be sent up, and I shall lay back the covers on the bed. Doubtless a nap shall revive you. Have you a lady's maid I may call upon?"

"No, for Mrs. Murgatroyd did not wish to go to the expense of an extra chaise. I shall be perfectly fine in a few minutes, truly."

But the butler did not appear to hear, for he led her up one further flight of steps, then threw open the rose chamber. It was very prettily decorated in a delicate fleur-de-lis pattern, with tiny pink rosebuds at the skirtings of both floor and ceiling. Amy looked longingly at the comfortable bed, with its sweet-smelling sheets and cherry-striped drapes that hung from their mahogany posts.

The duke set down the envelope and busied himself with the tinderbox, waiting silently for the fire to flare. The chamber, though clean, was nonetheless suffering from the same deficiency as *all* his rooms: biting cold.

"Leave that!" Amy's tone was sharp.

"Beg pardon?"

"Your . . ." she stopped, in confusion.

"Yes?" The gentleman took up a poker and began stoking the small blaze. When he moved to the coal scuttle, however, Amy showed renewed signs of agitation.

She colored up helplessly, but continued, nonetheless. "Your breeches. They shall be ruined."

A certain gleam appeared in Pemberton's eye. He continued with his task, though, until the cold room was perfectly cozy, and his offending nankeen breeches—cream, and utterly without crease—*were* a trifle blotchy from the exercise.

"See! I told you! Lighting fires is no work for a gentleman!" Amy scolded, for she was now hideously embarrassed at finding herself alone with this elegant nonpareil who, she was perfectly certain, had never worked a day in his life, never *mind* been butler to His Noble Grace.

"Ah, but I am not a gentleman, Miss Amy. The lower orders, you forget, do not count. It is therefore *perfectly* permissible for me to get my breeches dirtied in your service."

Despite her predicament, Amy's eyes twinkled.

"You are a rogue, sir, for drawing my attention to those unmentionables. Yes, yes, save your breath! I *know* it was I who first brought up the subject, but it was certainly *you* who chose to pursue it!"

Pemberton made some placating noises which included such humdrum phrases as "Begging the miss' pardon" and "no offense meant," he was sure, and "only doing his lawful duty," so that Amy wanted to either laugh or shake him. Certainly, he was an excellent remedy for her headache, for it had vanished completely.

"You can stop shamming it, sir! I may look in my first youth, but I assure you I was not born yesterday! You cannot—no matter how superior your talents— bam me into believing you are a commonplace butler." She laughed as he regarded her comically and said something whimsical under his breath. "No, no, sir! Not even a duke's butler. Not even, let us be blunt, a *king's* butler! Now, tell me, please, what—and I mean *what*—in the world happened to Lady Caroline's *actual* manservant? You have not, I trust, *murdered* him?"

"Murder? *I?*" His Grace contrived to look hurt even as he thought on his feet.

"Don't look so innocent, sir, or I shall certainly suspect the worst."

"Very well, then, I shall be plain with you, Miss Amy." His Grace straightened his shoulders and slightly—infinitesimally—regained something of the air of authority that Amy had first noticed about him.

She shook her head. "Miss Mayhew, you mean."

"Oh, very well then, if you must stand on ceremony . . ."

"I must." Amy's tone brooked no nonsense.

His Most Noble Grace cast her a glance of rueful appreciation.

"The flat truth is, Miss Mayhew, that Hedgewig, the Darris butler, is sadly under the hatches."

"Drunk, you mean?"

His Grace's eyes twinkled at her instant understanding of cant. She had brothers, then, the little Mistress Amy.

He nodded. "As a lord, madam, as the saying goes." He looked cheerfully unabashed as he set about drawing back the starched white bedcovers.

Amy flushed.

"Stop!"

"What *now?*"

"Surely you see how unacceptable it is for you to be performing such tasks? Indeed. . . ." She looked about her in sudden mortification. "Indeed, we had best return *immediately* to the guests! I shall be horribly compromised if we don't and you shall doubtless—"

"Be turned off without a character?" His voice was silky, smooth and a trifle laughing as he stood up from this, the most delightful and unsuitable of all chores yet assigned him.

"No! Worse! You shall be forced to marry me. I may be only of the merchant class, but I was reared as a lady and my Aunt Honoria has horrible hopes for me."

"Oh! Is that all? Then climb in, little Miss Mayhew, and I shall most *certainly* tuck you up."

Her lips twitched. "Sir, if you refuse to recognize the gravity of our situation, then I, at least, must be sensible!"

He moved away from the bed, closer to her, so that their eyes were level, although she was just slightly the shorter, so that where he looked down, she must needs look up, straight into those brilliant dark eyes, deep, perceptive and infinitely dangerous.

"Sensible?" His tone mocked her, for he could see her lips trembling, and the pulses racing about her pretty neck. Miss Mayhew may *pretend* to a serene calm, but her eyes betrayed her, and her fingers would not be stilled.

"Yes. Now, if you will excuse me, sir . . ."

"You do not even know my name!"

"No, for we have not been introduced. Do we move in the same circles?"

"Possibly. I think not."

"No, I am certain I would have remembered you."

He smiled. A little too jauntily, she thought.

"I shall take that as a compliment, madam, for I must tell you I am the greatest coxcomb at heart."

"Truly? Then it is as well you eat humble pie, today. A butler's life must be rather dreary."

"It has its compensations."

He was still looking down at her, and had not made so much as *one* move to release her gaze and exit the door, as must surely be the most admirable—and *sensible*—course.

"You are flirting, and I cannot abide flirts."

"You are teasing, and I cannot abide teases."

"I am *not* teasing!"

"Yes, you are! You *must* know that your hair is tumbling delightfully from your bonnet and that your lips curve in the most subtle manner imaginable. You are, in short, a menace, madam."

"A menace! Good God, I am nothing like it! My aunt calls me pert, at best. At worst, she calls me an intolerable bluestocking who is blessed with *none* of the gentler arts!"

"And which might *they* be?"

"Oh, the art of fascinating and driving sane men wild, and—"

"Your aunt lies."

"Beg pardon?"

"You heard me."

"You mean that *I* . . ."

"Precisely, Miss Mayhew."

There was a stunned pause. Then, ever honest, Amy regarded the duke.

"You are not exactly inestimable yourself."

He smiled at this faint praise and bowed. "I cannot say how you relieve me, Miss Mayhew!"

"Relief? I thought you said you were a coxcomb!"

"And so I am, in the ordinary way of things. But you forget, of course, that my unmentionables are filthy and that I am not standing on my credentials, which of course give me a decided advantage."

Had he said too much? His Grace did not altogether *want* Amy to guess who he was. It was fascinating, he found, to conduct a flirtation without his blasted rank standing in the way of everything.

"Are your credentials so unimpeachable, then?"

"Oh, decidedly so! They give me entrée into *most* drawing rooms."

"How felicitous."

"Yes, is it not? Though I am usually condemned to talk to either the companion or the potted plant."

Amy's lips twitched.

"How sad, and what a terrible waste! You must have very poor hostesses!"

"Alas, the lot of *all* impoverished gentlemen!"

"Ah, so you are impoverished."

The duke bowed, a little mockingly. Well, he spoke no more than the truth. And if it misled the fair Amy a smidgen, so much the better.

He expected her to withdraw a little. He *braced* himself for this, in fact, for Miss Mayhew was clearly a sensible girl and encouraging impoverished gentlemen masquerading as butlers was neither sensible nor prudent.

In his wildest dreams, he did not expect what happened next. It happened so quickly, too, that it was all over before he had collected his wits sufficiently to respond in a satisfyingly enthusiastic manner.

Miss Amy Mayhew, late of the emerald green traveling dress, flung her arms skyward, thereby tangling them in his excellently tied cravat, tilted her head slightly—thereby touching the shadows of his clean-shaven cheek—and kissed him. Not brazenly, not wantonly, not even carelessly or exotically. No, just swiftly and deliciously, with a rare smile of sweetness that knocked the duke out more decidedly than even the gesture itself.

"There! *That* should make up for all the potted plants! And now, my dear sir, you really *must* allow me to rejoin my party."

She seemed to have no fears that he might have any wicked designs upon her person. Indeed, the thought had not crossed her mind. Or rather, if it had, it had been entirely in the sense of her being a willing participant in all this debauchery. Which of course was nonsense, just as it was to suggest that the impoverished gentleman would not be all that was perfectly chivalrous, if not entirely proper.

"No so fast, Miss Mayhew! Has no one ever told you that you cannot do that to a gentleman—however poor his pocketbook—and not expect repercussions?"

"Repercussions?" Miss Amy regarded him blandly, but it was quite clear to both that her pulses were racing horribly and her smile, though pretty, was undoubtedly a trifle wobbly.

"Repercussions." Demian was quite firm as he made this remark. Then, flinging all thought of the Honorable Lady Raquel Fortesque-Benton to one side for a moment, he took Miss Mayhew's chin in hand and regarded her thoughtfully.

Miss Mayhew did not wriggle, or slap him, or any of the undeniable things she ought to have done. Instead, she stood perfectly still and regarded him stare for stare with as much composure as she could muster with a heart that was spinning cartwheels.

"Step a little closer, Miss Mayhew."

"If I were any closer I would be nestled in your arms, Mr. . . . ?"

"Hartford." The duke conveniently supplied her with one of his lesser titles.

"Mr. Hartford, then." Amy said it softly, as though tasting the name to herself. The duke could not help but smile, though his eyes never left Amy's for an instant.

"You are obviously blessed with no mean intelligence, Miss Mayhew. Your assessment of the matter is entirely correct."

"That I will be nestled in your arms?"

"Precisely."

"I must tell you, sir, that this is very improper behavior for one raised such as myself."

"Is it, indeed? How very unfortunate. Nevertheless, you shall do it."

His Grace's voice was quietly compelling. Amy was just about to comply when a shadow appeared at the half-open door. The duke looked up in annoyance, only to find Miss Bancroft bustling about in a fever of agitation, flushing to the roots and murmuring something unintelligible about "counting linen."

The moment was lost, and neither, truth to tell, was entirely sorry. Amy was relieved that she had not been so foolish as to lose all her carefully nurtured decorum, and the duke—though struggling a little with his breathing—was glad he had not committed the unutterable social solecism of finding himself betrothed to *two* young ladies of inestimable quality. For there was no doubt in his mind that had Miss Bancroft not timely intervened, his heart would have ruled his passionate, curly, dark head.

This did not stop him from *glaring* at poor Miss Bancroft, who had been sent on this particular errand by a laughing Caroline. It had just struck his naughty sibling that while ordering him there in the first place had been the greatest of good giggles, compromising Miss Mayhew's virtue—not to mention his own—was another matter entirely. So, she had excused herself from the amble through the Gothic library—all banisters and curves and dark, arched windowpanes—and hurried to find Martha, who could be relied upon in just such an emergency.

Thus it was that Miss Bancroft now appeared, and by the look of her stormy gray eyes, the duke would be in for a *thundering* scold when the delectable Miss Mayhew had been returned to the bosom of her party.

Now, however, it was *his* turn to glare, for truly, a less suitable moment to be pouring over lists of bed linen he could not imagine.

"You forget, Your—"

"Mr. Hartford." He spoke quietly, but with such rigor that even dear, dithering, entirely respectable Martha took his meaning at once.

"You forget, Mr. . . . er . . . *Hartford,* that it is imperative we look over the bed linen! Then there are all the blankets to be aired and we will need to organize hot bricks. The kitchens will be in a spin to get pails of hot water up here at a moment's notice—"

"Pardon me for interrupting, but I believe your concerns are all groundless. The party, as I understand it, is leaving before dark." The duke's tone was even, so Miss Mayhew was not able to read what was behind the inscrutable words.

The lady in the dark stuff seemed more agitated than ever. Poor Martha had encountered the combined forces of Mrs. Murgatroyd and the equally overbearing Mrs. Corey in the gallery. Though they considered her of little account, they had nonetheless made it plain to her—and to all who could hear—that they had precious little intention of removing to the inn.

"The snow seems to be halting, for the moment, but Mrs. Murgatroyd fears for another flurry."

"She *would!*" the duke said this under his breath, but there was no doubt that Miss Amy's eyes lit up in sudden appreciation.

"We can put three of the young ladies in the west wing chambers with—"

"No!"

"No?" Martha looked up in some surprise. "They have the sunniest aspect, Your . . . I mean, Mr. Hartford. . . ."

"That they might have, but I forbid it, nonetheless. The west wing is reserved exclusively for His Grace. I cannot think that he will be happy to return to residence and find Mrs. Corey ensconced in his private wing."

Martha smiled at this vehement understatement, the last traces of her frown vanishing.

"How true!" Then she smiled at the duke, as if daring him to countermand her next unarguable phrase.

"But I fear His Grace will not return for a sennight at least. Lady Caroline mentioned something of the kind to me."

What Lady Caroline had *mentioned,* of course, was the impudent letter she had penned practically *ordering* Demian to stay away. Demian knew this, for his eyes twinkled outrageously, so Miss Bancroft was hard put not to either blush or give the game away completely by proceeding with her scold.

In the event, neither calamities occurred, for Demian took the lists from her hand and consigned them all to the devil, remarking that if the weather turned foul, they would have no option but to house the party in the south wing.

"But that has been in holland covers for a year at least!"

Demian took up the envelope full of banknotes and slipped it in his jacket pocket.

"Then I fear it shall be dusty." The duke's tone was suddenly unsympathetic. Martha looked up at him sharply. Though his eyes were hooded and entirely unreadable, she could swear his lips quirked. It was just a fleeting notion, gone quite suddenly, and almost as swiftly, she could swear, as it had come.

Eight

Mr. Thomas Endicott was not quite certain how to proceed. For once in his life, he was at that interesting kind of crossroads that could lead him anywhere, and frankly, for the life of him, he was not certain where he wanted to be led. This was both annoying and charming to him, for it stripped him of his natural arrogance—annoying—but it also promised of adventure—charming. So, he tossed back an excellent glass of Madeira, shook hands with Lord Darrincourt—whom he had just beaten to smithereens in a game of chance—and checked the time.

Ten past eleven. Early, perhaps, but if he was to beat the snow he had no time to waste. Consequently, he returned to his town house in Grosvenor Square, where he lost no time at all in donning a casual—but becoming—pair of doeskin breeches. He also tossed on a hunting jacket of elegant crimson with brass buttons, rummaged through his drawers for a cravat—despite his enormous wealth he did not hold with valets—and came up with something that was remarkably well starched for its habitual level of abuse. Mr. Endicott was no fool. Though he shunned the services of a valet, he very gratefully accepted those of his housekeeper and several upper chambermaids. They all spoiled him horribly.

At noon, precisely, he left his calling card for Lady

Raquel Fortesque-Benton. He was permitted to kick
his heels in the receiving room for quite a quarter of
an hour before he was honored with her presence. She
wore a spencer of turquoise jaconet with dainty little
half boots to match. Her hair, he noticed, was elegantly
braided, though a little too severe for his taste. Despite
this defect, the matching ribbons that curled gaily down
to her waist were delightful, and softened her classical
features admirably. She cast a sheer silk shawl of azure
blue carelessly across a chaise longue and folded her
arms.

The hardened Mr. Endicott, quite used to all variants
of feminine beauty, was startled.

"Good day, Mr. Endicott! You have come, I hope, to
account for your disgraceful manners last night!"

His lips curved in an appreciative smile. So, it was
to be daggers drawn, then. Very well.

"No, Lady Raquel. Quite the contrary."

Lady Raquel flushed. Mr. Endicott was the most disconcerting, unaccountable, boorish man alive. She had
been expecting sonnets and received an insult for her
pains.

"I apologize, Mr. Endicott. For a moment I'd forgotten, of course, that you are not . . . high bred."

For an instant, Thomas's eyes flashed. Then they became as cold as the ones surveying him. If her lips had
not been trembling, he might *well* have been deceived
into believing the woman was heartless. But those
beautiful, perfectly pink lips *were* trembling, so Mr.
Endicott stayed the biting retort that had risen instantly
to his tongue. Instead, he surveyed her as if she were
a mere cockroach, or at the very least, a thing of no
interest.

Lady Raquel burned with anger, but also with something quite foreign to her: the desire to gain Mr. Endicott's complete respect. She told herself this was only

so that she could gain the upper hand over him, but of course, as was her habit, Lady Raquel was not always quite honest with herself.

"I beg your pardon. That was ill judged of me."

"Yes, it was." Thomas did not give her quarter. He stared at her hard, until the flush rose to her cheeks and the angry fretfulness returned in full force.

"I expect you called for a reason?"

"Indeed, yes. I have left a bouquet of winter florals for you with the butler. A confection of mistletoe and snowdrops, I believe."

"Oh!" Surprise mingled with pleasure on Lady Raquel's handsome countenance. Thomas thought that if she smiled more, she could be very beautiful, indeed. Outrageously beautiful. He caught his breath. He was not, he remembered, to get emotionally tangled.

"How very fine of you, sir!"

"It will be just one of a dozen, I am certain."

"Yes, but . . ." Lady Raquel stopped in confusion. Thomas stepped toward her. "But . . . ?"

"Nothing. Oh, nothing." Her eyes grew wider still at his closeness. She could smell tobacco and soap upon his person. It was a fascinatingly masculine combination. He tilted her chin up in his fingers. Raquel's breath caught.

"Ah, I see. How charming. We are back to 'nothing' as an acceptable form of discourse."

For a moment, she did not understand him, for his lips were achingly close to her own and he spoke in a wry whisper that she had to strain to hear over the sudden beating of her normally, *extremely* well-modulated heart.

Then she saw the mockery in his devilish blue eyes once again.

"You are a beast, sir!"

"Yes, so you have said. The conversation grows tedious." He released her chin from the palm of his exquisitely gloved hands.

Instantly, it tilted defiantly and she stepped back a few paces.

"You have delivered your little posy. Please don't let me keep you from any of your pleasures."

"Is that a polite way of dismissing me?"

She curtsied, a small glint of triumph entering her sapphire eyes. "I believe so, sir."

"Well, *I* believe it is nothing of the kind. It is damnably *impolite*, not to mention impertinent. But *whilst* we are on the subject of impertinence, my lady, I take leave to inform you that you are *not* keeping me from my . . . uh . . . pleasures."

She eyed him suspiciously. Mr. Endicott was not like any other gentleman she knew. She could not guess immediately either at his meaning or his intentions. He was like an annoying wisp of quicksilver. Lady Raquel was at a loss to know why she cared.

"I am not?"

"No, for there is nothing that gives me greater pleasure than taming a woman, Lady Raquel."

His eyes held a fascinating light that Lady Fortesque-Benton was somehow compelled to explore. She was not sure she *liked* what was in their depths, but she could not dismiss it with the haughty abandon to which she was prone.

"Don't gaze too deeply, Lady Raquel. You are like a moth—a beautiful moth—to a golden flame."

"Beg pardon?"

Mr. Endicott smiled, but the curve of his lips was dangerous rather than tender. "Often, the fascinating is also the deadly. I give you fair warning, Lady Raquel."

Again, the dark, silky tone that sent tingles up Lady Raquel's spine. Somehow, she liked this more than the complete indifference she had detected earlier. Perverse! Totally perverse, of course, for what could she care what an untitled nobody thought of her when she was about to become the foremost peeress of the realm?

She tossed her head. "I have no notion of what you may mean, Mr. Endicott."

"Have you not? I am tempted to show you, but of course, your own parlor, in the presence of your butler and your house staff is not a particularly felicitous venue. I am surprised there is not a chaperon."

"There *would* have been, had I known the company I was going to be subjected to!"

"Come, come, Lady Raquel! You are sulking, and I cannot abide the sulks."

"Can you not? I shall endeavor to remember that and practice my most *sullen* of pouts for your edification."

Thomas was torn between shaking the girl and laughing.

"Not advisable, Lady Raquel, but there, I have already warned you once. Practice all the sulks you like—it will keep me in your mind the whole day, I warrant."

"Oh, you are insufferable!"

He bowed. "That, I believe, is true."

"Don't you care?"

"Not particularly." He afforded her a handsome smile. She tossed her head.

"Do you still wish to view the castle at Darris?" His turn of conversation startled her. She dropped the theatrics, therefore, and turned on him questioningly.

Thomas had to step back, for the moment could not have been more perfect to catch her in his arms and kiss her thoroughly. This, of course, he was pledged not to do, so he stepped back and placed his hands in the pockets of his hunting jacket, an offense that would have had Weston, its maker, in fits.

Lady Raquel, for once, did not reproach him. Her thoughts were not on the cut of his rather handsome crimson coat, but on the sudden change of conversation. She was surprised at the pang she felt when Thomas spoke of Darris. Almost, she had forgotten.

"Of course I do." Well, she did, did she not? It was her most *earnest* desire to see the castle she was to become chatelaine of. It was the culmination of all her girlish dreams, in fact. To become a duchess, to be loftier in rank than even the Countess Esterhazy, and Lady Sefton, to be received in all the royal houses throughout Europe . . . oh, yes, quite *definitely* she wanted to see it!

"Yes, yes, of course I do. His Grace must have spoken to you of it."

"More than that. Demian asked me to convey you there."

"You!"

"Don't look so revolted, Lady Raquel! If we leave now, we should be at Darris before midnight. Eleven hours in my company is not, I assure you, too hard to endure."

"It is too late to travel!"

"If we do not travel today, then *certainly* it will be too late. I'll warrant that the first snows are already falling up north. If we leave it any longer, Darris will be snowbound and you will have to remain in London for the remainder of the season."

"No! I most particularly wish to view Darris. I believe I made that plain to His Grace."

"Yes, I believe you did. That is why he has charged me with conveying you there. If you wish to change your mind, however, I am perfectly amenable."

Mr. Endicott schooled his features to a studied indifference. So well did he succeed that Lady Raquel could almost have sworn he wished her to Jericho. It was all very unnerving, especially to one who was used to her every whim being attended to with due reverence and devotion. She wished very much to tell the arrogant man that she would find her *own* way to Darris, but she did not dare. It was likely her mama would fret and make a hundred objections and then the whole scheme would have to be shelved on account of the detestable weather. Mr. Endicott, she felt perfectly certain, would not have the decency to organize a thing on her behalf. Then there were the horses that would need changing. . . . Oh, it was impossible!

She played for time. The rain, to her, did not look too severe. It was certainly chilly, but snow was probably a figment of plain Mr. Thomas Endicott's overactive imagination.

"I can't simply take your arm and step out of this house. I shall need to pack."

"Certainly you will. But Demian says not to worry about more than a simple portmanteau. Doubtless there is all you will require up at the castle."

A flat lie, Thomas knew, but Lady Raquel did *not*, he thought, know the true extent of Demian's finances. He would authorize Lady Raquel to spend what she willed at Darris—there were several very expert seamstresses in the village—then charge the lot to himself.

"But a chaperon . . ."

Thomas smiled. "Very wise, Lady Raquel. I see you are heeding my advice to be wary. Very well, then, you may choose whatever chaperon you please, but be ready in one hour precisely. I don't like to leave my horses waiting and they have already been strutting their paces in the forecourt this half-hour at least."

"Oh! Well, if your horses are more important than me . . ."

Thomas quirked an irritating eyebrow at her. Drat the man, he was not possessed of the commonest civility!

"I will be ready in half an hour." She kept her voice as cold as ice. She hoped it would freeze his very marrow. But Mr. Endicott seemed amused, rather than chilled.

"I said an hour, child. That will be perfectly acceptable."

Oh! He was *so* annoying! Lady Raquel inclined her head regally and moved toward the door. Mr. Endicott admired the white pearl buttons that started at the nape of her neck, then ambled their way gently down the full length of her spine to the very arch of her delectable back.

"Lady Raquel . . ."

"Yes?"

"Do try not to wear a gown with such a plethora of fastenings when we travel. It will take you a half hour at least to get dressed."

Thomas wondered, silently, how long it would take her to get *un*dressed. That was the point, he supposed, of those innumerable, enticing little pearls. They made any full-blooded male wonder . . .

"I have said I will be ready, Mr. Endicott. What trimmings I choose will be my choice entirely."

Lady Raquel's voice was sweet, but Thomas was not fooled. He was positive that if she had been a man, he would even now be feeling the sharp side of a very dangerous sword. Thankfully, however, she was *not* a man, for if she were, Mr. Endicott would have been at a loss to describe his sudden soaring spirits.

Well! Feeling that she had got the better of the detestable man at last, Lady Raquel caught up her shawl in an elegant movement that caused the length of silk to billow after her in a fashionable swathe of azure.

She then firmly shut the door on his obnoxiously hand-some person. He did not open the door after her, but she felt her heart beating as fast as if he had. When she recovered her composure, she looked at the hall clock and gasped. Two minutes gone already. For the first time in her well-bred life, Lady Raquel threw cau-tion to the wind and actually *bolted* up the stairs.

The door to her chamber was already open. An under housemaid bobbed a curtsy as Raquel entered, her sheer shawl trailing behind her in soft flurry of satin trim. She hardly noticed, for her piercing eyes were already upon the tall, competent-looking woman within.

"Where is her ladyship?"

Lady Raquel's dresser looked up from the assort-ment of gloves she was critically reviewing. By her expression, none seemed to find the smallest degree of favor.

"Your mama?"

Raquel nodded impatiently.

"She has called on Lady Dantry. I really think we should discard the lilac. I cannot think the color favors you."

For once, Lady Raquel paid her no heed. "Never mind that. Did she say when she would be back?"

"No, my lady. Only that Stevens is not to wait up, for she might take a day trip down to Astley's with Lady Dantry's niece."

Raquel nodded as the gloves were all scattered about her bed and her expert dresser—a gaunt, thin lady with steel-colored hair—glided toward her. Raquel offered her her back, so that the poker-faced minion knew at *once* what was expected. It did not take long before the elegant Lady Fortesque-Benton was reduced to her smallclothes. She stepped into a fresh, sweet-smelling hooped petticoat and nodded thoughtfully.

"Very well, then. Maria shall have to be my chaperon. I am going out of town for a few days. To Darris."

Raquel's tone was crisp, but a small, rather satisfied smile hung over her lips.

There was a little gasp from her dresser, who was not so behind hand with the world as not to *immediately* fathom what this might mean.

"Oh, your ladyship! Has His Grace . . . I mean . . ."

"Now, now, Anders, you know I don't hold with gossip!" But there was a certain sparkle about Lady Raquel that spoke volumes. The dresser would have been astonished to learn that the sparkle had more to do with the infinitely tiresome gentleman belowstairs than with any intended betrothal. Consequently, she drew her own conclusions and laid out Lady Raquel's most modish rose satin. It was not, perhaps, the most suitable as a carriage dress, but it had style. Lady Fortesque-Benton's dresser was in no doubt that style was more desirable, in these fortuitous circumstances, then serviceability.

"Not that one!"

"But it is the very latest of Madame De Haviland's creations! It shall look charming on you! See, here, we shall add that tortoiseshell comb to the arrangement."

"I want the blue organdy." Lady Raquel's bow-shaped lips closed firmly. It was not that she did not *like* the rose satin, indeed, she had positively longed for her first opportunity to wear it. It was just that it fastened in the front with a confection of bows, and she most particularly desired buttons. Yes, of all things, she wanted rows and rows of shining buttons. And they must, of course, all fasten—every little one of them—at the back.

The dresser did not argue. Rather, she set about finding the appropriate garment and searching out the matching traveling bonnet of delicate straw. This she did with great efficiency, even as Lady Raquel pulled on a pair of delicately wrought silk stockings. Then, it was the turn of a pair of long, powder-blue gloves so that it was practically no time at all before the gown and bonnet were laid out and ready.

The dresser rang for Maria, barked a few orders at an upper chambermaid who was charged with the business of packing, and began the finicky matter of the buttoning. Lady Raquel eyed the ormolu clock on her mantel. She refused to acknowledge how terrified she was of being late. She was perfectly certain Mr. Endicott would leave without her if she kept him waiting a moment longer than the hour.

When Maria entered, her face was looking suspiciously puffy, and her eyes were pink, as if she had just been crying. Lady Raquel had her face to the mirror, so she did not immediately perceive her maid's difficulty.

"Maria, you are to chaperon me to Darris. Mr. Endicott informs me that though it is a long carriage trip, the roads are pleasant. We leave in half an hour, so make all haste, if you please."

Maria cast a miserable glance at the dresser, but *that* formidable lady was too busy fastening her ninety-first button to pay her the smallest attention.

So, Maria turned in miserable silence to her mistress. Lady Raquel turned from the mirror to smile at her, for though she was undoubtedly selfish, she was not unkind.

"Maria! You look positively hag ridden."

Maria had no notion of her mistress's meaning, but she sensed, by the tone, a smidgen of compassion. So she sniffed into her handkerchief and bobbed a small curtsy of confusion.

"Are you ill?"

"No, milady. I am just bothered with the toothache."

Lady Fortesque-Benton smiled surprisingly gently. "A little, or are you in agonies, Maria?"

Maria, who thought she could suffer any sort of agony when her mistress smiled at her so, lied bravely and muttered that it was "nothing that some tooth powder and a little of Cook's gin could not solve."

"You are certain? I could take Anders, here, if you are *very* unwell."

The dresser glared, for there was *one* thing she hated above all others and that was being dislodged from her lady's changing room and being forced to gad about the countryside in all weathers. Besides being uncomfortable, for however well-sprung a chaise might be, it did *not* shield one from bumps and lurches, and the whole suggestion was beneath her station. Ladies' dressers were hired exclusively for that occupation. They did *not,* under any circumstances, double as chaperons.

Maria was no match for Anders. She positively quailed under her glare.

"Yes, milady."

"Good!" Raquel breathed an inward sigh of relief and glanced at the maid sympathetically. "Ask Cook for a cold compress, but go easy with that gin. And hurry, we have precious little time."

The hall clock chimed, so Raquel had no need to consult the ormolu clock again. Her fingers flew through her hair as she swept it up into a topknot. Her dresser could have wept.

"Mind your precious curls, milady! Here, I am on the last catch. I shall do that myself."

"No, no, there is no time, no time. Pass me the bonnet."

"Not before you have put in several more of those hairpins, I thank you!" Anders sounded outraged. "You cannot go jaunting about the countryside with your hair spilling all over your face. Your father—a great man, Lord Fortesque-Benton—will have my head. No, no, not there. Leave the pins, my lady, I shall have to brush it through myself. Maria . . ."

But Maria had gone. And Lady Raquel was grabbing at the silver-handled hairbrush and tossing it onto the bed with scant regard for decorum.

The dresser stared.

Lady Raquel's mouth curved. "I am in a hurry, Anders! I believe I may have *mentioned* that fact!"

And so it was that precisely one hour and two minutes later, Lady Raquel Fortesque-Benton, one traveling companion, three portmanteaus and a bandbox, several baskets of fruit and a novel from Hookham's lending library trailed down the polished stairs.

Mr. Endicott's fob snapped shut. His eyes caught Lady Raquel's, who quailed before their stern glint. She braced herself for some morsel of scathing reproof, but heard none. Instead, he inclined his handsome head politely, so that Lady Raquel did the unthinkable. She turned all missish and blushed, much to the amazement of Maria, who despite her toothache knew enough to know that Lady Fortesque-Benton was fabled for her icy composure.

Then, without comment, he helped with two of the baskets and signaled to the attendant footmen. They instantly stepped forward and strapped the luggage to the back of the carriage.

"Have you a pelisse and muff?"

"In the bandbox."

"A pity. You shall need them, the roads will get icy."

"I shall be perfectly comfortable, thank you."

Mr. Endicott surveyed her proud stature with some amusement. He showed no indication that he had noticed the stream of golden buttons down her excellent back. Lady Raquel looked annoyed.

"Nevertheless, we shall retrieve them at the first posting inn."

Her ladyship's eyes flashed, but she said nothing, merely seating herself in the farthest corner of the supremely comfortable chaise.

Mr. Endicott helped Maria in with great politeness. His brow raised slightly as he caught a sniff of what his expert palate determined immediately to be an illegal variant of some form of King's gin. He said nothing, however, for the girl looked ready to weep. Doubtless Lady Raquel had been bullying her mercilessly.

"Good. We are ready, then." A swift word to the postilions up front and he was upon them again, this time taking up a seat directly opposite from her ladyship, so that if she did not want to catch his eye—as doubtless the little minx wouldn't—she would have to continue gazing out of the dull, rain-soaked window all afternoon.

Mr. Endicott hoped, rather politely, that she would not strain her neck. In response for his kindness, he received something very close to an unladylike snort. Being a charitable sort of fellow, he ignored the choked response and settled peacefully into considering himself entirely mistaken. Lady Raquel, he was certain, had merely delicately coughed.

Nine

"I shall return you, now, to the guests, Miss Mayhew. Doubtless they are engaged in inspecting the cellars, for I would wager a farthing they were rated high on Lady Caroline's interesting itinerary."

The duke cast a wry glance at Miss Bancroft, whose hands were fluttering in disorganized panic to the starched white ruffle at her throat. She coughed, then frowned severely at him for his levity. The duke, *most* unfortunately, appeared not to notice.

"They were, were they not, Miss Bancroft?"

The rotund lady in the prim ocher gown found herself forced to reply.

"Yes, among other things."

She glared at Demian, Lord Darris, repressively, for he was clearly enjoying himself at Amy's expense. "I believe the herbarium and the turrets at the east tower were also considered to be of passing interest."

The duke made a small movement. "Then we shall start at the top."

Again, a panicked flurry of hands. "No, no! You shall remain here, my lor . . . eh . . . Mr. Hartford. *I* shall locate the others and return Miss Mayhew to the company. There is no need—none at all—to trouble yourself any further."

If Miss Bancroft could look fierce, she would have. Instead, her face creased into a million charming wrinkles, though her eyes appeared determined. She had not forgotten, after all, the reason Caro had sent her here. She was to separate the duke and dear Miss Mayhew before any further calamities occurred.

"Oh, but there is *every* need, Miss Bancroft."

The duke was not to be put off so easily. A soft smile hovered about his eyes as his gaze rested upon his guest's charming, dark fringe.

Amy met his stare evenly.

"I must ask you a tremendous favor . . . sir."

"Must you?"

Glowing dark hair nodded in decision. The duke noted with approval that though it was cropped, it nevertheless looked decidedly feminine as it brushed against merino-clad shoulders. Her color was still distressingly high, he noted. She was flushed, but he doubted, now, whether she would actually faint. Removing her from the company had certainly been justified.

"Is it far to the nearest watering post?"

The question startled him.

"Not terribly. Some few miles to the Lion and Anvil, I would imagine."

"Is the snow likely to hold?"

"It is hard to say, Miss Mayhew. I would say that this is certainly probably the lull before the storm, but the storm itself may not break until tomorrow."

"Yes, I see that. If I leave now, I shall make it before any further flurries."

"You *can't* leave now. The grooms are all resting and the horses would need to be harnessed again."

Demian, who had been mentally cursing these necessities a moment before, for he had been calculating how soon he could get rid of his *other* unwanted visitors, now looked alarmed.

"Does . . ."

"Yes?" The duke looked into troubled eyes inquiringly. They were slate gray, again, and had lost all the fascinating hints of silver. For all that, though, they remained compelling.

"Does . . . do you think . . . I mean, would it be an awful imposition of me to borrow a horse?"

There was a moment's stunned silence.

"A horse?"

"Yes. It doesn't have to be a very fine one, for I understand His Grace's stables were . . . are . . . I mean . . ."

"What I think you mean to say, Miss Mayhew, is that it is well known His Grace has had to make a few economies. Is that it?"

She nodded.

Miss Bancroft interjected at this moment.

"Oh, my dear child, you cannot think to be out *riding* in this weather! It is impossible!"

"Not so impossible as staying, madam. I am accustomed to riding, but I beg you to believe I had no notion that . . . that . . ."

"That the Murgatroyd woman could be so unscrupulous?"

She flashed him a piercing look. "I did not say that, sir!"

"No, but you *should* have. Miss Mayhew, do you think you have received your two hundred pounds worth?"

"Beg pardon?"

"You heard me. Have no fear, I am entirely in Lady Caroline's confidence in this matter."

"Sir, the money should never have changed hands. I regret it was ever so." But now her eyes dropped, and the telltale flutter of her lashes told His Grace that Miss Amy, though undoubtedly very beautiful, and adorably fetching, was nevertheless not being quite truthful.

The stern expression vanished from his countenance.

"Regret, Miss Mayhew? Regret? That is an extremely harsh word. Have a care that my feelings are not too wounded!"

Then the silver returned to her eyes as a small smile curved her lips.

"Oh, not meeting you, sir, but *pushing* my way into the household! It is truly untenable to me. My only relief is that His Grace is presently out of town. I could not have borne the mortification if he were not. No, *nor* the triumph in Mrs. Corey's eyes!"

"It is as well that he is gone, then. But come, think a little. You have had an excellent repast, it is true, but you nibbled like a bird." Here, the duke turned to Martha, who was eying both Demian and Miss Mayhew with a thoughtful expression. His Grace, quite fortunately, did not appear to notice. He was teasing.

"It is true, is it not, Miss Bancroft? She nibbled."

Martha could only shrug her shoulders. She was finding the whole conversation fascinatingly beyond her comprehension, but the strange thought that had struck her earlier prevailed. She nodded, a small smile lurking behind her very proper exterior.

"There, I told you. Let me see, now . . . a smidgen of grouse, two carrots glazed in Cook's excellent sugar cream sauce, a tiny—*tiny,* mark you—nibble of veal, and two glasses of champagne. Let me work at this. Even calculating in the nobility of the residence, the attendance of one fake butler and two bona fide footmen, the outstanding vintage of the champagne and the undoubtedly regal settings—Sevres china, you understand—I cannot tally the total expenditure to be worthy of more than forty of your excellent pounds. Naturally, you took in His Grace's outstanding marble statues, the most notable of these being Venus and Androcles at the entrance, and some of the lesser works within, throw in, perhaps, the charm of the chandeliers and the honor of the freezing receiving room . . ."

The duke had the felicity of hearing a giggle.

"Must you be so nonsensical!"

"I am only showing you, quite properly, my dear, that you have not yet had your money's worth of the entertainments."

"Oh, I have! You forget, sir, my glass of freshly squeezed lemonade. Be assured I would have sipped more had I known that my every morsel was being observed. And by the by, I did *not* have the grouse. I merely passed the plate on to Miss Amanda Simmons."

"Very wise. I shall credit your account with one further pound."

"Why?"

"Oh, I have it on the best authority—myself—that the grouse was tough."

In spite of herself, Miss Mayhew laughed. The duke found the sound quite delightful and was tempted to dream up more nonsenses for her edification.

He was prevented from doing so by a squawking Miss Bancroft, who gazed anxiously at the door. Much as she was inclined to *encourage* this unlikely couple, Lady Caro's trust hung heavily upon her shoulders. If Miss Mayhew was compromised by any lack of diligence on her behalf, she would never forgive herself.

"Perhaps I can show Miss Mayhew His Grace's private collection of the Masters. *That* shall make up for any deficiencies in the meal, one would hope."

"One hundred and sixty-one pounds worth? I doubt it. You will have to escort her to the library, I am afraid. There is an original copy of *Pilgrim's Progress* to be found there. I believe His Grace also collects first editions."

"Oh!" Amy's eyes widened. "How I would *love* to see them! But it is an absurdity, of course. I would no sooner encroach on His Grace's private collections than on his castle."

Mr. Hartford adjusted his immaculate cravat. The effect was so breathtaking it constricted Amy's throat.

"Have it your way, of course. But I venture to suggest, Miss Mayhew . . ."

"Yes?" The eyes were definitely silver, now, and the lips were parted just slightly.

The duke hesitated. "I would suggest, Miss Mayhew, that it would be quite unkind of you to leave."

"Unkind? How so?"

"Contrary to what you may have heard—and by the by, a pretty female like you should *not* be gossiping— His Grace is a very honorable gentleman. If you have not had your money's worth, he will naturally be compelled to return your purse."

"Oh, what nonsense! Consider the remaining one hundred and sixty-one pounds compensation, then, for the loan of a horse."

"Utter balderdash! There is no horse, save one, in His Grace's stables worth the price."

"Then I will take *that* one!"

"You will not, for it is Season's Glory, the duke's personal mount. He goes nowhere without it." Demian could have bitten his tongue for this obvious slip, but Amy did not seem to notice. The fact that the duke was supposedly in London while his mount was stabled at Darris did not immediately register.

"Botheration! Then I *am* in a fix."

"Precisely. Why don't you join your party and make the best of it. You will be doing the duke a favor, I assure you."

"Just as I was doing my *aunt* a kindness in acquiescing to this ridiculous excursion. Do you know, she wanted me to sparkle at dusk like a sylph, solely, I am told, for His Grace's edification?"

At this, Martha gasped in horror, but the duke could not suppress an appreciative grin. This naturally brought down the wrath of heavens from a proper spirited Miss Bancroft, who knew very well that the duke was engaged in precisely the wild imaginings she had been sent to dampen.

"Come with me, Miss Mayhew! Mr. Hartford is being *very* unchivalrous in keeping you from your amusements! I believe, if we go swiftly, we shall not miss out on the fabulous gargoyles, though the weather is unfavorable for any of the more interesting *outdoor* pursuits. . . ."

Amy smiled. "Miss Bancroft, you are shamming it, too! You are no lady's maid, however superior!"

At which Miss Bancroft looked so rosy pink and flustered that Demian had to kiss her cheek gently and allow that she had been unmasked.

"But do not be afraid, Miss Bancroft! I doubt whether Miss Mayhew will betray you!"

"Indeed, no, though I never thought to be so entertained. Good Lord, I think I have now had my money's worth, for I have not been so surprised, amused, or . . . or . . ."

"Or?" His Grace looked deeply into those lovely eyes.

"Or moved, Mr. Hartford, since I first saw Kemble on the stage." There was a moment when the duke thought he might kiss her. Then it passed away, as fleeting as the tiny drifts of snow floating in the crisp air outside.

"You shall have your way, then. I shall escort you to the posting house."

"No!" Both ladies uttered the same alarmed protest, but for different reasons.

Demian smiled. "Yes, for I fear that whilst we have dallied in speech, Mrs. Honoria Murgatroyd and her denizens of hell have been using up the remaining eight hundred pounds. By the time they have finished their tour of the ice, eh, house—which I fear shall be rather uncomfortable given the current temperatures—and dropped a few more of the priceless Sevres plates, His Grace's obligation will be complete. At that time, Miss Bancroft, you may escort the whole tedious bunch of them to the south wing, holland covers or not."

"Oh! How *unscrupulous,* Mr. Hartford!" But Amy's eyes were laughing again.

"Yes, isn't it? The Darris butler shall return to bow and scrape, then he shall disappear forever whilst plain Mr. Hartford escorts the charming Miss Mayhew to her favored destination."

"No!" Again, the chorus of disapproval, for while Amy's heart was soaring quite wildly despite her every attempt to still it, Miss Bancroft was still looming like a benign black cloud, if such a thing could ever exist.

"It is not fitting, Your Gr . . ." The duke glared at Martha, who remembered, just in time, that he was masquerading as a commoner.

"It is perfectly fitting that, as a representative of His Grace's household, I escort her to her destination. It is a common civility in this weather!"

"It is a common madness," Martha muttered under her breath. She was not heard, however, for Amy was engaging Demian's august attention.

"If I cannot saddle up a horse, I shall return to the party. If we are to be foisted on the dreaded south wing, then my conscience, I suppose, can rest easy."

"That is *all* that will rest easy! The south wing, I assure you, is positively uninhabitable! The chimneys have not been used in a decade, so the chances of lighting a fire will be abysmal."

"If it is good enough for Mrs. Corey, then it is good enough for me!" A defiant tilt to Amy's chin should have warned the duke, but he was too used to going his own way to take any heed.

"You miss the point, my darling little innocent!" At which Miss Bancroft started looking around for the reticule. If *ever* she needed her smelling salts, this must surely be the moment!

"I am not that!"

"Oh, but you are!"

Martha tried to weave herself between the pair of them, but they seemed not to notice her, despite her bulk. So, despite her hero worship of the duke, she decided something must be done. "Wait! I am going to fetch Lady Caroline!"

"And leave us unattended? Martha, dear, you shock me!" The duke's tone was light, but already he had allowed his gaze to travel back to the travel-stained green merino.

"The point, Miss Mayhew, is that the lodgings will be decidedly below the standards to which I hope you are accustomed."

"I am not a flower, Mr. Hartford, I shall not wilt. The worse, the better, in my opinion. Mrs. Murgatroyd will be in hysterics and Mrs. Corey will be silenced, at last."

"And you?"

"I, my dear Mr. Hartford, shall have the satisfaction of standing in debt to no one, least of all to the duke of Darris. I hope, when he hears the tale, he has a hearty chuckle at our expense. We deserve it."

"Not you, Miss Mayhew."

"Yes, I. For being so foolish as to agree to this expedition in the first place. I knew very well that the guests had only one small matter on their minds."

"And what was that?"

"Capturing the interest, if not the heart of, our noble host."

Martha's jaw dropped open. This was plain speaking indeed! She opened her mouth to say something, then clamped it shut again. No one, she knew, was listening. There was a rapt stillness about the room that lent itself to the brief silence that ensued.

"But surely it was known he would be away?"

"It was known, yes. But it is also commonly known, I am afraid, that he is sadly in need of a wife."

"Really? You interest me greatly." Now. Mr. Hartford assumed a studied expression of bored disinterest that was decidedly at odds with his words.

"I have offended you."

"No, why should you have?"

"I don't know. I should not have spoken so openly, perhaps."

"It is the thing about you, Miss Mayhew, that I most admire. Or perhaps it is the charming way your hair gleams in the sunshine. I have not yet decided."

"Flirting again."

"Teasing again. You should not allow tiny lights to enter your eyes when you smile. Very disturbing. And you are heading off the point."

"That being?"

"That being that His Grace is in want of a wife."

"Oh, not any wife. A *rich* wife. That is why we are all being paraded about in the hope of catching his attention. It is believed that although his rank would ordinarily cast him quite out of our grasp, his current circumstances are felicitous. He *might,* Mrs. Corey speculates, consider marrying into the merchant classes."

Miss Bancroft gasped and threw a startled glance at His Grace. He, it must be said, was engaged in procuring a pinch of snuff from an exquisite box designed for this purpose. It was wrought in the purest of silver, but he did not, at that moment, seem to be diverted by this fact.

"Might he just?"

"Indeed, so. Mrs. Murgatroyd seems to think it is *Daphne* who will achieve these heights, but I rather think that Mrs. Corey has the advantage over her. Whilst Amelia is a trifle stout, her great uncle was a baron, and that *must* cast her in the superior mold."

"Oh, infinitely!" Demian's lips twitched.

"Personally, I favor Miss Fletcherson, but . . ."

The duke interrupted. "Does no one favor you?"

"Why, of *course* someone does! My Aunt Ermentrude thinks that because I am the daughter of Lord Dalmont—a very august gentleman, I am told, though he died when I was only three—I must surely have the advantage. Nothing I say can rid her of the opinion. I am afraid to say, she cherishes some quite *spectacular* hopes."

"Ah, yes. The sylph at dusk."

"Precisely." Then came that delightful gurgle the duke found so entrancing. "Did I tell you it was a *jeweled* sylph?"

"Jeweled? But how dazzling. Miss Mayhew, your merino—however elegantly serviceable—begins to disappoint me."

"Beg pardon for that. I reserve the gems exclusively, you see, for the duke."

"Ah. And the sylph . . . ?"

Amy's eyes danced. "That too, Mr. Hartford. Now, I beg you grant your thoughts a new direction before you overset me entirely."

There was a moment—a trembling moment—when Amy thought he would not. Neither, one might add, did Miss Bancroft, who more clearly knew what fire the lovely Miss Mayhew was dabbling with than she herself. Amy might tease poor Mr. Hartford, but she had no notion she was addressing the duke. Miss Bancroft rather thought that if she *did*, she would have stilled her lively tongue. Still, despite several frantic warning glances at His Grace, no one was paying her the smallest heed. *Again.*

"You . . ."

"Miss Mayhew, it is my turn to ask you a favor."

"Yes?"

"When this is over, when you have spent your freezing night—it might even be more than that—I fear a week—in mortal discomfort in the bowels of the south wing . . ."

"Yes?"

The duke continued, regardless of the heightened tension. Amy snapped open a pretty fan. He took it gently from her hands, hushing her apologies.

"When you have been returned to the bosom of your family . . .

". . . with lurid stories to tell of our great misfortunes . . .

". . . with lurid stories of your great misfortunes . . ." the duke unblinkingly echoed her humor. "Then, Miss Mayhew, *then* might I call on you?"

"Then, Mr. Hartford, you may."

"You have not forgotten I am merely an impoverished gentleman?"

"Not for a moment. You've not forgotten I am merely an upstart merchant chit?"

"Hardly that, Miss Mayhew, hardly that."

"You have not yet met Aunt Ermentrude."

"But I have met her niece. I believe that suffices."

Ten

It was impossible, of course, not to peek. There was only so long a young lady of excellent lineage could crane her exquisite white neck through a dreary, open window. It was open, for Mr. Endicott had decreed that whilst the weather held out, they could do with fresh country air. Her ladyship disagreed, for the roads were muddy, and long wisps of straw and dandelions kept floating in up off the carriage wheels. Still, she was not so mawkish as to disagree, for she was perfectly certain Mr. Endicott would blithely disregard any views she might harbor on the matter. Besides, she had determined not to speak to him.

The detestable man seemed not to notice and instead, occupied himself with staring at the elegant scalloped sleeves of her deliciously blue organdy. At least, Lady Raquel *hoped* it was her sleeves he was concerned with, for his fascination was apparently avid as his gaze rested upon her person.

Lady Raquel flushed, for whilst she had disregarded the matter at the time, the gown was daringly cut despite its excellent preponderance of buttons at the back. Oh, if she had only worn the rose satin, with its nice, safe neckline and its girlish ribbons! She peeped crossly at Mr. Endicott through entrancing blue eyes. If she took care to keep her neck facing the window, it was very likely he would not notice a brief glance.

Oh, how wrong she was! Mr. Endicott noticed at once and grinned quite disarmingly, despite her annoyance.

"Good! I thought you would weary of the view. You will find, I believe, that I offer a much more interesting prospect."

To her annoyance, she realized at once that he was correct. A foolish girl could look upon Mr. Endicott's rakish countenance and excellent physique for a lifetime. Fortunately, Raquel was not foolish. She broke the stare they had somehow become locked in and announced that she abhorred coxcombs.

"Ah, you speak! I feared that you must have sustained some injury to your tongue."

"None, I assure you." Raquel felt that this was a rather paltry response, but her heart was suddenly playing dangerous tricks on her and sadly, she could think of no better rejoinder under the circumstance.

Mr. Endicott could, though, and he murmured, just loud enough for Raquel, but not poor Maria, who was holding her tooth with a vinegar-soaked handkerchief, to hear.

"I am relieved. It is a delightful tongue."

Raquel's glance shifted to the red velvet of the carriage floor. Her color, by now, was quite high, and she had certainly lost most of the calm, cool, self-control that she was famed for. There could be no mistaking Mr. Endicott's meaning. Or could there? Could she be placing too much construction on his words because of her *own* wayward desires? Surely not. No, she could swear he was teasing her, flirting in some abominably deplorable manner that had all her senses quite at sixes and sevens and poor Maria looking from one to the other in miserable suspicion.

Raquel could not look at the crimson carpeting forever, so she was forced to look up, once more.

"Do not be fooled, sir. My tongue can cut like a whip."

"Can it? Yes, I believe it can. Demian told me so."

"You should not be speaking of me in that fashion!"

"We were not speaking of *you,* merely of your tongue."

"Most improper and quite absurd."

"Yes, but I delight in absurdity, and impropriety is my middle name."

"That is patently obvious, sir!"

Mr. Endicott ignored her.

"So it cuts like a whip?"

"Yes."

"Intriguing. Does it also taste as sweet as nectar? And is it as warm and soft as . . ."

The coach jolted forward. It was not a moment too soon, for Lady Raquel was becoming mesmerized by his lips and the dark smile that played at the corners of his wholly illuminating eyes.

Maria, aware that there were strange undercurrents on this trip that doubtless Anders would blame her for, took another tiny swig at Cook's gin, then moaned.

Lady Raquel stopped herself from catapulting into Mr. Endicott's lap, but at the expense of having his firm arms steady her. They were strong and appealing, and dizzyingly warm. They also released her almost instantly, which came as both a relief and a sublime shock.

"We shall stop here." His tone was crisp.

"Why?"

"Why?" He echoed her words with a faint rise to his brows.

"Yes. Why? I assume you have some *reason* for this dictatorial decision? Darris is hours from here. And if you think I need to rest, I am made of sterner stuff." Raquel forced herself to be brisk. If she wasn't, she would probably throw herself into his arms and disgrace herself utterly. If he read those thoughts, he showed no sign of it. He did, however, allow his features to soften and a small smile to enter his impossibly blue eyes.

"It's not rest you need, Lady Raquel." This he murmured, so possibly she did not hear, though her nose rose a little higher in the air.

"No, we shall stop here because your maid needs her tooth pulled. See, her face is swollen."

Stricken at her self-absorption, Raquel noticed that the odious man was right. Not all of Cook's gin could numb the pain of poor Maria's tooth, nor slow the swelling around her jaw. By now, her eyes were wet with tears, and though the vinegar-soaked handkerchief was efficacious, it was not large enough to muffle the small moans that were escaping into its folds.

"Maria! Is this so? Do you need us to stop?"

Maria, overcome by the concern of her superiors and by the possible ire of Anders, moaned even louder.

"I should have known. It is my fault. Oh, Maria, *why* did you not tell me how severe it was?"

For answer, the little maid sobbed the more.

"There is doubtless a sawbones in the village. He will have to attend to her, but if you want to make Darris we shall have to press on."

"Alone?" A flicker of alarm crossed Raquel's face. Mr. Endicott's expression was shuttered as he confirmed her fears.

"Indeed, my lady, I believe that to be the case. If you are squeamish, I can have the horses turned round. There is still time to return to London at a respectable hour."

"No!"

"No?"

"No! We will push on to Darris. I am determined to do it."

"Without the maid?"

Maria tried to say something, but instead, clutched at her offending jaw.

Lady Raquel looked directly into Mr. Endicott's eyes. *"Without* the maid. I rely, completely, on your honor."

Thomas laughed. "Is that quite wise? I warn you, Lady Raquel, that I am a rake."

"I have inferred that, Mr. Endicott."

"And still you come?"

Lady Raquel Fortesque-Benton took one of the deepest breaths of her life. She was strangely exhilarated despite being cast in such a scandalous position.

"And still, Mr. Endicott, I come."

The tension in the chaise was dangerously high when the carriage drew to a halt. Maria, too concerned with removing her modest traveling case from the equipage and then with thanking Lady Raquel a dozen times or more for pressing a guinea into her hand, did not notice overmuch. But then, Maria had always been singularly unobservant, especially so as she was afflicted with an ailment so dire as the toothache.

Besides, she would escape lightly on the grounds of the excellent piece of gossip Anders was even now spreading around the upper hallways. Her ladyship was entertaining the duke of Darris's suit. It would not have dawned on Maria that Raquel might, therefore, be flirting—or coming dangerously close to flirting—with society's most notable rake.

He laughed out loud at Lady Raquel's determined words. He also noted, with approval, that so far from blaming Maria for what was essentially her own fault, she had actually looked stricken. Further, she'd pressed a *very* handsome amount into those flushed, handkerchief-bearing hands. Better yet, there was a blush upon her cheeks he found promising. *Definitely* a thaw in Lady Raquel's coldness.

"Bravely spoken. Now, Maria, you shall tell me which box holds my lady's muff and pelisse, and you shall be off."

"I am not cold."

Mr. Endicott ignored the suddenly plaintiff tone.

"Which one, Maria?"

"That green one, sir, what is banded up wiv lilac cords." It was fortunate Mr. Endicott could hear her through the handkerchief, which she now quite convulsively clutched in two woolen-clad fists.

"Very good, Maria, I shall attend to it. You run along, now."

Maria knew a moment's hesitation despite her pain. Anders would have her head if she had been derelict in her duties.

Lady Raquel remained in the carriage and ignored the excellent doeskin breeches that partially obscured her vision from the window. It was harder to ignore their *contents*, of course, but this she did, and quite nobly, though her errant heart was still playing ridiculous tricks.

"Yes, hurry, Maria. I should not like to think of you in agonies much longer. You may take tomorrow morning as a half day off, and offer up my compliments to her ladyship. Mama will be anxious to know that I am traveling safely."

Maria bobbed a clumsy curtsy.

"Oh! And don't have anymore of that gin. It will make you ill. Barley water is better, ask at the inn."

"Yes, milady." The maid bobbed again, grabbed her case and stepped out of the way of the carriage wheels.

"Go!" Mr. Endicott waved her away, for it seemed likely she would dither forever over the flagstones.

Clearly, in spite of her pain, she was in two minds over leaving her charge.

"Yes, sir." And with a last, uncertain glance at her ladyship, Maria obeyed.

Then Mr. Endicott's fascinating doeskin breeches disappeared from view as he strode to the back of the chaise. Lady Fortesque-Benton could hear several muttered curses as he tried to extract the correct portmanteau from the three she had brought. He evidently succeeded, for it was not long before he was back in the lady's line of vision. Through the window, he made an excellent sight, though Raquel would rather have had her tongue cut out than make such an admission.

Then she gasped in outrage. The man was actually opening her portmanteau, quite oblivious to the stares of his coachman.

"You can't do that!"

Lady Raquel's voice trembled between alarm, amusement and indignation.

"Whyever not?" Mr. Endicott asked idly as he continued to do just exactly as he pleased.

"You are a detestable man! I said I could live without my pelisse."

"And I said that you can't. Ungrateful girl, I should make you shiver with cold when the paths turn to ice."

"Oh! You unspeakable . . ."

But Raquel's voice trailed off as the portmanteau snapped open to reveal, among the dimities, several delightful pairs of clocked stockings, two excessively delectable undergarments of crisp white linen, a mountain of petticoats, a satin slipper of pale cream, and a tangle of ribbons. For some reason, Mr. Endicott felt a strange tightening in his stomach that could not be attributed to these trifling things. Heaven knew, he was a connoisseur in the matter of lady's undergarments. Lady Raquel's were undoubtedly excellent, but rather

plain for his customary taste. Perhaps he was responding to the sudden intake of breath behind him. He felt
it soft and warm upon his neck.

He denied himself the impulse to turn around, so
that the breath would become flesh. He had little doubt
that if he did, Lady Raquel's sweet bow lips would be
his undoing. Instead, he rifled idly through the under-
dresses and lace spencers and allowed a shadow of
amusement to cross his face.

"Perhaps if I dig deep enough I shall find the promised pelisse."

"Perhaps if I scream, someone will save me from
an obvious barbarian. You are no gentleman, sir!"

The gentleman pulled out a pair of exquisite pantalets, raised his brows faintly, then placed them on top
of the growing pile. They were smooth and long, and
looked like they housed only the lithest of limbs. He
valiantly tried not to think of that, but his thoughts were
distressingly errant. It was therefore some several moments before he answered Lady Raquel's accusation.

"Lady Raquel, you are spoiled, arrogant and ob-
structive. You are also excessively pleasing on the eye,
and you test my manhood to its limits. If you don't
want me to show you what I *mean* by that singular
statement, don't try me any further. Be pleased that I
am a gentleman, Lady Raquel, for almost certainly,
were I not, you would have either been soundly repri-
manded or thoroughly kissed by now."

Thomas waited for the storm, but to his surprise, it
never came. Only the breathing against his neck became more ragged. He wondered why, with a faint stirring of masculine interest.

Then he was all business, clicking the portmanteau
shut with such firmness that several pieces of lace were
sadly crushed and one particularly interesting petticoat
flounce trailed tantalizingly from its confines.

He fingered it for a moment before turning to face Lady Raquel through the open window. Her eyes were bright and burning, but for all his experience, he couldn't read them. He longed to trail his fingers along the slightly parted bow of her lips, then desisted. Some unaccountable part of him wanted to goad her. He told himself he was merely taming her, for Darris's benefit.

"Speechless again. How edifying. What is it, the thought of the kissing or the thought of the upbraiding—I'd be decidedly thorough in both, I assure you—that silences you?"

Lady Raquel leaned forward in her seat. She wished she could feel as cool and controlled as she always did. This untitled upstart was heating her senses and meddling with her mind in the most intolerable manner. She was perfectly certain that she hated him. No one before had ever offered her anything but reverential respect, and not even the most *daring* of her suitors had ventured to kiss her in quite the manner Mr. Endicott suggested.

"Both. You are quite insufferable. If I were a male, I would kill you."

"But you are not a male."

"More is the pity."

Mr. Endicott smiled and a sudden warm light of amusement lit his severe features.

"I take leave to disagree. Now, shall I go through all your portmanteaus—Maria was obviously mistaken about their contents—or shall we cry quits and agree to share my greatcoat?"

Lady Raquel glared. The thought of Mr. Endicott opening all her luggage did not appeal. He was quite apparently without shame and would do it, she knew, in the twinkling of an eye. She blushed to think of the pantalets, bought on the spur of the moment and very infelicitously fast. Anders had had very prim fits, but

Raquel, always the height of calm etiquette, had for once been defiant. It amused her to think that beneath her very proper skirts lay nothing but a few frills between her and flesh. It was all the rage in France, and she could quite see why. The pantalets were cool and did not incommode her nearly so much as the traditional swathe of petticoats. These, she thanked heaven, she was very properly wearing now. But Mr. Endicott's unnerving smile told her he doubted it.

"Well? The horses are growing frisky. Personally, I would prefer rifling through your undergarments, but . . ."

Raquel's fingers clenched. "Very well, we shall share your greatcoat."

"Good. Beautiful and biddable. Take care I do not fall in love with you."

With this cryptic remark, Thomas stowed away the lilac corded portmanteau and took a few brisk strides up to the carriage door. The lady, he noted, was silent. She'd stopped calling him all manner of detestable things and was staring, stony-eyed, from the window. Thomas might have thought her indifferent to his last, flippantly made comment, but for the sharp intake of breath and the dwindling of her color to a satin pale cream. For an instant, he wondered whether he had goaded her too far. It was not his custom to bully young ladies, but Lady Raquel positively invited such treatment by her imperious, icy manner.

A sharp glance at the lady reassured him. Doubtless her silence indicated disdain rather than remorse. He hoped so. He was beginning to enjoy these spats. Besides, if it was remorse she was feeling, he might easily be led to comfort her. He was not sure he *wanted* to comfort the elegant Lady Fortesque-Benton. She was already wreaking far too much havoc with his self-control.

He nodded to the coachman, and with a swift, sleek movement, hoisted himself back into the chaise. It seemed much bigger, now that Maria was not taking up half the leg room. Still, for all its spaciousness, it was strangely intimate, and Raquel could not help the slight shiver that crept up her spine and kept her from peering out the opposite window as she had intended.

Mr. Endicott contemplated her quietly. Her hands lay still in her lap, and her back, though straight, curved a little at the arch. His thoughts were not pleasant, for while he had the most overpowering urge to take her in his arms and kiss away the cross pout and the arrogant incline of her chin, he had promised the duke of Darris that he would resist just these impulses. For the first time in his life, he cursed Demian. She was looking at him now, which made a change from her previous tactics. He wondered if it was boredom, curiosity, or something else that drove her. Her eyes were quite intoxicatingly blue.

"You are looking at me now. Does that mean you acknowledge me as a person?"

"Would you care if I don't?" The words were softly spoken and slightly more whimsical than he would have expected. He smiled.

"Good technique, Lady Raquel. A question for a question. Always keep the opposition guessing."

"Are you the opposition?"

More questions! He eyed her speculatively, all the while wishing he could take up the sudden challenge he detected in those heavenly eyes. Did that golden curl fall by accident or by design? It looked superb across her brow. He wished to thread his fingers through it. He cursed, wondering if she knew.

"I shall allow you to formulate your *own* opinion on that, my lady."

She viewed him suspiciously, her blue eyes widening

a little in thought. Mr. Endicott found her delectable when her icy manner flagged, as it did now. Cursing the duke, he had to clench his fists to retain his mocking demeanor.

"I think you *are* the opposition, for you disapprove of me."

He cocked his brow quizzically, neither confirming nor denying her assertion. Disapproval did not rank highly in his thoughts, but then, neither did chivalry. The very honorable Lady Raquel Fortesque-Benton would probably shriek and run ten miles in the snow if she knew what he was thinking. And so she should.

A flicker of amused frustration reached his eyes. How singularly trying that he should find this stiff-rumped shrew so intriguing. She was begging for a denial, but he would not give it. He *did* disapprove of her. More specifically, he found he violently disapproved of her in relation to a wife for Darris. The fact that she would make a well-bred, beautiful and appropriately regal duchess made things worse, not better. He kicked a tasseled Hessian against his elegantly crested door, then cursed.

Lady Raquel raised deliciously arched brows, which only made Thomas wish to repeat the offense. He didn't, but his bearing became stiffer than usual and he almost resorted to staring out the window. Fortunately, his innate dislike of such stratagems came to the fore, so he settled on gazing at the lady in question with great beetling brows of his own.

She sighed. Mr. Endicott was being uncommonly restrained, but his very silence spoke volumes. Raquel was piqued. She found she did not favor being disapproved of. She answered his stare with a bold one of her own, though she feared it presented itself more as a flush than as cold scrutiny. Annoyed to find how much she *cared* about this arrogant, untitled man's opinion, she nevertheless pressed on.

"Can you honestly deny you do not wish me to marry Darris?"

Thomas, who was at that moment wishing his good friend the noble duke of Darris to the devil, could answer promptly and most truthfully. His eyes, it must be said, never left the lady's for an instant.

"No, my lady, I cannot. *Decidedly* I do not want you to marry Darris."

Had Lady Raquel been used to receiving subtle rather than overt compliments, she may have dipped her eyes flirtatiously at this obvious double entendre. She was not, however, accustomed to such subtleties, the bulk of her suitors being ruthlessly unrestrained in their praises. Her fortune, after all, demanded it.

So she took the statement at face value and felt her face flame with mortification. Since he obviously did not regard her as marriage material, his odiously flirtatious manner must now be construed as insulting. Oh, he *was* a beast! A flagrantly attractive, heart-stoppingly handsome beast. He trifled with her merely to pass the time and divert her attention from Demian.

Raquel bit her lip and allowed her eyes to flicker to the silver carriage cushions. Impossible to avoid a glimpse of those elegantly clad knees, but at least she had avoided the broad, compelling chest and the unnerving stare she had endured for quite long enough.

Arrogant sapskull! She concentrated on this thought for quite two seconds before noticing the knees move a little. The silver cushions became more fascinating than ever.

She had never wanted, in all her life, to be kissed so much as she did now. Her color deepened even further, for the thought was decidedly unsettling. More annoying still, she doubted herself. It had become a habit to see herself as others did. The Lady Raquel Fortesque-Benton, modishly dressed, always, in bonnets of prettily trimmed straw, was a diamond of the first water, a prize beyond compare. Now she saw herself as this nonpareil must: a passing beauty with a bad temper and a cold aspect. She felt bleak.

Mr. Endicott, watching her closely, divined some of these foolish feelings. He steeled himself against the crushing urge to kiss them away. Demian, he thought with wry humor, would probably not thank him for his concern.

Tears glittered in the delicate blue eyes. He could only just see them through the tangle of lashes. He wondered what it was about his silver squabs that was so fascinating. Perhaps, if he reclined her against them, he would know. . . . His jaw hardened.

And the haughty, cold Lady Raquel with her endless lists? *She* was at a loss to know why she felt so bitterly bereft. She couldn't care a *farthing* for what plain Mr. Thomas Tyrone Endicott felt. He was merely a courier, after all. A courier charged with escorting her to her betrothed. She must be *mad* thinking of him as a nonpareil, just because his charm was effortless and he looked . . . oh, he looked beyond compare. He could not have the air of command she credited him for—he was not even a baron, for heaven's sake! True, he had the ear of the highest in the land, and had commanded His Majesty's tenth division of Light Brigades into battle, but *that* was not to compare with the luster of a duke! Oh, if only she had not been so hasty! Stepping into his chaise was the stupidest, most scatterbrained thing she had ever done in her well-ordered life.

He watched her unravel her thoughts, amusement vying with something else in that picture-perfect countenance. Raquel thought she could hardly bear to look at him, let alone interpret the glance. Nevertheless, she

felt her lacings tighten as her body instinctively responded to . . . she knew not what. Mr. Endicott, after
all, had not moved. Her imagination was playing tricks.
But, in a rush of consciousness, she knew that Mr. Endicott, courier or not, stirred her with one mocking
thrust of his jaw in a manner that the duke did not. She
was never more annoyed—or flushed—or flustered—
in her life. It did not help that the mocking smile widened as if it understood every fluttering cause of her
confusion.

"You are beautiful when your eyes mist up." Lady
Raquel's heart turned over as the words, smooth and
silky, caressed her. There was a moment's silence.

"Does it require a lot of practice?"

Lady Raquel took a moment to understand the insult.
"Oh!" Her face flamed again, but this time with outrage. She did not have to lean far forward to bridge the
gap between them. If the carriage had jolted forward,
she would have been across those annoying knees. Fortunately, it did not. Very properly, it swayed from side
to side. Lady Raquel was therefore able to lean forward
and, with stunning aplomb, slap his mocking face. The
sound reverberated between them in the closed carriage.

Lady Fortesque-Benton sat back in her seat. Two of
the silver squabs landed on the floor in her haste. Neither picked them up. The sound reverberated between
them, magnified out of all proportion by the tension
of the moment.

Stunned by her momentary loss of poise, Raquel
thought wildly that the slap must have been heard for
miles. Breathless, she peeked out of the carriage. The
coachman seemed not to have noticed, for though she
could not see him for the horses, he was murmuring
something gloomy beneath his breath. It was something
inconsequential about the weather. Peaks of white

drifted softly across her face. In a dreamlike state, Raquel noticed that her very breath was forming smoky wisps on the carriage frame. Patches of frost alternated with small, fragmented pools of water on the spokes. And her gloves were wet. Slowly, she stopped clutching at the frame and drew them inside again.

Eleven

Meeting his eyes was unavoidable. Mr. Endicott, nursing his cheek with a gloved hand, was curiously silent. Raquel's heart beat all the faster. She was not so henwitted as to believe him indulgent, for he had already shown himself to be otherwise.

She therefore tilted her chin defiantly, noting with some alarm—and a good deal of satisfaction—that the singularly handsome face was streaked with red, fading, as she watched, to a dull pink. Her pulses raced. She did not feel *nearly* so icy as her reputation, despite the thrill of shivers that beset her.

Outside, the coachman watched the skies and slowed the horses down to a simple trot. The first flakes of snow brushed gently on the carriage roof before slipping silently to the ground. Neither person inside the gay, well-sprung chaise noticed. Regardless of the telltale signs of winter, *both* people were decidedly warm.

The carriage was cast in shadow, but Raquel could still see the mark she had produced on that amazingly virile countenance. She could only *imagine* at the consequences and sank back in her seat. It was hard without the squabs. The silver winked at her from the carpet of red, but she did not pick them up. Instead, as calmly as she could, she folded her arms and waited.

Thomas surprised her. He did not, as she'd half expected, retaliate with a stinging blow of his own. Neither, as she rather feared, did he take her in his arms and kiss her senseless.

She breathed a little sigh, half relief, half maddening disappointment. There was still a silence. Then she noticed the tilting of Mr. Endicott's lips as though he were fighting back waves of laughter. She glanced quickly at his eyes and noted that they were twinkling with a sudden, quite glorious light. In spite of herself, Lady Raquel found her own graceful bow lips twitching quite infectiously. The next moment, both she and Mr. Endicott were laughing, though neither quite knew why. When they stopped, both were a little self-conscious, but a new understanding seemed forged between them. Thomas did not know whether this was good, or decidedly bad.

"You little vixen! I shall inform Demian to think carefully. He is doubtless marrying a shrew." But his eyes smiled.

"I am only a shrew when the company is disagreeable." Raquel flirted with her lashes. Mr. Endicott noticed, but did not succumb.

"I am only disagreeable when the company is a shrew." He deftly turned the phrase to suit himself. Lady Raquel understood the insult a little quicker this time. "Oh!"

Thomas was alert. Lady Fortesque-Benton's hand was already raised.

Their newfound amity appeared to evaporate like the mists.

"No you don't!"

Raquel raised her brows, *furious* that her hand was being so forcefully held. She refused to allow herself to enjoy the sensation, as the faint, traitorous whisper in her being so tantalizingly demanded.

"Next time, you see fit to slap me, my lady, be warned. I shall answer in kind."

"It is fortunate I am marrying into the peerage, Mr. Endicott. Gentlemen, I believe, do not slap ladies' faces."

"I said nothing about your *face,* Lady Raquel." Thomas's words were silky.

"No?"

Lady Fortesque-Benton looked puzzled, though her words challenged. Her hand was still a prisoner. Mr. Endicott leaned over, without warning, and in a single twisting movement pulled her forward and positioned her indelicately across his knee. His palm, warm and hard, lightly pressed itself against her pert day dress with its fathoms of petticoats and excellent French lace.

Lady Raquel eyed the red velvet carpet and the gleaming black Hessians with misgiving. She refused to wriggle, but, despite her layers of fashionable undergarments, she felt excessively alarmed. Mr. Endicott's meaning was now patently apparent to her. Her dignity did not permit her to scream, but she *did* manage an icy command.

"Let me go!"

Thomas laughed, admiring her spirit. No milk-and-water miss, this. "Certainly, my lady. I was merely making a point."

"Well, you have made it, you brute. Now let me go." But Mr. Endicott had already begun the process of tilting her upright and depositing her on the seat beside him. Raquel breathed a sigh of shuddering relief, though her dignity was as much offended as her derriere had been. Despite its unexpected reprieve, it tingled. She shifted, as if to return to the other side, but his gloved hands stretched out lazily. They prevented her, maddeningly, from doing so.

Lady Raquel summoned her most scathing of glances.

"Are you *bent* on compromising my virtue?"

Mr. Endicott appeared to consider the question as he propped her back beside him. Then he leaned over suddenly and retrieved the squabs. Raquel wondered if it was an accident that his thighs brushed against hers. She shocked herself by hoping not, for despite her protestations, she felt herself intolerably in Mr. Endicott's tantalizing toils.

Now, he answered her question. She was annoyed that she couldn't see his eyes without turning. She refused to do so.

He grinned, as if divining her thoughts. "How excellent! You neglected to add 'beast,' after those prettily spoken words. And to answer your question, the theory tempts me, but no, I am not. I have promised your virtue to Demian. See? Even *I* can be foolish."

Raquel ignored the innuendo and the sudden gleam that accompanied it.

"His Grace should challenge you to a duel for the insults you have offered me."

"He should, but he won't. His Grace has a partiality for me, I fear."

Raquel wished she could say the same. But, meeting Mr. Endicott had opened her eyes a little. Lord Darris did not look at her as if he wished to devour her, with burning dark eyes and a silky smile that refused to be banished. His Grace had been all that was proper, but nothing more. Casting her mind back, she did not think he had even commented on her ravishing looks—and they *were* ravishing, she'd been told so a million times—nor had he composed her a simple sonnet. But she was being absurd. Theirs was palpably a marriage of convenience. The duke needed funds and she needed a title. Which reminded her, of course, that Mr. Endicott, for all his airs and supreme address, was entirely ineligible. Perversely, the thought made her wish to slap his handsome face again.

"Perhaps he won't be so partial to you when he knows you have taken liberties with his fiancée."

"I have *not* taken liberties. I have not even *begun* to take liberties. Shall I, though? The idea is intriguing."

Raquel was glad that he was not facing her, for she was flushing like a schoolgirl. It seemed a maddening coincidence to her that his thigh was again brushing softly against her skirts. Possibly, if it were not so unbearably well proportioned, it would not have mattered.

"I don't take liberties with a libertine. Now let me return to my seat."

"No, for the temperature is now approaching freezing, and though I am loath to remind you of it, we have a deal. You are to share my greatcoat."

Raquel eyed the greatcoat with disfavor. It was being removed unceremoniously from Thomas's shoulders, affording her a glimpse of broad muscles and a light, cream-shaded waistcoat. The fact that it emphasized his waist annoyed her, for this was no time to notice how obviously attractive he was, or that no tailor had been required to pad any of his many interesting areas of anatomy with lamb's wool. Possibly if one had, she would have been able to muster up some kind of amusement, or even, better yet, contempt. Now, however, she kept wishing that the abysmal man would kiss her, and this caused havoc with her calm, ordered senses.

The coat slipped over her shoulders. It was warm, and softer than it looked. She felt an impulse to snuggle in, but arched her back stiffer yet. She could feel Mr. Endicott's breath on her hair, for he was pulling the other side tightly around himself. A hopeless case, for the carriage coat had been made to mold to his body, not to float like a bag about his elegant person. Sharing was going to offer more of a challenge than he had bargained for. Still, with an impish smile, he made a valiant attempt to snuggle into his share, an event that pulled Raquel closer than she cared to be, so that she gasped, both with annoyance and with sudden, unexpected pleasure.

The warmth made her realize just how cold it was, for where the coat missed its mark, she was freezing, and even her hands, through her gloves, felt icy. For an instant, she wished Mr. Endicott had found her muff, but the thought was banished as the entire thing slipped about her person and Mr. Endicott changed seats.

"You are freezing. I am a villain not to have insisted on finding your pelisse."

"You would have been a villain if you *had*."

He smiled, then, the curve deliciously lighting up his features.

"Bravo, my lady! I think that is the first kind word you have had for me. I shall treasure it."

"Now you are being ridiculous. And you freeze on my account. I will not have it."

So, beneath the starch and the ice, there was a tender heart. He had suspected it when he saw her concern for the maid. Some other ladies of his acquaintance would have turned the servant off for the dire inconvenience. Further, they would have submitted to a fit of hysterics upon finding themselves without chaperonage. Lady Fortesque-Benton, for all her evident faults, had done neither. Thomas had liked her the better for it. He did not think he would lust after her as much as he did if there was not some raw degree of admiration. He had had beauties aplenty in his lifetime, and he knew all too well that dewy eyes were skin deep. He always reacted the strongest to character, though well-formulated curves never went amiss. Lady Fortesque-Benton apparently had both in abundance. Demian was a fool if he called her cold.

"Even so, you shall have to, madam. The coat was not made for two, and though you have several times called me a brute, I am *not* a cad. I will *not* wear my cozy carriage coat while a lady freezes."

"My pelisse, then . . ."

"I'll not stop the horses a second time. They need to keep moving to retain their warmth."

Raquel nodded, for once without argument. She wrapped the coat around her, smelling the pleasant scent of . . . she knew not what. It was indescribable, but most decidedly reminded her of the man gazing at her darkly. She relaxed into it, acknowledging that it was more than the warmth of the cloth that elevated her spirits.

Mr. Endicott, she noted, did not complain, though his arms must have felt quite frozen against the icy wooden panels. It was too bad that there was no hot brick at their feet, but then she would have had to share, and sharing was dangerous with the likes of the man opposite.

The horses, plodding now that the snow was a little thicker, ground to a halt. Thomas was prevented from doing anything decidedly rash by the obvious advent of his coachman, who had deserted his perch and leaped into the snow, to the bewilderment of six perfectly matched bays.

"The snow be right deep, sir. Reckon as we had best stop afore the wheels are stuck."

"We are not far from Darris. Indeed, I would be surprised if we have not already crossed the southmost border. Can we not push on, Mallard? I most particularly desire to reach our destination before nightfall. It is possibly no more than five miles, ten at the most."

"No sayin', guv. I reckon as I won't like to take any chances wiv them 'igh steppin' beauties."

Thomas frowned. "No, you are right, of course. How far back was the last posting inn?"

"That be the Lion and the Anvil, sir. Reckon as it was six miles."

Thomas nodded, his eyes alert and alive in thought. They flickered over to her, tucked snugly in his capes, then back to the whitening lands.

"Too far. If we turn back, we will be holed up there for a fortnight. I can't risk that. Yes, yes, I am aware of the horses." He gestured to the coachman, who seemed about to interrupt.

"There is a sentry's cottage not far from here. I will escort her ladyship there by foot. The snows are still light enough to take that risk. You, my friend, shall have to turn this rig around. Stable the horses at the inn and make sure they are rubbed down well. Check Applewhite's left hock. I think she might be pulling to the left."

"Aye guv, wot I thought too. But the missus . . ."

". . . will be fine. Take this for your board and the stabling expenses. I believe it should keep the innkeeper happy a while."

Mr. Endicott drew his purse and laid it carelessly in the coachman's hand. The man nodded as if it were of little consequence, so Raquel surmised he must indeed be a trusted minion, quite used to the queer starts of his employer. He doffed his dark, speckled hat and turned toward the bays. Thomas shouted after him.

"Wait, I will help you. There is a bit of an incline. You will have need of the extra hands."

The coachman lifted his gloved hands in grateful response before disappearing from view. The sky seemed to darken a shade. Raquel heard the cry of a bird—possibly a falcon—and the quick rustle of a small animal darting to some burrow. Otherwise, the world was quiet. Even the horses were still, their hooves no longer beating steadily across the path.

Raquel saw but could not hear the coachman muttering. His words were blown forward on the breeze.

"I should not have brought you here." Thomas's tone was rough from concern. In the closed chaise, he sounded abrupt and impatient. Raquel nearly agreed with him, for his simple assumption that she would "be fine" rankled. Still, she could see he was not quite as sanguine as he would have her suppose, for he eyed her appraisingly—despairingly—and brushed several disheveled hairs from his forehead. The glance he flickered at her held warmth and annoyance and unusual sincerity. Perversely, Lady Fortesque-Benton, who had been thinking *precisely* the same thing for half the journey or more, shook her golden head.

"I would have come anyway. I am notably head-strong."

She was rewarded with a slight smile for this, but Mr. Endicott's thoughts had moved on.

"Stay here. I shall see to the horses. The path narrows from here onward, so if this confounded chaise is to be turned around it has to be now. You do understand?"

Lady Raquel nodded. She had been brought up with horses and understood perfectly the need for caution. But Thomas had not stopped to see her response. He'd already opened the door and alighted. The cool rush of air made her gasp for breath. Outside, she could hear the coachman's exhortations to the horses, then the grind of carriage springs as she lurched across the chaise, back to the seat Mr. Endicott had just vacated.

It was still warm from his breeches, and despite the cool air, Lady Raquel flushed. She was so close to Darris! So close to the end of this strange, unsettling episode. And yet, it appeared to be only beginning. She held her breath, hardly knowing whether she was pleased or sorry to see the coach thus summarily dis-

missed and diverted. Certainly, there was no question
that night was now dangerously imminent.

Mr. Endicott had promised she would reach Darris
by nightfall. He was with an ame's ace of his promise,
but two miles or six miles or seventy miles was all the
same when a young lady was about to lose her reputation.

Raquel bit her lip. Tears were for fools and she was
not a fool. So she calmly placed her hands in her lap
and watched what maneuvering she could from the
window. What she couldn't see she felt, for despite the
excellent springs, the carriage jolted considerably, so
she was certain she would be stiff in unmentionable
places.

She concentrated on not allowing her teeth to rattle
and on averting her gaze from each flicker she spied
of a white lawn shirt outside. It looked grievously thin
in the cold, but Raquel knew better than to distract her
escort by beginning the greatcoat argument all over
again. He was a hard man. He would not thank her,
she thought, for her trouble. So she pulled the coat
firmly about her person—no point in them both freezing—and awaited his pleasure.

Twelve

The horses had long disappeared down the path leading to the Lion and the Anvil. The snow was not thick, but slippery and wet and cold to the ankles. Lady Raquel's skillfully selected carriage dress was sodden, and she was forced to concentrate on every step to avoid the indignity of slipping. Delicate flakes of snow clung to those fiercely masculine capes, but safe beneath the greatcoat's folds, Raquel was shielded from the worst of their biting frost. She wished she could say the same of Mr. Endicott, who was silently forging a path. She could see his muscles plainly beneath his shirt, which was now so soaked it was practically transparent. Raquel allowed her thoughts to wander immodestly over his form.

If she was forced to endure this drudgery, she might just as well afford herself some pleasure. *Most* unmaidenly, but then, Mr. Endicott never had brought out her maidenly instincts. When she was with him, she wanted to curse and pummel and . . . no, she would not allow herself to linger long over such nonsenses. And his shirt was neither wet nor deliciously transparent. It was as stiff as a board and freezing. In shock, she realized that he must be suffering a great deal more than he seemed, with his jaunty walking stick broken from an old, gnarled yew, and a stride that was far longer than her own.

"Stop!" She panted, trying to catch up. Mr. Endicott stopped, eying the state of her dress with critical calm. "We are nearly there, I can see the gray quarry stone walls."

Lady Fortesque-Benton nodded, catching her breath. It had been slightly uphill all the way and she was unused to such exertions.

"Shall I carry you?" The question was so at odds with his dismissive manner and brusque stride that she thought he was mocking.

"I am not a doll. I can manage, thank you."

He nodded stiffly. "A pity. Pretty as a doll, of course, but sharp-tongued. I keep forgetting."

"I am *not* sharp-tongued!"

Mr. Endicott did not stop to brangle with her. He shook his head and walked on, but Raquel noticed that his steps were slower to match her own. She wondered if it was because he was tiring, or because he was trying to be considerate. She decided he must be tiring, and rather gloomily squelched on. Her bonnet was frozen and she had little doubt that the several pastel-colored feathers that adorned it must be suffering a similar fate. In short, she looked, as she felt, a complete dowd. The thought did not console her wet feet, but she trudged on without comment or complaint.

If Thomas thought the better of her for it, he did not choose to say. Instead, he pointed to the welcome sight of the sentry's cottage and strode on ahead to open the door. It took some minutes to pry open, but thankfully it was not locked.

"Come in." He held open the door so that she had to walk past him to step inside. She did, blinking at the darkness of the interior.

"Dank and musty, I am afraid. The sentry, such as there is, was moved up to the castle years ago."

Raquel nodded. She did not need to be told why.

The house was in obvious disrepair and the duke's finances bleak. *That,* she knew, was why she had received his handsome offer.

"I shall have the house restored when . . ."

Her eyes dropped. Thomas was regarding her dryly. Raquel flushed. "Don't look so superior! It is not uncommon for the bride to have funds. I believe it is perfectly respectable."

"Oh, perfectly. But I would tread carefully, if I were you. Demian may not like a hundred plans put to him before you have even seen the castle."

"Why should he not? He surely cannot wish his estate to continue this obvious decline?"

Thomas shrugged and rubbed his fingers together. They were aching with cold and his entire chest felt numb. It was bad enough when they were walking, but now that they were stationary the cold seemed to bite deep. He eyed his greatcoat longingly and checked the pile of firewood. Not much, but enough to sustain a reasonable blaze. Without answering Raquel's question, he knelt by the hearth and reached for the tinderbox, concentrating on creating some warmth, if not much in the way of light. It was several moments before he was successful.

Raquel took in her surroundings with distaste. There were corners thick with cobwebs, and though there were several chairs, they were all hard and entirely devoid of padding. She dared not inspect the larder, for she was certain it would be empty. The well outside looked far too ancient to be of any use, though there was still a wooden bucket that looked serviceable. If she filled it with snow, water would not be a problem.

"Where do you think you are going?"

She had not thought Thomas was still aware of her existence. Evidently he was, for he turned from the fire and regarded her with suspicion.

"I am going to fill the pail. We may need water."

"Very true, my lady, how provident you are!"

Was that amusement or sarcasm in those eyes? Raquel did not know, and frankly she did not care.

"You are frozen. Take the greatcoat and I will search out some blankets. There must be some somewhere."

"Only horse blankets. The rest of Carlew's possessions were sent up to the manse."

Did he think she would shudder at the thought of horse blankets? Certainly, the grim satisfaction of his tone made her think so. Raquel ignored him and removed the coat wordlessly.

His brows raised.

"That is for you, my lady. It is freezing here, and I have no wish to argue."

"Do only ladies freeze? Not the masculine sex? How interesting. That was an aspect of anatomy which my governess failed to teach me."

"Did she teach you anatomy? How shocking! I thought water-colors and dancing were more suitable lessons."

"Well, you are wrong. I had a very superior governess and have learned several of the more masculine studies—which, by the way, I find fascinating."

This came with a quaint little glare that was meant to be arch and cool, but rather lighted Thomas's soul more than the paltry fire flickering in the grate. He did not give her the satisfaction, however, of gaining the upper hand.

"Excellent. Then if you have had anatomy lessons, you can have no objection to my removing this frozen, confounded shirt. No, take that thing away. It is pointless brandishing a greatcoat when I am soaking to the bone."

So saying, he nimbly—for one with such frozen fingers—undid his cravat and began on the small fastenings of his shirt with practiced ease and none of the self-consciousness that suddenly flooded Raquel's being.

"You brute! You deliberately provoke me."

"Ah, brute, again, how delightful. And did you say I provoke you?" He moved closer as his cold white shirt touched the cobbled floor. Raquel gasped, for she had never before seen a man naked to his waist, nor so unutterably beautiful. Nor so intolerably rude, insolent, overbearing and thoroughly annoying.

She stepped back.

"Yes, I did. But I did not mean . . ."

"What did you not mean, my lady?"

He was dangerously close to her now, close enough to kiss her.

There was a brief moment when Raquel thought he would. She felt quite faint at the prospect, and had to will herself not to sway toward those dark, fearsomely blue eyes.

"I did not mean provoke in the way . . ."

". . . a man provokes a lady. How terribly disappointing." But Mr. Endicott did not look disappointed. Rather, he looked amused and sanguine and rather disbelieving.

"You lie very badly, Raquel. Is that a failing or your fortune, I wonder?"

But he did not stop for an answer, and he ducked neatly when the only earthenware pitcher in the entire place was hurled at his head.

"Temper, temper, my lady!" Leisurely, he reached out for one of the horse blankets and handed it to her. It was gray and scratchy but quite dry.

"I shall take up your offer. Not the one in your eyes, Raquel, but the one of my greatcoat. I shall need it when I head up to the castle."

"Head up . . . you are not leaving me here?" For the first time, alarm entered her voice.

Thomas sighed. "You are dry and warm here. You are also safe. If you step up with me to the castle, you shall be neither of those things."

"Why not?"

"It is cold, snowing and wet. There is only one garment of any use between both of us. You shall also be horribly compromised if we arrive together without a chaperon."

"Oh!" Evidently, that thought had not occurred to the poised, cool, society heiress. It seemed eons ago that she had ever been poised or cool.

"But safe!"

He looked at her quizzically. "I think not, Lady Raquel. There is a limit to a man's endurance, I believe. And though I hesitate to mention it at such a time, your ankles are delectable even if your hems are not."

"Oh!" Suddenly, her face was warm, though the chill air told her the cottage was damp. And he had been eying her ankles as they walked, not her dowdy bonnet feathers or her sack of a greatcoat! Why did she want to hum and grin foolishly when she should scold? And why did she do neither, just stare at him with her eyes wide and her lips parted idiotically?

Thomas laughed. "So you see, Lady Raquel, it is best I depart immediately for the castle. Doubtless Demian will then send a brigade of people down to tend to you. As the newest duchess-to-be of this region, I suppose it is all you deserve." But the laughter left his eyes and the faint contempt crept back into his voice.

"Yes, I see. Thank you." Raquel quelled the urge to beg him to take her with him. It would be no more than an hour or two, surely, that she would be left to her own devices in this godforsaken cottage. It was not exactly the reception she had imagined for herself, but then neither was worrying herself sick about a man whom she detested heartily and who was entirely ineligible. Or was he? It was not as though he had no power, or social entrée, or . . . but no, he had no rank. The obstacles were insurmountable and she was being ridiculous thinking in such terms. The duke awaited her.

Slowly, she handed him the coat that had proved so warm, so comforting, so masculine, even. The horse blanket seemed a poor swap, but she was comforted by the knowledge that Thomas would be a little warmer. *And* he would be covered. She blushed at her missish reaction to his near nakedness. He probably thought it was *nothing* to flaunt himself in front of young females. He shrugged himself into the coat in a single second's movement that would have astonished any self-respecting valet, and moved to the door.

"There is wood enough for hours yet, my lady. If I don't see you again before your betrothal, I wish you adieu."

"Won't you be staying? I am sure Demian would wish it."

"Would he?" The lips twisted a little. "Well, I won't. And I think I have already exceeded myself in pleasing my lord Demian. You are meek and untouched. Both miracles."

He left before she could hurl the pail at him.

It was several moments before Raquel's gaze left the open door. He did not look back, though she willed him to. Feeling flat and defeated, Raquel shut the door and settled to await the carriage Demian would probably send down. It would not be a team of six, she knew, but one or two horses could probably brave the distance. She wondered how she would feel when she saw her betrothed again. Certainly, they would make a handsome couple, for he was dark where she was fair, and though she could not *quite* recall his classical features, she knew them to be tolerably handsome, though not devastatingly so, like Thomas's.

Oh! She must not think of him as Thomas, it was not proper. Mr. Endicott. *Mr. Endicott,* she repeated firmly to herself, then again and again, until the name buzzed annoyingly in her head and she had to sweep the cottage of every cobweb vigorously with an old broom before she could think of anything else. What she thought of *then* was that while the cobwebs were gone—along with a dark, long-legged spider that had caused her to gasp—the dust was not. She coughed a little and opened the door cautiously. The sun was just setting, lemon-pink against the blue-white shadows creeping up with dusk. Though the flakes were not falling nearly so wildly as she had feared, the snow was thick around her. Thomas's tracks were almost frozen into the landscape, but they were disappearing fast. Raquel had never felt so forlorn. She stepped outside and bent to trace her finger over one. Foolish girl, for all she achieved were wet gloves.

There was nothing for it but to return indoors and wait.

Mr. Endicott's progress was neither swift nor easy. Many times he had to stop himself from breaking into a run, for that would be foolhardy beyond permission. If he were to break a leg, it would not just be he who waited for help in the wintry shadows, but Raquel, too. No one would think to look for her in Carlew's sentry cottage. Indeed, he was perfectly certain Demian would be astonished to learn he had undertaken the trip at all. In this weather, he would have been forgiven for bowing out of their previous arrangement.

Not that there had *been* much of a previous arrange-ment—just him acting more the coxcomb than usual. Thomas grimaced. He had blithely undertaken to teach Lady Raquel Fortesque-Benton a few manners. He had *not* anticipated wanting to run Demian through with his sword merely because His Grace had the dubious felicity of being her betrothed. He had *not* expected his heart to hammer like a schoolboy when her soft, infinitely feminine scent assaulted his nostrils and made a mockery of his breathing. No, indeed, he had not bargained for any of these things. Lady Raquel was sharp-tongued, but she was also witty and vulnerable. Anyone thinking her aloof and cold was seeing only the outermost layer. Thomas imagined he had glimpsed more than the outermost in his short acquaintance with her.

And bother! It was *not* just that! It was the blatant attraction he felt for her, the sort of physical yearning that made him want to throw her to the floor in her hideous horse blanket and play out the piece that seemed to tremble between both of them. Yes, she felt it too, he had no doubt about it. Again, his arrogance reasserted itself in a somewhat livelier tread. A faint half-smile still hovered about his mouth as he reached the castle stairs.

He would nip round the back. Hedgewig—he knew the sour-faced old creature—would probably slam the door in his face if he made his appearance in soiled Hessians, muddy unmentionables and nothing more than a greatcoat between him and near nakedness. Probably quite correct, too, for he would make a most unedifying spectacle for Lady Caroline Darris—though she was a hoyden herself—or, more pertinently, dear old Martha. Martha, he was certain, would be shocked.

He would try the servant's entrance, for Cook had a

certain fondness for him. The corners of his wide lips twitched. *All* cooks had a certain fondness for him! He could wheedle his way round housekeepers and cooks with the crook of his little finger. As for maids . . . well, he would not digress down that idle but decidedly pleasant path.

He rapped loudly on the stout oak door. Unlike the main castle door, it was not blessed with a shining brass knocker, but the leaden one, green with age, served its purpose more than suitably. Thomas did not wait for an invitation to enter, but strode in purposefully, slamming the door shut with his back.

There was no one about, but the aromas coming from the larder were irresistible, so, heedless of his dripping boots, he ambled across and helped himself to a partridge pie. Demian must be less under the hatches than he had thought, because there was evidence everywhere of a banquet. Huge platters of cheeses sat on a board waiting, he presumed, to be served. He was just toying with the idea of ditching the pie in favor of some Stilton, when some footsteps behind him made him jump.

"Don't you dare touch that!"

Thomas whirled round. What he saw made him nearly whoop with laughter, but as a gentleman, he did not. Possibly the events of the day were causing him to hallucinate. He decided to humor this apparition of his.

"May I eat the pie, then?"

"Oh, yes. There are piles of them. I fear, in fact, that I made too many. But the Stilton was appallingly expensive. I wish *I* had had the management of it, not Cook. I am certain I could have driven a better bargain."

"Oh, undoubtedly, a seventeen-year-old robed like a dowager and wearing . . . *is* that a coronet? You must excuse my stupidity in these matters, but I find your headpiece quite fascinating."

Lady Caro's eyes danced. "Yes, hideous, isn't it? I rummaged through the ducal jewels but everything was so austere. This seemed just perfect."

"Pardon my sublime ignorance, also my shocking state of undress—though I suspect, you scamp, that you have not even noticed—but perfect for what?" Thomas bit into his pie and eyed her thoughtfully.

"Oh, I am masquerading as the lady of the manor as in some Minerva Press novel and Demian is the butler and . . ."

A chunk of partridge pie hovered precariously at the back of Thomas's throat. It was only by dint of very careful swallowing that he did not actually choke.

"What did you say?"

Lady Caroline chuckled. "Oh, I know, isn't it the greatest jest? Demian dismissed Hedgewig just when we needed him most vitally, so the role just somehow got assigned to him, and, oh, he should be down any moment to take in the first remove. I hope he hurries, for we are hopelessly short-staffed and Martha is busy chaperoning him . . ."

Now the pie was put down altogether.

"What did you say?" His voice thundered in Caro's ears.

"Hush! Have you an ear complaint, Mr. Endicott? You seem to be quite deaf today."

"And you seem to be hovering perilously close to lunacy. Explain yourself fast, young lady, or I'll not answer for the consequences."

"I am seventeen. *Way* too old to threaten. Go away, Thomas, unless you want to be an under butler or a second footman?" For the first time, she eyed his great-coat doubtfully.

"If you are seventeen, you can no longer take liberties with my name. You will shock London with your scapegrace ways, Lady Caroline. And, yes, I can."

"What?"

"Threaten." He advanced toward her from round a long, heavy beechwood table. Caroline squealed and darted away, but *most* unfortunately tripped over her regal hem. Mr. Endicott caught her, then shook her, then set her down upon a bench and hovered over her menacingly.

"Now, talk!"

"The cheeses . . ."

"I shall put a cloth over them."

"Very well, but when Demian arrives—"

"When Demian arrives I shall shake *him*. In the meanwhile, talk."

And so, *much* beset, but still with an irrepressible smile playing about her lips, Lady Caroline did.

Thirteen

Caroline had stopped sitting as soon as she could see by Mr. Endicott's thoughtful frown that he was not likely to bite her bejeweled head off. Instead, she made herself useful by putting a great copper cauldron onto the fire. It smelled heavenly to Thomas, but he was thinking of a great deal more than his stomach at that moment.

"Are you certain Demian was taken with this chit?"

"Smitten! I tell you, Thomas, it is a godsend! She looks to be the nicest creature and you have no *idea* the set down she gave that vulgar collection of chits!"

"Is she beautiful?"

Caroline regarded him scornfully. "Of course! When has Demian shown the smallest interest in anyone who is not a diamond? She might not be so in his usual way, for she has cropped hair and is less . . . less . . ."

Thomas was amused to note the flush appear on Caroline's cheeks. The little minx was growing up, then.

"Voluptuous?" He supplied the word with bland amusement.

Caro eyed him suspiciously, then nodded. "Yes, though indeed I do not think she is actually *lacking* . . ."

Thomas chuckled. "Caro, if you were *my* sister I would spank you! Has no one yet taught you what is and what is not a suitable topic of discourse for young ladies of quality?"

Caro waved her hand impatiently. "Of course! And really, it is the stupidest thing, for gentlemen talk all day long on such matters and no one berates *them.*"

"Yes, very unfair. Now tell me quickly. Has Demian said nothing about his betrothal?"

"Betrothal?" Caro stared at him blankly.

Thomas sighed and took a large ladle down from its hook. "Yes. I assume he told you he has offered for Lady Raquel Fortesque-Benton?"

"Yes . . . no! I knew it was his intention, but not that he had actually done it! Oh, Thomas, this is dreadful!" Great, round eyes looked up at him. He stirred the pot, then tasted some of the liquid with a serving spoon. It was heavenly, as he had suspected. Caro was too distracted to scold him as she would have, if she'd noticed.

"Is it gazetted? I cannot believe it! I could swear he was smitten with Miss Mayhew! So much so that I had to send Martha off to fetch him, for when he escorted her up to her chamber . . ."

Thomas burned his tongue.

"He did *what?*"

"Well, he *is* the butler." Caro looked defensive. "Besides, when I sent them off—"

"Ah, so it was your little scheme, was it?"

"Yes, but only because Miss Mayhew looked faint and I took pity on her with those old tabbies staring daggers and—"

"Demian making moon eyes."

"Well yes, but—"

"Lady Caroline Darris, I take leave to inform you, you are a meddler! I also take leave to inform you that when next I lay eyes on your brother, I shall personally strangle him!"

"But why? No one wants him to wed some spoiled creature who cares more for her rank than for his person! But if he has already offered . . ."

"Precisely. And I take leave to inform you, Mistress Caro, that that spoiled young lady is at this moment shivering in the sentry house."

Now it was Caro's turn to echo Mr. Endicott. "Shivering in the—"

"Yes. shivering." Mr. Endicott's words were suddenly curt. "And she is *not* spoiled, merely proud. She has the courage of a man and the beauty of . . . but no, I will not discuss such matters with a little slip of a schoolgirl not yet out! Get Demian!"

"I can't! The ladies will just be returning from the gallery—I got two of the housemaids to escort them—and will be expecting dinner shortly. They will think it passing strange if I am not there to greet them."

"Caro, I could not care two straws for what a dowdy parcel of chits think when—"

"Oh, they are not dowdy, Thomas! Did I say they were dowdy?" Caroline's eyes twinkled again. "They are as fine as peacocks and more brilliant! I swear I need my parasol inside for I can't see for the glitter of gems."

"Very charming, I am sure," came the dry retort. "But my point remains. Get me Demian. And a trap. I am going to throw a few provisions in this sack and take them down to her. Is there firewood anywhere?"

"Yes, Williams chopped some the other day. It is stacked in the scuttle outside. But you cannot be thinking of—"

"I cannot bring her up to the castle. It is bedlam here."

"Lord, yes! You *definitely* can't bring her up here! Good Lord, what in the world would she think? If she is truly Demian's betrothed . . ." She regarded him narrowly.

"Cut line, Caro! Why would I lie about a thing like that? Though you may as well tell Demian with my compliments that if he continues dangling after this Miss Mayhew, then my bond is no longer in effect."

"What bond?"

But Mr. Endicott did not think it necessary to go into details. Keeping Raquel pure in the snowiest of senses had proven a harder task than he had blithely imagined. If he was set to spend a night of snowbound bliss with the creature, it was well he had matters straight with Demian. Lord Darris had every facility to arrive forthwith and demand his betrothed. If he did, Thomas would no doubt have to offer her up meekly. But if he did not. . . . Mr. Endicott closed his eyes for a brief second. He would not dwell on this last matter. All he knew for certain was that the lovely Lady Fortesque-Benton did not deserve to have her honor compromised. A night alone with him would accomplish precisely that. Already, if rumors filtered out about their unchaperoned trip . . . but no, between Darris and himself they could scotch that.

Thomas prayed, in a half second, that the unknown Miss Mayhew was captivating, enticing, and lovely beyond imagination. He could not bear it, he thought, if she was not. Yet Demian could not simply cry off. It was a coil. But not one he could blithely ponder whilst a lady relied on him to return.

"Thomas?"

Caro was still regarding him intently. "A man's business, Caro. Just tell him. Can you stock this up? I am going to negotiate the trap and stack it with firewood. I presume there are no servants about?"

"None. They are all engaged in removing holland

covers and such. It looks like they are going to have to stay here overnight, after all."

"Overnight? Probably a week. You were mad, Caro."

"I know, but it did seem a good idea . . ."

"Godsend I am never the recipient of one of your 'good ideas!' You are going to be hell to marry off, Caro."

For the first time, Lady Caroline looked hurt. Thomas raised his hands helplessly. "Oh, hang my vile tongue! Come, don't cry. Doubtless there is someone out there mad enough to want a scapegrace wife! Why, I would marry you myself if—"

"Fustian, Thomas!" But the tears had stopped welling up in her bright eyes. She was laughing again. "I will get a hamper sorted for you. Leave that filthy sack—I will find something better and include a tinderbox and some flint . . ."

"Good girl!"

"Is a trap enough? There is Demian's barouche, but it is probably hemmed in by all the other carriages. The party came in three at least."

"Not a problem. Can I get to the trap easily?"

"Oh, yes, for it is stabled for the dower house. Easier for the servants—such that there are left." This, a little gloomily, so Thomas understood something of the reasons why Demian had been in such agonies to shackle himself.

Mr. Endicott nodded briefly. "I will organize it, then. Has Demian any fresh shirts handy? Mine is ruined, this greatcoat is hideously scratchy and I've sent the chaise off to the Lion and the Anvil."

"Lady Raquel's things too?"

Thomas grimaced. "Indeed, we are a sorry pair, for she has sacrificed this greatcoat for a horse blanket."

"Good Lord, Thomas. How *could* you! I don't *care*

if she is a poker-faced icicle, the wretch must be miserable!"

"The 'wretch,' as you inaccurately put it, is admirable. She has actually managed to fling an earthenware pot at me, melt . . ."

Thomas stopped. He had nearly said "melt my heart," which would *not* be a felicitous thing to say to the sister of her betrothed. Besides, the thought amazed him as much as it would have her. He said nothing, therefore, but Caroline was no fool.

"By Jericho, Mr. Endicott, I detect a romance!"

"Save detection for your betters, Caro." There was a subtle warning in his voice. It was going to be hard enough to scotch scandal as it was.

"Very well, but if she threw an earthenware pot at you she must have some redeeming qualities. Mind you, Demian *said* she was a shrew."

"Your brother Demian has a lot to answer for. I hope it does not come to pistols at dawn, for I am a very good shot."

"So is he. But you intrigue me, sir."

"I am only 'sir' when you wish to wheedle something from me, Caro. I would stop and indulge you, but there is a lady who deserves and needs some attention. If it cannot be from Demian, than it shall be from me."

Caroline sighed. "Very well. Go on, then, I shall nip upstairs, smile at the tartars, fob them off—though heaven knows, they must all be simpletons if they haven't smelled a rat by now—grab some laundry and scuttle down again. By then you should have Charlie the job horse trotting around nicely."

"Charlie, is it?"

"Yes, and he responds well to carrots."

"Caro, I may be beggared and shirtless, but I will

be *damned* if I dangle a carrot on a stick. Next you will be telling me the animal is a donkey."

"He is."

Lady Darris reached into a casket of vegetables. There were several potatoes and parsnips, but she had to scratch around fiercely for anything so much as resembling a carrot. At last, she felt one and wiped it down hurriedly with a calico cloth.

"Here." Her lips did not quiver as she handed the vegetable to Thomas. Then she perched her gemstones carefully upon her head, pinned them helter-skelter with a few frightfully loose hair clasps and scuttled off with as much dignity as she could muster. If she heard Mr. Endicott hurl all manner of oaths at her retreating back she did not reveal so. Only a tiny gray mouse, hiding behind a cherry wood hall clock, heard her mischievous chuckle. By the time she had reached the stairs, it was drowned by the first chimes and several high-pitched titters and exclamations of interest. It seemed that the duke's ancestors had found favor.

Amy walked in on several loo tables. The guests were nibbling on sweet frappes and squabbling over numbers. They pounced on her gleefully, for she made up even numbers, despite the fact that she *detested* the game and avoided gambling whenever she could. Mrs. Corey made some snide remark behind her fan that Lady Caroline bobbed up more frequently than a cork, and had they but known her propensity to vanish into thin air, they may have chosen to stay at home.

At this, Amy inferred that they were all thoroughly disgruntled at the duke's continued absence and growing bored. She smiled, but avoided the obvious retort that rose to her soft, sweetly becoming lips. Instead, noticing that when Lady Caroline *did* appear she looked distracted, Amy slipped into her seat and took up her cards, muttering platitudes in a soothing way.

If she could head off the ire of Mrs. Corey—or even Honoria Murgatroyd—that must surely assist the lady in some small way. It was obvious to her that His Grace's finances were bleak, and that it must be rather hard on Lady Caroline to be entertaining in such a manner. To be entertaining at *all,* for that matter. She hardly looked above sixteen despite the languid manner and the worldly air of sophistication.

So, kind as always, Amy gently drew attention away from Lady Caroline and assumed it herself. When there was tea to pour, she poured it, when there were ruffled sensibilities to soothe, she soothed them. No one seemed to remember that she had been pale and faint, but everyone seemed to remember that the servants were tardy and that the corridors were drafty. Miss Riverton even so far forgot herself as to mention that parts of the castle were "positively shabby"—and this in full hearing of Lady Caroline, whose cheeks flushed, but who somehow pretended not to hear.

Still, in the thrill of winning and losing great sums of money—all carefully inscribed on little debt of honor bills—they squabbled about as though they were *not* all heiresses swimming in merchant-made money, and the afternoon soon progressed to dinner. Miraculously, every lady but Amy had packed ball gowns for the occasion. Amy wondered wryly how it was that five debutantes and two chaperons had all been able to accurately forecast snow. Still, she supposed she was merely foolish for not entertaining the possibility. This time of year the weather *always* was intemperate.

"Amy, *do* ring for the dressers. They must be made available at once." So Amy, with a cautious glance at

Lady Caroline, who sensed a friend and did not at *all* mind her assumption of control, rang for the dressers, gave orders for the portmanteaus to be brought up from wherever they were being stored, and generally acted as dogsbody and genteel companion to all her social peers. No one seemed to notice in the slightest.

Then Honoria, at her most cloying, turned to Lady Caroline. "My dear, *such* an inconvenience! I do assure you, had I known we would have to rely on your hospitality, wild *horses* would not have dragged me from London! I *do* hope we will not be inconveniencing His Grace?" This last, with a faint, quizzical question attached.

Lady Caroline coughed. She wondered wildly where His Grace was, and what he could possibly have to say to the addition of eight undesirable guests in his household. He would probably strangle her in private, no doubt . . . but here was Martha, resuming her position as upper house servant and thankfully removing the tray of sugarplums. If Miss Fletcherson stretched out her sticky hand for one more, her French-lace gloves would surely be ruined. As Martha turned, Caroline tried to catch her eye, but the older lady merely frowned, then curtsied, fluttered about a bit, then bobbed another curtsy before leaving.

"Odd servants. Lady Darris." Mrs. Murgatroyd was growing bold. Caroline wanted to plant her a very indelicate slap upon her bony cheek, but instead, scrutinized her with an ancient monocle she had plucked from Demian's wall. The treatment seemed to have its effect, for Honoria modified the comment with a faint titter and some disclaimer that this was naturally often the case in noble households.

"Yes. Miss Bancroft is an old retainer. Very loyal. More friend than servant."

Now it was Mrs. Corey's turn to titter. She tapped

at Caroline playfully with the stem of her fan. "Oh, my dear, how *droll!* How naughty, naughty to tease us with such humor! But you must not talk too loudly, my dear." She moved a little closer and whispered loudly, "Might give them ideas above their station."

At this fortuitous moment, His Grace himself ar-rived. Not one of the guests—save, of course, for Amy, who trembled slightly and refused to meet his inviting eyes—seemed to notice. No, that is not quite true. Miss Fletcherson did, for she inquired rather querulously when they were likely to be shown to their rooms. But since she did this with a haughty toss of her shoulders and a slight frown upon her otherwise quite passable face, the duke was given to understand his masquerade had not yet been suspected, much less actually discov-ered.

"I am sorry for the inconvenience, madam. The south wing is being prepared, but unfortunately, since it is still in holland covers from . . . uh . . . recent reno-vations, this might take a while. I assure you, the entire Darris staff is working on the matter."

"Humph! One would think . . . but there, we *heard* Darris had his pockets to let." Whilst the ladies whis-pered loudly to themselves, Caroline shot her brother a startled look. She had expected many things, but not the south wing. He slipped out, after bowing to no one in particular and sneaking a *very* hazardous wink at Miss Mayhew, who had finally brought herself to look at him. No one but Caroline observed this exchange, the significance of which buoyed both her spirits and her curiosity to bubbling point. So much so that when the butler quietly signaled for the loo tables to be re-moved, she slipped past the footmen and followed him from the room.

"Caro! Ladies do not chase after butlers. Get back in there."

"Butlers do not wink at ladies! Tell me what is going on, or I shall—"

"Scream? Not, I think, very wise, Caro, dear. Now, save your hysterics for later."

"Easy for *you* to say! *You* did not just find out that your sibling was betrothed."

"Lady Raquel? I am sorry, Caro, but there was simply no time." Demian picked up a silver platter that awaited removal to the kitchens.

"No time to tell me that that same betrothed was on her way to Darris?"

The salver dropped with a crash.

"Ow!"

"Hush. You are not telling me . . ."

"Yes, I am. I sent Thomas away to the old sentry cottage. It is freezing and pitifully stocked, but she could not come here. Not now." The duke was appalled. "God, I should say not! But the sentry cottage! I will never hear the end of this!"

"And serve you right! How *could* you go and betrothe yourself when I've gone to so much trouble for you?"

"You?" Outrage oozed from every pore of Demian's body. Then he picked up the salver and laughed. "Had I known, Caro, I swear I would not have done it! But you only wrote to me of hats and peacocks, remember?"

"Yes. And foxes."

"And foxes. I've brought the confounded liniment that you require. What does Thomas say?"

"Churlish. Particularly churlish. He wished, I believe, to slam you into a wall. Or was it simply to knock you down senseless? I can't remember. Anyway, he seems remarkably taken by your betrothed. I gather she is prettier than you disclosed, and a great deal more charming. Or so I infer."

"Tommyrot! She is poker-faced and spoiled. Thank you, Betsy." This, as Betsy, returning to the kitchens, picked up the salver and placed it back into the duke's hands. His gloves were in danger of becoming soiled, so he made a face and looked beseechingly at his minion. Betsy, enjoying the prank taking place in the ducal household, grinned boldly, just resisted curtsying, and took up the platter once more.

Lady Caroline waited for her to disappear into the bowels of the scullery, well out of hearing. Then she shrugged in a very unladylike manner, but the gleam of mischief had reappeared.

"Your good friend Thomas *also* sends you some garbled message that he was infuriating enough not to explain."

"Which is?"

"Which is that his bond is no longer in effect. Particularly if you are dangling after Miss Mayhew."

A speculative look entered Demian's eye. "Did he, now? I wonder which bond he was alluding to? The one not to strangle her, or the one not to . . . great good gun, it might be the very thing!"

Caro tried to look patient. "Demi, I don't like to inquire into the intricate workings of your mind, but—"

"Then don't." Demian was singularly uncommunicative as he pinched his sister's cheeks—thereby eliciting an undignified squeak—and adjusted his cravat. Too elegant for a butler, of course, but a man *did* have his pride. Then he took off after Betsy, behind the great oak door and into the cozy, aromatic, cocoa-smelling kitchens. It was the warmest place in the castle.

Caro did not stop to watch him. Rather, she tossed back her head, swept up her skirts and adopted her pose with miraculous dignity. She pushed open the door and gazed, poker-faced, at a particularly splendid chandelier. The tapers had all been lit—a shocking waste—but she concentrated on them carefully. She had sixteen querulous eyes to avoid. She feared if she did not take this precaution, she would fall into a foolish fit of the giggles.

"Ladies, I suggest we leave off ball gowns. The chambers are not yet ready and I am sure the exigencies of the weather outside makes a slight deviation from protocol understandable. If I may say so, your current attire is quite admirable."

Miss Oliver seemed inclined to pout, for her gown was of an apple-blossom green and very becoming, by all accounts, but she was silenced from an unexpected quarter. Miss Corey announced scathingly that since His Grace did not appear to be at home, they might just as well traipse about in their rags—at which she received a dig in her tightly pulled-in corset, for Mrs. Corey was a shrewd woman, and not altogether unaware of Lady Caroline's influence. If she were to put in a good word for Amelia . . . but Amelia was compounding her sin by declaring that she was famished in a most indelicate and unladylike manner.

There were several audible gasps, for all the young ladies had been tutored to think of themselves as very genteel indeed, and "only ever ate like birds, veritable little sparrows." Of course, Miss Corey's girth indicated otherwise, but this was entirely beside the point. There was, therefore, much tittering and significant little nods as Caro led the ladies down to the second floor. She was heartily sick of Demian's Gainsboroughs at this point, but nevertheless managed to dutifully point some of these out along the way, although a much-loved statue of Hermes she described as Pan, but no one seemed to notice this scatter-witted mistake, for which she was thankful. Well, it is true that *Amy's* features relaxed into laughter, but then, Amy, she had decided, was a friend. She never minded being corrected by friends. Martha did it all day, when it came to that.

At last, they turned into the breakfast room, refurbished a little, from lunch, and sporting green silk drapes and elegant flowers drifting out of silver epergnes. Martha, it seemed, had not been idle. His Grace was already positioned behind a laden serving board where the cheeses Mr. Endicott had seemed ready to swipe were prominently displayed.

Demian moved over to Miss Amy and murmured something inaudible in her ear. She colored up delightfully, Caro thought, but frowned severely upon her sibling and ordered him across the room for a glass of ratafia.

He complied, and dutifully filled the glasses of all the guests, but not, Caro noted, with Madeira or even port. Mrs. Murgatroyd was startled to find lemon barley cordial in her glass, and was inclined to cough. A similar occurrence occurred with Mrs. Corey, although she was clever enough not to comment on the matter. The young ladies all seemed dubious upon their first delicate sips, but Caro regaled them with stories of how His Royal Highness always refused to drink anything very strong with the first remove. This patent false truth seemed to mollify the guests, who were delighted to think of themselves hobnobbing one step from such elevated company. Each spent a delightful few moments concocting such phrases as, "Oh, when my good friend Lady Caroline Darris and I dined, oh, the funniest thing, she is close to the Prince of Wales, you know, so when he . . ." and that sort of thing.

Mrs. Corey dryly remarked that she was unaware of such restraint on the part of His Royal Highness, but Caroline quelled her with a crushing glance that caused Miss Mayhew to stare at her cutlery and the butler to very suddenly quit the room.

Miss Bancroft appeared then, laden with dishes, and the company set to with relish, Betsy's trout being considered with particular favor. By the second remove, conversation was genteelly resuming, and Caro's composure was sufficient to allow her to preside over the meal with decorum. She engaged Miss Mayhew in some interesting conversation, always noticing how Demian seemed to linger close, as if to catch every syllable.

"By Jupiter, he is smitten!" she thought in surprise, for her brother, whilst renowned for his liaisons, had never before shown any decided preference for one maiden in particular. She wondered what Mr. Endicott was up to and frowned. Her brother seemed to be in even more of a coil than she, herself. If Lady Raquel sued for breach . . . but no! Demian was not a common jilt. But to go through with a loveless ceremony. . . . Her eyes softened as she watched Miss Mayhew. Now *there* was an estimable bride. Beneath all that decorum she wagered lay a well-nurtured sense of the ridiculous. Well, it stood to reason, when she plainly suspected, and blushed every time the wretched butler approached. Since *she* could not help herself, *he* must stop lurking in that manner if he did not want to be instantly exposed!

"Pemberton!"

"My lady?" The voice was servile, but there was a lilt of devil-may-care laughter in the tone.

"You are excused. Go see to the . . . uh . . . the . . . the . . ."

"Fox?" he suggested, softly.

"Yes! Fox! And don't come back with the third remove. Send in the under butler." This, with an imperious sweep of the hand when she knew full well there was no under butler to be had for hair or hide. The duke did not blink.

"Very well, my lady." He bowed subserviently, then allowed a wide, private smile to cross his face. Miss Mayhew was privy to this, and felt that her cutlery was suddenly *terribly* interesting.

"Miss Mayhew, shall I escort you to the south wing? I see you have finished your dinner, and you might like to speak with the servants who accompanied you. I have comfortably housed the coachmen, I believe, but the dressers and—"

"My good man, *that* is no job for a pert young miss! Are you quite bereft of your senses that you refer to her, rather than I? *I* shall accompany you to our quarters. I trust that the sheets have all been aired? And I will need to see that the hot bricks—"

"Honoria! You are nothing but a meddlesome widgeon! It is *I* who should see to these little niceties. Shouldn't I, girls?" And Mrs. Corey beamed at the six young ladies who were in varying stages of their repast.

"Nonsense! It is plain, Hyacinth, that your plate is still laden! What shocking manners to desert your place in such a manner! I cannot imagine what dear Lady Caroline will think. It is fortunate that I, of course, eat like a little cock robin. Naturally, I am finished." She stood up and glared expectantly at the butler. There was nothing he could do, of course, but bow rather glacially and murmur that she follow. He nearly made the fatal mistake of offering her his arm, then caught himself up short in time. There were, after all, compensations for being merely a manservant. He was spared the bony clasp of Mrs. Murgatroyd's gloved hand. Other than that, he could think of few.

With his departure, Caroline's composure was completely restored. Three servants tripped in with candles, for the light was almost gone and the cold was creeping in gloomily. Though she could not see it, something told her the flurries were worsening. Mrs. Corey's sharp eyes darted to the window. When she noted the same, she took a long draft of the offending lemon cordial and sighed in satisfaction.

Fourteen

Thomas threw off the greatcoat and buttoned up one of Demian's shirts. It was too tight, for the duke had a smaller frame than he, though both physiques were impeccable to the eyes of any interested beholder.

Nevertheless, His Grace's tailor was obviously a scrupulous gentleman, for the fit was exquisitely molded to Darris's form and thus rendered hopelessly tight across Mr. Endicott's shoulders and chest. Still, it was better than nothing. So was the carrick coat of soft kerseymere and wool that Caro had thoughtfully provided, though that, too, was tight.

Thomas discarded his own greatcoat upon the kitchen slates. It was too wet to be of use any longer. Caro had provided a basketful of smallclothes for Lady Raquel, but had been too scatter-witted to provide much else. A nice gown might have been handy, or even a decent pelisse. But that was Caro all over! Kind to a fault, but not brainy.

Since beggars could not be choosers, he bundled up what he could, snatched several macaroons cooling on the table, and the basket Caro had provided. That, at least, was heavy enough to be regarded as ample. The skies were certainly darkening and the winds were up again. Thomas's only worry was that he would not make the cottage. The weather could turn foul in seconds.

He loaded up the trap, eyed the donkey sternly and bade it go. It wouldn't. He tried again, but the wretched animal refused to budge, despite having walked down from the dower house quite reasonably. Thomas wished to kick it, but instead, pleaded a little, removed a precautionary carrot and pushed a lump of sugar into the lazy beast's mouth. Both offerings were accepted, but made singularly little in the way of difference. It then dawned on Thomas that today was not his day. Cursing, he removed the basket from the trap, gasped at its weight, scowled at the ass, cursed it, muttered dire and unlawful threats and proceeded to walk. The cottage seemed a great deal farther than he remembered, he could not see a trace of it on the horizon and night was now decidedly falling. Only the thought of the Lady Raquel, alone, frightened and cold, made him walk on. It would have been an easy matter, after all, to bade Demian do his own dirty work. But there was the crux of it: He did not *want* Demian anywhere near his own betrothed. And for the life of him, he could not admit why.

He ignored the pain in his chest and the terrible difficulty he had gasping for breath in the frigid air. None of it mattered, at that moment, for the vision of glorious golden ringlets and sapphire eyes and bow-shaped lips spurred him on. Not in lust, either, for what kind of man, laden with a deadweight basket, shivering in snow and almost numb with cold could be driven by such a delightfully warm tormentor? No, lust—though decidedly it had been his companion the greater part of the day—was now, sadly, extinguished. So what was left? A drumming in Mr. Endicott's head and a dull determination to beat the cold, the dark, the teasing moon.

Inside the castle, Lady Caroline peered past her dinner guests. What she saw outside the frosted window did not cheer her. The flurries were definitely imminent, and though the castle was cold, they were all undoubtedly safe from the elements. Thomas, she knew, was not. Neither was the detestable Lady Raquel Fortesque-Benton, though now she was removed from her brother's immediate sphere, possibly not that detestable. But what of her reputation? A night alone with Thomas would ruin all vestiges of it, she was certain. Guilt crept over her miserably, for if she had not meddled, it would have been perfectly acceptable to bring her ladyship up to the castle. Even now, surely, she should do something to prevent that lady's ruin. She did not, however top lofty, deserve to be compromised. But Thomas was with her. Thomas could be relied upon to preserve her honor. Or could he? Assailed with doubt, Lady Caroline nearly made the fatal error of chewing on her fingernails.

Then she thought of Thomas's bold challenge to Demian and stopped her woolgathering. Mr. Endicott, she knew, had never yet been at a loss. If the matter could not be elegantly hushed up, he would marry her himself. The thought made her brighten considerably, but when she nodded augustly to Miss Kirby and murmured something about "squeezes and crushes and fatiguing presentations," the gloom returned. More likely Thomas would force *Demian* to marry the chit. Then all her hard contriving would be for naught.

"I can't help but feel that the weather is worsening. My dear, dear, *dear* Lady Caroline. What can I say? How *gracious* of you to house us in this splendid manner. Perhaps you would like to call on . . . what was his name . . . Masterton or Pemberton or whoever, my dear, to stoke up the fire. But of course, you await the under butler. Perhaps *he* can perform the trifling task. I am only dropping a delicate hint, you see, for I have

been mistress of a great establishment for *many* more
years than your youthful self, though I am sure you
would not guess it, for what with Mrs. Moorleigh's
wonder lotion . . . frightfully expensive you know, but
Mr. Corey is always saying as how I must needs get
the best of everything, and really, the poor dear spoils
me sometimes. Anyway, I am perfectly certain you
don't at *all* mind my pointing out a few little errors,
for though you are noble born, you have never actually
had the *means* that some of us are blessed with. And
I, too, am nobly born, my dear, being the relative, twice
removed, of Rear Admiral—"

But no one was to hear of the rear admiral, for Miss
Daphne Murgatroyd, asserting her rights now that her
dear mama had departed, interjected that she was sure
Lady Caroline did not need to hear about distant relations so far removed. "Some people," she added, "are
far richer than the Coreys, being directly connected to
Murgatroyd, Murgatroyd and Parsons Inc, which everyone knows to be—"

Here she was interrupted when a lively skirmish
erupted between two vehement and one lisping young
heiress. In the end, it was reluctantly agreed that the
Coreys had *much* more of a right to point out matters
of etiquette to dear Lady Caroline, though the younger
Miss Murgatroyd was sure *she* would never be so brazen as to point out that the servants were slovenly and
that the butler looked far too *comely.* Indeed, she
pointed out, *"That* was His Grace's task, and no doubt
one that he would undertake directly when he returned . . . ?" Now there was a definite question mark
lingering genteelly about the end of the sentence.

Caroline did not have to bite back her scathing reply
to these little impertinences, for Miss Fletcherson immediately took it upon herself to make some few com-
ments herself, rather coyly remarking that she expected

His Grace would return at once to Darris Castle to assure himself of his sister's safety in the inclement and unkind weather.

Caro could not resist. She shook her head innocently. "Oh, no, my brother has several engagements in town. I doubt we will see him for a fortnight at least."

"Oh, you are funning Lady Caro! You don't mind me calling you that, do you? I feel we have become *such* friends! Surely he is not so unnatural a sibling as to leave you in this . . . this . . ."

But she subsided under a slight lofty tilting of the brows. Lady Caroline could never tolerate any criticism of her brother, and was *anyway* fast losing her patience.

Fortunately, Miss Bancroft appeared to smooth things out, acting the role of upper house servant to perfection and fussing over the company as if she actually *cared* whether their feet ached and whether mustard baths could be prepared for one and all immediately after the repast. She curtsied respectfully to Mrs. Corey, who had returned and taken up her ample seat, and Miss Amelia Corey, and Miss Oliver, and . . . well, the list went on.

The cottage was now clean. Raquel, fearful of catching her death in the miserable cold, decided that some exertion was required. For a young lady who had never done anything more physical than snap her fingers for a housemaid, her efforts had been remarkable. She had also shown singular presence of mind, for certainly, had she huddled next to the fire in nothing but her horse blanket, her fingers might have numbed along with her nose. Then, if she had drifted into uneasy slumber. . . . But she would not dwell on unhappy might have beens.

The embers did *not* catch on her horse blanket, nor

the fire extinguish itself entirely. Raquel was diligent in stoking it, and when there was no more wood, she sacrificed half of her best linen petticoat to the blaze. The other half she tore into rags, the better to restore order to this haven for spiders. She tried not to think of mice, though her heart beat painfully. She did not use the well, for it was iced up, but she melted snow, and the resulting water was put to good use, though it soon became patently clear that more than one petticoat was required. When neither His Grace nor his staff, nor even, dared she think it, *Thomas* returned, she refused to entertain the thought that Mr. Endicott had deserted her, but rather dwelt on the magnetic effect of his eyes, such a handsome blue, so akin to her own . . . then she allowed her thoughts to take a rather more immodest path as she balefully wiped at the windows and forced grime from the sills.

She had never wanted a bar of lavender-scented soap so much in her life. But there, she was not really thinking of soaps, but rather of a certain Mr. Endicott, who looked so shocking in nothing but his unmentionable breeches and a faint, mocking smile upon his infuriating lips. She scrubbed harder, and searched about for candles. She thought she had worked an age, and indeed, for a young lady unused to such burdens, it must have seemed like a lifetime instead of the rather mundane hour that it was. When Lady Raquel was satisfied with the results—but not with her soiled gown and tattered undergarments—she sat down by the hearth. There was not much more to stoke and she began to become seriously worried. It was too late to head for the castle herself, for the dreaded snow was now falling too hard for such calculated madness.

She wished she knew what time it was, for if dark fell, frankly she would rather have her reputation ruined then spend the night alone. Which just went to show, she scolded herself crossly, how her wits were scattered and she was losing her mind. And what Lord Fortesque-Benton would say when he heard of this! Raquel had been treated like a delicate porcelain doll all her life. She was *not* reared to dance about the room merely to shrug off the cold, which she was sorely tempted to do, or to wrap herself convulsively in a motheaten horse blanket, which was precisely what she *was* doing.

There was an old grandfather clock in the humble bedchamber, but since this had not been wound for three years at least, it was hardly much good. After about a half hour of patient, concerted waiting, Raquel conceived the notion of winding it anyway, so that even if it was inaccurate, it would at least give her an idea of how fast time was passing.

Or how slowly. She concentrated on the task, for this, like everything else that had fallen to her lot that day, was new to her. When she heard the familiar ticking, she was so relieved she actually chuckled. That she was reduced to thinking of a clock as a companion! She would regale with future dukes of Darris for years to come.

The notion depressed her spirits a little, for when she thought of these little dukes, she could not help thinking of them as diminutive Thomases, and for the life of her she could not imagine dark-eyed Darrises at all. She wished Demian would arrive to brush away all her doubts. Perhaps, if she let him kiss her . . . but he *had* kissed her! Over the table in an odiously confident manner. She had permitted it, but his kisses were *nothing* like what she imagined mocking Mr. Endicott's might be. *He* would not kiss her chastely on her cheek—Raquel conveniently forgot that it was *she* who had turned her face at the crucial moment. Mr. Endicott, she was sure, would explore her lips delightfully, slowly, teasingly. . . . Well, if nothing else, reflections down that wayward path were keeping her from freezing, which must be considered a plus.

But thoughts, however intriguing, however much they brought a flush and a smile to her beautiful face, were not enough. The fire demanded more, and there was precious little left in the way of petticoats. The chairs would be good, but there was no convenient ax. Raquel searched about thoroughly, but life seemed to be conspiring against her. So she picked up the smallest—and finest—of the seating arrangements and dumped the entire thing onto the miserable flames. They appeared to enjoy this treatment, for they perked up at once and offered a little more light for her ladyship's entertainment. Sadly, after drumming her fingers on the windowsill and staring fruitlessly out the darkening misted window, she realized she was not entertained at all.

Then her new friend, the dear, ticking clock, her only companion, chimed the hour. Of course, if was probably not the hour at all. Nevertheless, Raquel decided it was proof that time was actually moving on. Not that she *needed* proof, for it was almost dark and her eyes were beginning to strain to see the shadows. Heartily sick of this enforced inactivity, she took herself and her horse blanket off to the bedchamber and lay down. No sheets, but there was a musty old pillow. She removed her bonnet—something she should have done hours ago—pulled out her pins so that her hair fell luxuriously to her shoulders, and found that her curls had vanished completely.

They had disappeared entirely—without the help of an expert dresser and curling pins. For once, Lady Raquel did not mind. She huddled in her blanket, closed her eyes and tried to sleep. She would have been surprised to know how quickly she achieved this blissful state, or, indeed, how foolishly she dreamed.

* * *

Thomas coughed. It seemed many hours since he had left the castle. There was not a man about to offer him a ride, or at least relieve him of his burden. This he obstinately clung to, for there was no purpose served in returning to the cottage empty-handed. Lady Raquel would probably place a curse on him, the little witch, and they would both starve. Not a particularly pleasing prospect, but then neither was the dead weight of the basket. He wondered what in the world Caro had stuffed it with. But then, of course, she had been reckoning with Charlie. Job horse indeed! If he ever saw the brute again he would kick it. But Thomas knew only too well that he would probably pat it and empty his pockets for him. He sighed, and pulled his beaver down over his face.

Squinting into the blue-white dark, he could just make out the cottage. Far, yet, but with long tendrils of black smoke to set it against the landscape. Welcoming. Raquel had done well to keep the fire going. Quite redoubtable, in the face of adversity. Something to remember. Unconsciously, his pace quickened as he imagined her wide-eyed greeting and her barely concealed relief at his arrival. Oh, undoubtedly the minx would try to conceal it from him, but he was not a fool. She *would* be relieved. And hungry. Suddenly, the snow did not seem so thick or so cold. He took the last mile or so at a glide, falling twice into the snow and oversetting some inviting little jam pies. Some he left, some he gathered up in a quick gesture of impatience. Then he was running again, out of the snowflakes and in through the sentry door.

The Lady Raquel was nowhere to be seen, but the hearth was ablaze, and so, too, were the remains of an oak chair. It crept from the grate and heated the stone tiles of the floor. Close to it, a second chair smoldered black. Mr. Endicott had barely time to register this fact before it finally ignited, dry to a bone, and lighted the room in an eerie orange. There was a crackle and a quick lick of flame. A third chair began to smoke from the legs.

"Raquel!" But there was no answer.

Fifteen

The south wing smelled as musty as Martha had feared it would. Though the servants had hastily removed the holland covers, they were still stacked in calico piles by the walls and added nothing to the decor. Not that there *was* much decor—the fourth duke Darris had sold the Egyptian hangings and the Chinese silks long before Demian succeeded him. Still, there were several very fine examples of eighteenth-century samplers and a collection of porcelain dogs that must be considered remarkable, if not exactly inspiring, to houseguests of the gentler sex.

The sheets, Miss Bancroft noted with anxiety, were yellowing with age, and all, except for His Grace's own crested ones, were darned in too many places for comfort. She deliberated over using these, but then quailed at the thought of tucking Demian into the dank, motheaten ones. Not that she would tuck him in, of course—she pinkened at the very thought—but sooner or later His Grace would need to sleep. She might be an old fussbudget but it was *not* fitting that he should have to recline on unaired sheets whilst the spiteful Miss Amelia Corey slept on the ducal bedding. The notion appalled Miss Bancroft's rather proper senses, which left the deplorable linen she was now confronting as her only choice. At least Caro had had the good sense to spend some of the deposit on those delightful feathered quilts which she *wished* they could have saved for Christmas . . . but there was no point wishing when there was work to be done.

If they covered the beds with the counterpanes, the deficiencies of the sheets might not be noticed. She was just directing this dubious operation when the duke himself made his handsome appearance. Mrs. Murgatroyd was in tow, so he frowned warningly at Martha and sailed past two of his faithful retainers, who did their level best not to giggle, but unfortunately did not succeed as admirably as they may have wished.

Mrs. Murgatroyd's cheeks seemed even thinner and bonier, if that were possible. Her nose was being born high in the air, which was just as well, for she missed seeing several meaningful glances being cast and a cobweb being squashed underfoot.

The butler seemed not to notice anything amiss, for he went blithely over to the drapes and pulled them open. Moonlight crept into the gallery area, which did not bode well, for any defects that were suspected in the gloom were now confirmed in the snowy half-light.

"My good man, are you demented? I did not seek a tour of the servants' quarters! I am freezing! Is there no fire in here? Come, come, make haste, if you please."

"We have arrived, madam. You will find the bed-chambers to the left, and I have instructed your maids—"

Mrs. Murgatroyd stared at His Grace as if he were a Bedlamite. She did *not* wait for him to complete his sentence, but tittered in outrage.

"What in the world do you mean? This is worse than the scullery at my own home! *Not,* I might add, that I have ever visited the scullery, but Mr. Murgatroyd never purchases anything but the very best. Which is more, I can see, than His Noble Grace, who apparently

has not a feather to fly with and who has brazenly—
brazenly I tell you—misled us! Or is it just *you,* Pink-
erton? Or Pemberton, or whatever your name is?"

Demian lazily wondered what to reply, for in truth
he had *forgotten* what he'd called himself. He rather
thought it was Pemberton, but he did not like to wager
on the matter. Fortunately, the question appeared to be
rhetorical, for Mrs. Murgatroyd then began a studied
denunciation of his talents, his manners and his address. She then announced that she was duty-bound to
report his abominable conduct to the duke, and since
he had not chosen to grace them with his presence,
Lady Caroline.

This threat, understandably, did not cow the butler
as much as Mrs. Murgatroyd had wished. Rather, His
Grace apparently had difficulty retaining his strictly
poker face. He only actually *succeeded* by dint of bowing low. This brought him to the sad realization that
his topboots were no longer satisfactorily gleaming and
that his valet would treat him to a rare scold. He so-
bered up completely when he realized that the self
same valet had not been paid for a week. Mrs. Murgatroyd was still ranting, but he did not think he had
missed much.

"Oh, too late to bow, my good man! I shall write a
letter of complaint directly to the duke. Fancy thinking
you can house us here! This is not the *first* time I have
found your discretion lacking."

"Madam, I was given to understand you were to be
day guests."

"Oh, tush! A ducal household, however poverty-
stricken, can surely manage better than this! Don't forget, my good man, I have seen all the marble and
alabaster and Gothic statues—"

"Roman, madam. In the classical style, I believe."

"Don't you dare to interrupt! I think your betters

can be relied upon to know a little more than you! Why, it was only the other day that Mr. Murgatroyd bought a splendid Gothic bust of Herculaneum. Straight out of China it is and constructed entirely of pink marble, so you can see, my good man, that I know a little bit more than you!"

Demian strove nobly not to correct the three glaringly contradictory elements in this pronouncement. It was an effort, but he managed. Mrs. Murgatroyd, convinced she had subdued the manservant with this display of obvious wealth and gentility, continued in an admonishing tone. "Hyacinth Corey was correct, for once. One should not allow oneself to be conciliatory to the servants. I made that mistake with you, I believe, and it gave you notions above your station. Be assured, it shall not happen again. Now, find us some suitable accommodation and commend me to the housekeeper, if you please."

"The housekeeper is unwell. I believe that once several fires have been lit, the south wing will be more than habitable. It used to belong to the third dowager duchess of Darris when she was in residence."

"But not, I trust, with frayed carpets, precious few furnishings of note and smoky chimneys?"

"That I cannot say, madam."

"Can you not, you impertinent jackanapes? In my day, they would take a whip to your back for impertinence."

Demian subsided into silence.

"There are no other rooms, then?"

"No."

"Ha! You lie! There is the duke's own suite."

"Ladies of quality do not enter gentlemen's suites."

"True, but His Grace is not in residence and the circumstances are different. . . ."

"Nevertheless, His Grace's quarters shall be reserved exclusively for him. He may return."

"Oh! *May* he?"

Mrs. Murgatroyd's eyes became speculative.

Full of gushing platitudes, she changed course at
once and wheedled Darris with a vulgar smile. He preferred the earlier treatment, but manfully did not entirely permit his revulsion to show.

"We shall compromise, you rogue. The party shall
take up this south wing. Only, as I am sure you will
agree, with the dressers and the maidservants and such,
it is a sad crush. Miss Daphne and I will therefore
sacrifice ourselves for the sake of the rest and allow
ourselves to be housed . . . closer, I believe, to the ducal apartments. A single chamber, I am certain, will
not be too hard to procure."

Demian stared at her openmouthed, though his
brows flew skyward at her blatant maneuvering.

"Do you have some problem with these arrangements? I fancy I have worked everything through most
admirably. Mr. Murgatroyd always says that a good
head is worth a thousand pretty faces, so . . ."

This was testing Demian rather too far. "How fortunate," he murmured. He did *not* say that Honoria had
a face like an overstretched pug, but sadly, his tone
implied it. Mrs. Murgatroyd nearly spluttered with offended sensibilities. Her meager bosom heaved dra-
matically and her eyes narrowed to outraged slits.

"That, my dear man, is it! I shall report you at once
for impertinence and levity! Why, fancy—Good gracious man, when the duke hears of this matter . . ."
The bluster continued over Demian's head as he wondered whether Amy's eyes would be silver or slate when
they first kissed. But, then, there was the Lady
Raquel. . . . He closed his eyes for a moment.

"You are not listening to a word I am saying! I have

never, never been so treated in my life! You may not
know this, but His Grace was paid thousands of pounds
to host us . . ." The noisome complaining went on.

Cursing Caroline's prank, Demian then came so perilously close to a shrug at this latest display that
Honoria felt compelled to turn on her heel and stride
out without further escort from him. It was left to Miss
Bancroft, throwing a fulminating glance at Demian, to
drop her counterpanes, emerge from the nearest of the
bedchambers and chase after Honoria. In an inspired
moment, she called to her.

"My lady!"

Mrs. Murgatroyd stopped. She *liked* being addressed
in this pleasant but erroneous manner. It reminded her
that some of the staff, at least, were used to all manner
of high-born guests. Her temper calmed enough to
complain bitterly to Martha. This, whilst striding
briskly back to join the others, and informing Miss
Bancroft in short gasps that she was used to being
treated with the *utmost* respect and that *her* butlers
would have to answer to Mr. Murgatroyd if they were
ever so pernicious as Pemberton or Pembercew or
whatever his name might be. She pronounced pernicious "pernaeshus," but Martha was made of sterner
stuff than Demian. She did *not* nearly give the game
away by laughing. Quite the contrary. By dint of many
soothing noises, she managed to consign the blame entirely to the duke's heartless beast of a butler. She also
was so adept as to soothe Mrs. Murgatroyd's outraged
nerves and produce a bottle of sal volatile for the megrims. She was wafting this delicately when Mrs. Murgatroyd reentered the breakfast room.

Mrs. Hyacinth Corey was finishing the last of her
sugared pastry, baked in syrup and a testament to Lady
Caro's time at Miss Apperton's Seminary.

"Well? I trust it is all sorted? The ladies are fatigued.

And Lady Caroline informs me that His Grace is shortly to be betrothed. Well! I fear we have been sorely used, for I am certain no one whispered any of this to me. . . . Are you sure, my dear?"

With a belated attempt at a conciliatory expression, she looked inquiringly across the table. Some devil had caused Caro to mention this salient fact carelessly, over a glass of sugared lemonade.

"Oh, perfectly! He wrote to me himself this morning. Naturally, it is not common *knowledge* of course. . . ."

"Mmph! Well he might have spared us an odious trip if it *was!*" Mrs. Corey glared as if it were Lady Caroline's fault Demian was engaged.

Caroline, heartily sick of the charade and not inclined to be charitable, rose her brows in an excellent imitation of Lady Jersey and remarked frostily that she could not conceive how the one circumstance could possibly have anything to do with the other. This silenced Mrs. Corey, who prided herself on the subtlety of her machinations.

Miss Bancroft shook her head silently at Lady Caroline. Only Miss Mayhew intercepted this glance, but she was delicately playing with her spoons again and did not contribute to the drama unfolding. Her mind, truth to tell, was not on some absent, unknown duke, but rather upon a certain masquerading butler. He was intoxicatingly handsome, and the very epitome of every one of her foolish dreams. And she rather thought he liked her. . . .

She blushed. She had never desired anyone to like her quite as much as she desired Mr. Hartford to. He might be impoverished, but he was respectable and kind, and, oh . . . he was a paragon! Aunt Ermentrude might be disappointed, but she could be brought round. It was not as if he wasn't a gentleman, after all, and if

he was related to a duke. . . . Oh, Aunt Ermentrude
would yield. For her part, she wouldn't care if he *was*
a common butler.

Upon such pleasant thoughts her recalcitrant mind
lingered, so she missed Amelia Corey's spiteful remark
about the lackluster drapes, and Miss Kirby's lisping
outburst that it was "thimply not fair that His Grathe
should not have met them firtht." As if he would *immediately* have bequeathed his name, his rank and his
titles to her if he had. Lady Caroline was hard pressed
not to make an inflammatory comment of this nature,
but her eye caught Miss Bancroft's, so she pressed her
lips firmly together, selected a coconut macaroon and
behaved.

The duke did not appear for the fourth remove. Miss
Mayhew did not know whether to be relieved or de-
flated, for his closeness seemed to have an unnerving
effect upon her person. Indeed, she had never been so
giddy in her life. She decided, therefore, to be relieved,
and smiled engagingly at her hostess.

"Shall we drink a toast, Lady Caroline, to your
brother's betrothal?"

Caroline's eyes danced. "Certainly, Miss Mayhew,
for I hope it will be announced within the week, and
to the loveliest girl imaginable."

"Hmmph! *I* heard Lady Raquel Fortesque-Benton is
insipid. All blonde ringlets, you know. Now Daphne,
here—"

Mrs. Murgatroyd had stopped blustering about the
accommodations and resumed her seat.

"Never mind Daphne! She is nothing to my
Clorinda, but if His Grace has decided—"

"I believe, ladies, that he has." This, a new voice
from the door. Amy felt her heart stop and her color
rise. It was just as well she had refused the fourth remove. She might have choked with breathlessness. Mr.

Hartford looked magnificent in fresh white gloves and a dark, almost plum-colored jacket. Too smart for a butler, but then, he was no ordinary butler. . . . His eyes locked with hers and Lady Caroline's. Looking from one to the other, Amy seemed to detect something quite extraordinary.

For the strangest moment, almost suspended in time, Amy glimpsed the truth. His air of autocratic arrogance was far more suited to a duke than to a second cousin a few times removed. But, then, the moment vanished as he was subservient again, pouring Miss Kirby some lemonade, begging pardon when Mrs. Corey hurled abuse at his head and admonished him tellingly for eavesdropping on the conversations of his betters. His mortification seemed short-lived, however, for he threw Amy one of his cheerful winks—not arrogant at all—and advised Lady Caroline that the weather appeared to be improving.

Mrs. Murgatroyd interrupted the smooth, toneless speech.

"You!" She cried in tones of loathing. The butler glanced at her coldly and bowed infinitesimally. Then he carried on his speech with the Honorable Lady Caroline. By the time he had a new set of imperious instructions, Martha had signaled for the footmen to step forward to serve the meringue anglaise with custard sauce. Miss Bancroft then trailed from the room in Pemberton's stately footsteps. Out of hearing, His Grace teased her.

"Craven!"

Miss Bancroft eyed him sternly and announced that she was brave, but *not* brave enough to hear what Mrs. Corey would say when she heard there was to be no hot water fetched up to the rooms. No newfangled water closets either.

Oh, she *did* hope the snows would let up soon! She was too old for these nonsensical pranks.

Sick with fear, Thomas threw off his kerseymere carrick coat and threw it over the second burning chair. There was no time to search for any more horse blankets, and no time to seek water from snow. If the coat did not extinguish the blaze, he would have seconds to throw himself from the cottage. But not before he knew where Raquel was. *Surely* she had not been such a simpleton as to go after him in the snow? It defied belief, but was precisely the type of thing a woman like her might do.

"Raquel! Raquel!" His voice cracked and sounded hardly his own. There was no answer. He moved toward the chamber at the back of the house and cursed. His chest ached, and despite the cold, he felt hot and feverish. In the dim orange light he saw a fresh pail of water. He grabbed it and soaked the third chair. It stopped smoking, but still emitted the same dry, woody smell he had detected earlier. The carrick coat was unrecognizable save for a few charred capes, but it seemed to have served its purpose. The fire, such as there had been, was out, only its embers smoldering on the charred remains of His Grace's furnishings and kerseymere coat. Thomas trembled a moment, for what might have been.

Then he opened the front door and threw the kerseymere and embers somewhere haphazardly on the duke's estate. Bending, he grabbed some snow and placed it at the nape of his cravatless neck. It slid down his back like ice meeting fire. Vaguely, he wondered how he could be so hot when it was white all around him and the wind was high, howling for him to return inside and slam the door.

But he couldn't; he had to find Raquel. . . . He wondered wildly where she might be, and in what straits. How could he have let Demian continue on with his masquerade? Matters were way beyond funning. Oh, how he wished he could sleep. . . .

A particularly large gust of wind seemed to argue with him, to urge him inside. He resisted, straining for some movement or call that might inform him of the Lady Fortesque-Benton's whereabouts. None came. He would have to search out a lantern—pray God Caroline had provided him with one—or at least with sufficient tapers—and check the southernmost borders.

She could have wandered into Monmouth, or back onto the Great North Road, for he had not passed her when he'd trudged down. Despite his feverish state, Thomas was certain of this, at least. His ears had been straining for any noise that might be useful. A passing hostler would have been heaven, but any extra pair of hands would have been heartily welcomed. There had been none of these, in the quiet stillness of the snow flurries. If Raquel had been out there, he would have known.

Unless she had frozen. He dared not explore *that* thought any further. An ancient horse blanket was no match for a winter carrick, so he allowed himself to be tossed back inside by a baleful gust. Then it was the matter of closing the door against the winds, bolting it, waiting for his eyes to adjust to the more molten darkness—the night outside was now blessed with a full moon—and finding Lady Caro's deadweight basket.

It was at his feet, for he had dropped it the instant his quick eyes had detected the blaze. Now he scrambled through it, praying for a lantern. There was none, though Caro had provided him with lint, several tallow tapers and a tinderbox. Thomas thought he'd had enough of fires, but he lit a candle and moved down to the bedchamber. Possibly there would be a lantern to be found, hanging invitingly next to the beechwood bed. *If* it was still there. The old man might have moved it up to the dower house along with his fishing tackle and other worldly possessions. It had been *years* since Mr. Endicott had been in the old sentry house. Still, he could not be idle, despite the pain he had on breathing, and the unnatural heaviness on his sultry lashes.

Nothing, he found to his half-startled thoughts, was so bad or so painful as losing Raquel. He felt like he had a brick upon his chest. If he could find her, he would endure a hundred such bricks. Then he would return her smartly to Darris. A man did not need such agonies. Savagely, lying *entirely* unconvincingly to himself, he entered the bedchamber and set the candle down in a holder. Moldering with dust, he supposed, but this was not a moment for niceties. Carlew would have kept his lantern near the bed. He moved purpose-fully toward it, buoyed by the fact that his eyes were now seeing most objects, although all were still bathed in the gray light of night.

The horse blanket on the bed did not startle him. There were hundreds like it in the stables of England. He supposed it had been there, lying in the middle of the bed like a discarded rag for years on end. When it moved, though, his heart beat a little quicker and he stopped in his tracks.

"Raquel!" In a sudden movement he whipped the blanket off the bed, his spirits rising with his fury. Yes, there she was, sleeping like a baby when she had nearly burned the house down and sent him delirious into the snow.

"Wake up!" But she didn't; she just moved her long, glorious legs, and smiled. Her toes were peeking from the remnants of her gown. Even in the half light, it was apparent that her ladyship was wearing far less in the way of petticoats than she had been. As a matter of fact, judging by her perfectly form-fitting shape, she was reduced to her shift.

Except, of course, for the recalcitrant lace that seemed to insist on remaining to preserve her modesty. Bits had been ripped from her petticoats. Thomas could perceive that at once. He wondered, idly, why. *And* why her gown was so adorably filthy. There was nothing left of her ringlets, of course, but she did not need them. Guinea-gold locks down to her waist seemed a fair exchange. Thomas wanted to touch them. He was certain they were silky. But Lady Raquel was not one of his flirts. He resisted the urge, cursed Demian again and brushed the perspiration from his brow.

Then he coughed. It was excessively painful. He coughed again, and flailed at his chest. Something was seriously wrong. He had the fever, he knew it. He had seen other men have it. He refused to dwell on it. He was not the dying type.

Quietly, he picked up the candle. It was not like him to be chivalrous, but Lady Raquel might not *like* to wake up to him in her chamber, however inviting the bed might look. More was the pity. Well, if he could still think lovely, lascivious thoughts like that, he was not dead yet. The flame flickered traitorously on several silver buttons.

Her ladyship stretched, turning slightly, so that he could see those proud little fastenings by their hundreds. He was seeing double, but doubtless if Raquel knew, she would be pleased. He was perfectly certain she would have liked to present, for his delectation, a thousand such buttons. They were her silent mutiny. He remembered how he had smiled when he'd first noticed them. Almost immediately, he recalled. But he had not pandered to her fit of pique. Doubtless she thought him a cad for ignoring them so completely.

But he had not ignored them; they had tantalized him the whole way through their carriage ride. How many times had he imagined unfastening them? As many times, he thought, as the carriage wheels had gone round.

Now, when he was too tired, too weak to any longer think sinful thoughts, her dress was damp against her creamy skin. It clung to her slender frame tenaciously. It should be removed. She could catch her death if it wasn't.

Thomas regarded the merry organdy dispassionately. It was a soft sea of blue that should be folded neatly, or discarded on the floor. It mattered not. What mattered was dry clothes for her ladyship. *Dry clothes.* He concentrated on the words, as if mouthing them would make the deed occur. It did not, of course.

And first there were the buttons. . . . They were sparkling at him. In normal circumstances, he would have attacked the matter ruthlessly. Possibly even with a malicious relish. Possibly merely with relish. Mr. Endicott tried to smile at his own humor but failed singularly. All he wished to do was sleep. But he couldn't. Not when Raquel could catch her death. He had saved her from freezing, he had saved her from burning. Now he wanted to save her from inflammation of the lungs. A pity, he was certain, she would be grateful for *none* of these small attentions.

The candle was set down yet again. This time, on a small occasional table—if such it could be described— near the bed. It had burned almost to the socket, but Thomas could see well enough. So he did *not* return to Lady Caro's basket of delights, but rather began on the buttons. His fingers were clumsy. How strange, when he had dutifully unribboned, unbuttoned, unlaced and undressed all his manly life. What was more, the ladies did not snore when he did so. Neither did their eyes flutter open in confusion, although he had to admit, their lips *did* tend to part, as Lady Raquel's were now doing.

"Don't scream. I am not ravishing you." Sick as he felt, Thomas thought such clarifications of his intentions were necessary. He was glad there was no earthenware pot to hand, much less a pistol.

But Raquel was strangely dreamy as her tongue slowly moistened her lips. If Thomas had any wits about him, which sadly, he hadn't, he might even have thought her content.

"Oh," was all she said before drifting off again.

Mr. Endicott would dearly have loved to explore the wealth of possible interpretations behind that simple syllable, but felt it more prudent to engage himself with the job at hand. He wished his chest did not ache so, or that the room did not feel so hot. He considered kissing her ladyship's back, for it was so delightfully creamy and cool to the touch. Then he thought that maybe her back was the incorrect place, for it was always so rigid and unbending. Perhaps her curves, for they molded delightfully—but no. Curves, he told himself sternly, were strictly forbidden. The lady was Demian's betrothed. The future duchess of Darris. He must keep thinking that, for it was virtuous, chivalrous and suitably chilling. He needed to be chilled, the room was so hot. . . .

He was somewhere between the thirty-ninth and forty-second button when his fingers betrayed him and his breathing altered to match Raquel's. It mattered not that his boots were still on, or that his intentions had truly been noble. Mr. Thomas Tyrone Endicott was sound asleep.

Sixteen

When Raquel opened her eyes, she had a most wonderful sense of well-being. The room was strange to her, and the biting cold froze at her toes, where there was no horse blanket and no golden-skinned man—who was draped across her stomach—to warm her. The drapes fluttered slightly, and she could hear a dripping on the drain pipe. It was snowing outside, she knew it from the white light.

Vaguely, she wondered where she was. Perhaps she was dreaming. Oh, she had never had such an outrageous dream before, where she was damp and warm and luxuriously lethargic. There was no maid tiptoeing across her chamber with hot water from the kitchens, there was no cocoa arriving on a tray, there was not even, she noted sleepily, a dour-faced Anders demanding to know whether she intended spending all day in curling papers, and brandishing a brush with businesslike intent.

Instead, there was soft breathing and that curious warmth, warmer than a hot brick, which by now would surely have grown cold. Raquel sat bolt upright and leaped from her bed as if scalded. It was *not* her bed, there were no sheets redeeming it, and worst of all . . . she gasped at the worst of all, her hands clasped to her lips in complete, unmitigated horror.

She had *not* dreamed about that delicious warmth

that crept about her waist and trapped her to a masculine body in the most possessive and . . . and . . . *scandalous* of ways! A feverish exploration of her person revealed her buttons were half undone. She flushed deeply. A young lady of her elevated rank and station did not misconstrue such a circumstance.

She was ruined, and the object of her ruin lay sleeping like a newborn lamb, perfectly oblivious to the havoc he had wreaked. Oh, how handsome he looked, with his brow smoothed of all expression and his lashes curled gently over his cheeks. Then there was his chest, neatly clad in a starched shirt that was woefully tight. . . . Raquel's fingers seemed to have a will of their own, for whilst *she* wanted to kill him, *they* wanted to explore the muscles that were almost visible beneath the flimsy fabric.

She flushed. She had never before felt so wickedly wanton. It would be an easy thing to climb back into the bed and shut her eyes, but fury battled with mortification and treasonous longing. She *refused* to listen to that alien creature whispering to her of disappointment and chagrin. If she had spent a night worthy of the scandal, she would at least liked to have remembered it. But try as she might, she could remember nothing. Nothing of his lips, or of his hands, or even of her struggle. She *hoped* that she had struggled, but there was no sign of it. Shards of glass about the bed or a blemish on Mr. Endicott's intoxicating face would have been promising. But there was nothing. And when she had woken, his arms had twined possessively round hers. *Not* a good sign.

Now would be a good time to awaken him and demand an explanation. Perhaps she should boil some water and pour it over his illustrious physique. But no, the fire was out and she had not the heart. Perhaps she was bewitched. Certainly, the Honorable Lady

Fortesque-Benton, diamond of the first water, cream of the bon ton, would undoubtedly have screamed herself hoarse by now. She owed it to her dignity, though she was a fallen woman.

But the shrieks never came. She wondered why, even as she wondered why there were tiny beads of perspiration on Thomas's brow. Her *own* brow furrowed as she noticed that his soft breathing was interrupted, at times, by a hoarse coughing. He slept, but now, regarding him with the fullness of awakened faculties, she realized that it was not a natural slumber.

"Mr. Endicott!" How ridiculous that she used that name, when they had spent a night alone together! But there was no reply, even when Raquel gingerly pushed his hair from his brow.

"Thomas!" The coughing worsened, but he opened his eyes. Raquel was amazed at how relieved she felt, though she was ready to kill him with her own bare hands.

"You are a rogue and a villain! I am ruined! My father will flail you alive, which is less than you deserve, you . . ."

But those dreamy blue eyes were misty, hardly seeing her.

"Thomas!"

Now, Raquel was seriously alarmed.

"Thomas! Wake up! Can you hear me?" But, apparently, he could not. Raquel took his hand. It was as warm as she remembered, but far, far too warm for the chilliness of the room. Raquel had little experience of such matters, but she was fairly certain he had a fever. Which was hardly surprising, when he had practically ordered her to wear his greatcoat and had trudged miles in the snow with nothing but a thin lawn shirt upon his broad back. If she had not been so selfish, or at least so self-absorbed, she would have worried earlier about such a possibility.

And now, he was seriously ill. Raquel did not stop to think of her future, which was now very different from that which she had mapped out for herself—was it truly only hours earlier? It seemed another lifetime ago.

Even if Thomas had *not* despoiled her, there was no gainsaying she had spent a night alone with him and in his arms. Her reputation was thoroughly compromised. There was no chaperon, no groom, and no spare, redeeming bed. She did not care.

This Lady Fortesque-Benton was a very different one from the proud creature who had scorned Mr. Endicott as common raff and scaff. *This* Lady Fortesque-Benton very much wanted him alive. The boot was on the other foot, too. For no matter what had occurred between them, passionate, romantic, scathing, conciliatory or not, it was *she* who was now the common raff and scaff. Her very name would be a mockery, whispered gleefully behind fans and held up as a lesson to silly little chits who were in danger of losing their heads to fortune-hunting rakes.

If Thomas survived, Lord Fortesque-Benton would demand satisfaction and very likely put a bullet through his heart. What a dreadfully foolish custom. It did not in any manner help *her*. *She* would still be cast out of society and branded a fallen woman. As for marrying His Grace . . . it was now out of the question. He would have to find some other willing heiress. A duchess-of-Darris-to-be did not spend unchaperoned nights with other gentlemen. Or not until *after* wedlock, in any event.

Somehow, she grieved less over this matter than over the other. She found, curiously, that she did not *want* Thomas dead. Something indefinable had shattered the golden image she'd always cherished regarding the nobility of rank. Which was just as well, of course, for such expectations could no longer be applicable. She could retire quietly to the continent, perhaps. Or hire a house in an unfashionable watering hole. Frankly, she couldn't care.

What mattered was concocting some story for Lord Fortesque-Benton's edification . . . and nursing Mr. Endicott through the fever. She knew if she could get it to break, he would doubtless recover his former jaunty self. And if he did . . . if he did, her father—and very possibly her betrothed—would be likely to run him through with a rapier.

They must be made to believe Thomas innocent of all wrongdoing. Perhaps she could fabricate some heroic story of chivalry, where he'd spirited her away from highwaymen and dueled with the devil himself for her honor. Raquel thought all this through as she tore the last of her hooped undergarments and dipped them in some of the fresh snow water she had dragged in yesterday.

She was still thinking as she reached the bed, rolled him over slightly and placed the cloth on his forehead. She sighed as she squeezed some of the water onto his temples. Highwaymen would *still* not explain why he had dismissed her maid and not turned back immediately for London. Toothache did not seem a very compelling argument in the light of day.

She wondered how long it would be before Demian discovered them. Why had he not come down himself? Why had he sent Thomas back when he must have known she would be compromised? It was a strange puzzle. Perhaps he worried about the propriety of hosting her himself. But Lady Caroline Darris would have lent them countenance.

Any situation must surely have been better than sending Thomas back, as he had. Demian must not be too damning: he had much to answer for himself. Raquel decided she would release him from his obligation at once, so that the task of defending her honor would not be one that fell to him. She'd heard disquieting rumors that His Noble Grace, the fifth duke Darris, was a crack shot with pistols. She would have been relieved to learn that Thomas had been his tutor, but of course, isolated as she was, this interesting snippet was out of her grasp.

But all this was immaterial. The cottage was freezing. If she did not find a way of lighting a fire very soon, they would most likely die of exposure, for the stone walls had trapped the cold inside with them. Raquel dipped the cloth once more into the melted snow. She must procure some more from outside. Thomas's wide, berry-red lips looked alarmingly dry. She laid the cloth lightly over his mouth, taking care not to trail her fingers across the soft flesh as she would like to have done. She may be fallen, but she was not wanton. Not yet.

Sternly admonishing herself, she moved to the outer room, where she noticed, for the first time, the remnants of the fire. So *that* was the acrid smell hanging about her nostrils! She supposed she could have died. And Mr. Endicott had sacrificed a glorious coat—His Grace's, she recognized it. So Demian *did* know of her whereabouts!

Raquel fingered it idly and focused on the trivial. What a waste! It was doubtless made from the purest of kerseymere, though the charred remains were no longer as enticing as the complete coat must have been. Then, since she could ignore the more important of the issues no longer, she found her mind wandering back to the fire.

So! She owed Thomas her life. How typical of him

to be heroic. Raquel tossed her head crossly. He made it *very* difficult for a lady to loathe him as she strictly should. And look! A basket of goods. How annoying. It made her want to thank him rather than rant at him as surely any self-respecting person must. He had actually made it to the castle, then come back for her. To *her.*

She knelt over the basket and felt a rush of cold at her back, where her buttons were unfastened almost down to her lower spine. Raquel wondered whether he had even noticed. He must have. *She* hadn't unfastened them. Ninety-nine buttons, she had chosen. Ninety-nine to annoy and confound him. He had looked neither annoyed nor confounded, tiresome man! Still, he had gone to the trouble to undo at least half of them. Her heart beat faster at the thought. What else had he gone to the trouble of, as she slept? Wicked thoughts crept into her mind unbidden. She scolded herself sternly. The man was near delirium. He must surely not have been thinking anything more lascivious than that she would catch her death. And so she probably would, if she did not slip out of the organdy soon. No point in them *both* succumbing to the fever!

So Raquel slipped off her gown and the remains of her torn-up undergarments. She could not regret their demise, for the crisp linens and calico had been put to excellent use, and, now that it was daylight, she could see that the room was spotless from her labors. There was no longer more than a single, spindly cobweb in sight. This she dealt with ruthlessly before inspecting the basket.

Underclothes! She could hardly believe her luck as she searched about for a new gown of sorts. None. Suppressing disappointment, she hung the organdy out to freeze—still maintaining a vestige of humor!—and donned the crisp shift. Clean and serviceable, but *not* stylish, or even frivolous, as she was accustomed. She supposed, with a wry smile, she had to hope Mr. Endicott did not recover too quickly. Or, at least not until the organdy had dried.

The candles and flint lifted her spirits, but when she started unwrapping and unpacking the pies, the cheeses, the sweetmeats and the ale, she positively glowed. She may be a fallen woman, but today, at least, she would eat like a queen. She had half resigned herself to starving as a suitable punishment for her sins.

What sins? She couldn't remember a *thing* about the pleasures of the previous evening. And doubtless, if Mr. Endicott had practiced half the sensuous charm upon her that he had unwittingly done on their fateful carriage ride, she would have remembered. Or *should* have remembered. She felt that strange warmth creeping over her again at the very notion. Ha! This scandalous immodesty must surely be counted as a sin in itself. Raquel, suddenly flushed, conceded so.

She tried scolding herself, reminding herself that she was compromised, fallen, foolish, and all manner of unpleasant things, but still there remained that incredible lightning of feminine spirit, that soaring of sentiments that was so at odds with her situation. She had never expected to see Mr. Endicott again, and she despised him. But he moved her. And he had come back.

It was unlikely that anyone would brave the weather to save her virtue. Whoever was up at the castle seemed to think it perfectly acceptable to send down smallclothes, but no physical help whatsoever. Curious. Unless they thought Mr. Endicott *himself* help enough. Curiouser still.

Her mother would doubtless await a politely penned missive describing the tedium of the carriage trip, but she would not worry unduly if this was delayed. The weather was notorious. So, for a few precious days she was probably safe from the inevitable pandemonium. Raquel threw on her half boots, laced them lightly and opened the door. The icy air almost stifled her breathing, but resolutely, she checked the well. Still useless.

Sighing, she fetched in more snow for water, then slammed the door tightly shut behind her. Thomas must be made to eat and drink. She rummaged in the basket for the vegetables she had glimpsed, regarded them dubiously, then set to work on a barley broth. A fascinating experience, for not only was she sadly short of cooking implements, but she had actually never performed so menial a task in all of her life. Still, she had learned the basic principles, as all delicately nurtured young ladies must, so she now applied them gingerly.

Lighting a fire from the ruins of the grate was probably the hardest of the tasks, her plain but pristine underclothes taking a fine smudging, but once done, matters progressed nicely. The broth simmered invitingly in a cast-iron pot that Lady Caroline had scrubbed the previous day. By the time an encouraging smell emerged, Raquel was inspired enough to steal some of the meat from the pies to add body to the brew. The crusts she ate herself, and was amazed by her unladylike hunger.

She was just licking her fingers and wondering what on earth she could do to break Thomas's fever, when a shadow fell over the slate floor and she knew at once, from the giddying rush of her pulses, that that gentleman was now awake.

She turned, but he was leaning against the doorjamb and looking very different from the arrogant, dictatorial gentleman it was her particular curse to be acquainted with. So her embarrassment and anger waned at once, leaving her tongue-tied with concern, and a whole plethora of other confused emotions she did not quite care to define.

"Get back to bed! You look shocking!"

Thomas tried to smile. "Touché. I might say the same of you—though delightfully so." He devoured her ensemble with a wolfish grin that was sadly lopsided. Raquel blushed, but it was too late to run for the damp organdy. She was ruined, anyway. She didn't think Thomas's eyes upon a bundle of ash-soiled petticoats could make much difference. At least they weren't the pantalets.

"Bed." She said it as firmly as she could, without flushing, though her eyes dropped to the floor and she stirred the broth as though it were of some particular interest, rather than merely barley, vegetables and pur-loined scraps. She had glimpsed the beads of sweat on Thomas's brow and the way his hand clutched at his chest. She wagered it was painful.

He ignored her and moved forward. His stockinged feet tripped over the broom handle. He swayed precari-ously, so Raquel left the broth and steadied him with her ungloved hands. The shock of warmth she felt had little, she knew, to do with his fever. But his skin *was* hot.

"Careless," he mumbled, in a failed effort to be jaunty. He tried to retain her hands, but she shot him a smoldering look and removed them the instant his balance was restored.

Ignoring her bed edict, he stumbled into the room and blinked.

"Clean."

"Yes, there was nothing to do yesterday." How strange to be talking common places when there was a wealth of unspoken dialogue between them. She un-packed the cheeses and tried to ignore him.

"No cobwebs." He was blinking rather stupidly.

"No. I hate spiders."

"Marry me."

So! She *was* ruined. She knew it, now, of a certainty. The rakish Mr. Endicott did not exactly strew his path with betrothals. If he offered for her, he obviously needed to. Raquel had never doubted his honor, or that he lived strictly by a gentleman's code. The code that stated that if you bedded a lady, you wedded her, no matter how tiresome the outcome.

"I am betrothed already." Too soon to tell him ladies had a code, too. She would not marry simply to assuage his masculine guilt. Further, she would *not* offer Demian spoiled goods. Besides, there could be a child. . . . She knew little of what happened between men and women, but she *did* know that. The dukedom of Darris would not—must not—be put in jeopardy because of her indiscretions. Oh, but how she wished she at least *remembered* those indiscretions! She scowled fiercely at the shadow on the floor. Mr. Endicott had discharged his duty by offering wedlock, but he should not come off scot-free by her refusal. She tried to think of some dire and wicked revenge she could wreak upon his person, but failed singularly.

What was worse, he was looking dizzy, so she took him firmly by the arm and led him back to the bed. It looked uninviting with just the horse blanket and no sheets, so she retrieved the remainder of her discarded underclothes, ripped them yet again—this time at their exquisitely stitched seams—and spread them over the middle part of the sturdy four-poster.

"Lie on the underclothes. They shall serve as sheets. I fear you have the fever, so I am going to nurse you."

"Raquel—"

"Don't you *dare* call me that. I am Lady Fortesque-Benton to you."

He nodded, unusually docile.

"I am going to get you some of that broth. Drink it."

"I am not hungry."

"Good. Then you won't mind if I eat the Périgord pies."

"Drink the broth, too."

"No, *you* are going to do that. And if you fight me, I am going to pour it down your wretched throat."

Thomas tried to sit up. "You are angry."

"Furious. It is not every day I lose my maidenhood on an unaired bed. My only consolation is that I cannot remember that particular pleasure. Salutary, I am sure, to a man whose amorous activities are legendary. Or so I am told."

Raquel wondered how she dared say such a scandalous thing. Yesterday, she would have stood on nails rather than repeat guttersnipe gossip. But she was a different person from the ladylike creature she had been the day before. So, without waiting for a reply, or hearing the slight chuckle emanating from the makeshift bedclothes, she turned on her heel and stalked off.

Mr. Endicott, sick as he felt, had just time to glimpse a particularly excellently turned ankle as it stalked from the room. Her words had been a revelation to him. So the little minx had misconstrued their situation! She thought herself outrageously used. Part of him was coldly furious that she should think such a monstrous thing of him. The other grudgingly admired her ladyship tenfold, for he noted none of the hysterics that would have been perfectly well-justified if her belief had been even faintly founded in truth.

Moments later, feeling strangely bereft without her acerbic presence, he sank back into the discomfort of her torn and rumpled petticoats and found oblivion once more.

Seventeen

Raquel sat rigidly by the bed and watched him. She had carried in the chair with the smoke-blackened legs. It was still damp from its dousing but since it was now the only stick of furniture available to her, it sufficed.

Her back ached from sheer physical activity—she had never spent an hour—let alone several—scrubbing in her life. Not to mention chopping up firewood, for whilst Thomas had dutifully loaded the trap, the crucial wood had been left behind. Caro had thoughtfully included a small ax in the basket, so the remains of the furniture had been sacrificed to its blade. Enough heat for a day, probably, before they either froze or were discovered. Raquel could not decide which event she relished least.

Mr. Endicott breathed as if in pain. Occasionally, he gasped for air, so Raquel had to roll him gently to ease his position. *Then* she had to climb up on the bed beside him, and though he was too ill to make any further inroads on her dubious virtue, she could not help blushing at her proximity to his deeply fascinating torso. Consequently, she regarded him with wary eyes and treated him as though he were some scorpion ready to sting at any moment.

The scorpion never stung, but his sheer closeness seemed to prove fatal, for Raquel could actually feel those muscles that had mesmerized her in the coach.

They were every bit as intoxicating as she had imagined. They worked like some annoying force pulling her to him rather than the reverse.

His sleep was uneasy, and occasionally he mumbled words that made no sense. Once she was foolish enough to think it was her own name he murmured. But then, he might, insufferable man, be riddled with nightmares. Raquel rather hoped he was.

It seemed like hours that she sat perched on that hard chair, staring at him, etching every aspect of his features in her memory. She had no idea *why* she felt so attracted to such an unsuitable man, but she did. This was probably her only opportunity ever to admit this to herself and take advantage of his weakened condition to enjoy him. For yes, she *did* enjoy him, despite being utterly ruined. Had he really asked her to marry him? Ordered, more like, except that he had practically swooned in the demanding. Not terribly convincing. When he woke, she would not remind him of it, but be as caustic and scathing as he deserved. In the meanwhile, he needed another cloth.

She rose, glad that she did not have to sacrifice her current petticoats. Whoever had provided the basket had also provided tooth powder, soap and washcloths. Raquel dipped two in the pail. One for his chest, and an especially wet one for his mouth. His lips were dry. He had fallen asleep before drinking the restorative broth, and he probably needed to drink, with the fever. But since he was sleeping, she would have to drop the water into his mouth, drip by drip. A time-consuming process, but that was one thing she *did* have at her disposal. Time. Time, in this strange state of transition, where her world was about to crumble around her but had not quite yet. She should either be horribly bored or fearful. She was neither. She just concentrated on her task and listened to the clock tick. It seemed in synchrony with her heart. Now and again, she pressed her ear close to his chest. Yes, his heart was beating still. She couldn't think *why* she was relieved.

Her lips just touched his stark, white shirt. She felt a tremor run through him and raised her head quickly. His eyes were open, and there was a gleam of amusement in them that made her wonder how long he had been awake and just how much of this fever he had been shamming. But when he coughed and a look of pain crossed his features, she knew that it was only heroic effort that caused him to look at her so and not sink back into his pillows.

"You should be sleeping."

"You make that difficult." His eyes, bluer than ever, met hers keenly.

"Then I shall sit in the other room."

"No!"

"No? Then close your eyes. Your fever has broken, I believe, but you might be suffering inflammation of the lungs. Are you having difficulty breathing?"

"Yes, but that may be from the sight of you in your shift. More delicious than I dreamed. I love you, Lady Raquel Fortesque-Benton."

"Don't be flippant, Mr. Endicott." Raquel would *not* let him see how his words affected her.

"I am never flippant when I am dying."

"You are not dying yet, Mr. Endicott, though I don't fancy your chances when you are recovered."

"You mean, I recollect, a duel. I am an excellent shot."

"How fortunate. But it is not pistols you shall have to face."

"Rapiers? I—"

"Not rapiers either. I have no wish to see either my

affianced or my father slaughtered in such a poor cause. Bare hands, Mr. Endicott. Mine."

Raquel spoke conversationally, but there was a hard edge to her tone.

Thomas stared at her, then relaxed back onto the nonexistent pillows. His head hit something hard, so he cursed.

"Don't curse when a lady is present. Common etiquette, but then, perhaps I should not expect you to know that."

"You are very beautiful. Even when you are cross-grained and shrewish."

"Save your flattery for unversed maidens."

"Rest assured, I *shall.*" Thomas glanced at her from under long, twining lashes. If she knew no better, she could swear his words had some significance. Some flirting, caressing meaning that escaped her just at present. She was no maiden any longer. And though she was unversed, Thomas did not—could not—know that.

"Good. Then we understand each other. Just as soon as you are well enough, I shall have my revenge."

"Why bother waiting for me to be well? You have a much better chance, if I may say so, of wringing my neck when I am as weak as a lamb."

"*Some* people play fair, Mr. Endicott."

Raquel removed the cloths and handed him the waiting bowl of broth. It was cold, but she did not offer to reheat it.

"Drink that. I believe it might do some good." Then, with her nose in the air and her bearing as proud as if she were wearing a ball gown of shimmering sapphire, spangled at the front with pearls and complemented by tasseled Roman sandals—which she might have been, had she actually made it up to Darris Castle—Lady Fortesque-Benton left the room.

She did not see the sudden anger blazing in Thomas's

eyes at her insinuation. Contrary to any prejudiced opinion on her part, he *did* play fair. Which is why she was still unkissed, never mind unbedded. He wondered how often she would throw his supposed sins up in his face before realizing this obvious fact. He wanted to laugh at the irony. Her murderous intentions were founded on a quite ludicrous lack of substance. But he *did* admire her! And he *had* compromised her.

He had compromised her on the first day, when he had dismissed the maid. He had compromised her by setting off knowing full well they were chasing the weather. Foolishness! Sane, rational gentlemen would have remained on in London. But *he* had the image of her pearl-white back, not to mention her intriguing décolletage, to spur him on. He had been acting from pique, not from chivalry. As for doing Demian favors . . . ha! Demian would not thank him for his interference.

Perhaps the Lady Raquel was justified in her parting remark. He had not raped her, as she intimated, but he *had* ruined her for Darris. He had forced her to fall in love with him. That was just as bad.

Thomas was honest. He knew all the signs of women in love, and Raquel had them. Tenfold. She trembled as she touched him, she nursed him, she threw pots at him. One day, she would kiss him. He hoped it would be soon. Confound it, there was still Demian. He prayed, as he had never truly prayed before, that the lovely Miss Amy Mayhew was all Caro claimed she was. A broken betrothal could mend faster than a broken heart. But then, Demi's heart had never been involved. Neither, he fancied, had the lady Raquel's. She would not have flaunted herself so consciously at the ball if it *had* been. She had been like a taut string under his amused scrutiny. From the very start, there had been an unspoken attraction. Only, Thomas had been experienced enough to recognize it for what it was. Lady Fortesque-Benton, on the other hand, had proven a mere green girl. For all her proud posturing. Thomas silently thanked the heavens for it.

He leaned forward and sipped the broth. The pains were still there, but he fancied they were subsiding. If he could live without being murdered, he might survive. The soup was terrible. And the vixen had given it to him cold.

Amid a chorus of protests, the ladies had been shown their quarters. Mrs. Corey raged and ranted, her great bosom heaving in indignation. Her dresser, already shivering in the antechamber, echoed her sentiments and pointed indignantly to the cheval mirror that had been brought in for their use. Eight ladies and one mirror! It was abominable!

Never *mind* the turrets and gargoyles and stained-glass arches—all very well, they were, but useless without common amenities. Then there were the porcelain wash stands adorned with nothing but common pitchers and water lugged up from the kitchens; the chimneys were smoking from disuse; and great clouds of pitch tar were soiling all the open portmanteaus and trunks. And the chairs! They were scant and hard, only two had any padding to speak of, and though they were in the fashionable Egyptian style, some of the gilt was chipping off. In short, they were sadly lackluster.

Some of the ladies shrieked when they viewed the chamber. They had to share—actually had to *share*— the bedchamber! Miss Bancroft had ordered four pallets to be made up. These, an astonished Miss Oliver announced, were actually intended for *their* use! She could understand if they were for the maids, but the maids were evidently to be quartered with the Darris servants. "These . . . these . . ."—she could splutter out neither "pallets" nor "beds"—"are intended for *us*."

Amelia Corey decided this would be a very good time to have hysterics, so she consequently opened her mouth and proceeded to wail. Not to be outdone, Miss Daphne Murgatroyd followed suit, though *her* hysterics were more pitiful, for they were accompanied by several gushing tears. They rolled down her cheeks and were allowed to drip upon the faded carpet. The cacophony was appalling, especially since *all* the young ladies, encouraged by their graceless chaperons, were inclined to follow suit.

"Where is Lady Caroline? I *must* see her ladyship!" Mrs. Murgatroyd bellowed at poor Betsy, who had been delegated the unenviable task of settling the party, stoking the fires and collecting up the crushed traveling garments so that they could be cleaned, dried and pressed in the duke's kitchens.

"Don't touch that, you stupid girl! It is made of the finest oriental silk! Put it down at once!"

Betsy tried to explain, but was brushed aside by an infuriated Mrs. Corey, who took up the gown, but in her agitation, caught it on a hook protruding from the bare wall. There followed a ripping sound, then shrieks of fury from the Corey dresser, Mistress Amelia and her mama as all three lunged for Betsy and shook her.

Amy, quietly coaxing one of the fires, lost her patience. She set down the leaden poker and glided past an army of females. They were all watching with interest and in relative degrees of swoons, ashen pallors and imminent hysterics. Without a word, she separated Betsy from her tormentors and delivered three sharp slaps. One on each startled face. None, of course, on Betsy's.

"Ladies! I have never seen such an unedifying display in all my life! You shame me and you shame our class! Is it no *wonder* no self-respecting lord or lady will give us the time of day or leave their visiting cards in our neighborhood? You ladies gristle all day about this unsatisfactory state of affairs. If I had the smallest choice in the matter, *I* would not acknowledge any of us either. We may all be wealthy, but we are neither courteous, civil or remotely noble. We should be ashamed."

"Well!" Mrs. Corey placed a hand on her pudgy cheek. It was still burning, for Amy had strength, if not the delicate pouches of puppy fat that were considered ladylike in some circles.

For once, Mrs. Murgatroyd stepped forward and echoed Mrs. Corey's tone, if not her words.

"Fancy!" She said in failing accents that nevertheless contrived to be spiteful. "We have raised a viper in our breast! I can assure you, Miss Mayhew, that you shall never grace *our* invitation lists again! I am sure Ermentrude Worthing must always be welcome, for there is no doubt that *dear* Froversham is worth a fortune, but you! My dear Miss Mayhew, were you heiress to ten times the sums you are, you will never darken my door again. And I have it on the best authority that though you are an heiress, your fortune is not so large as Ermentrude would have us think! I am perfectly satisfied that I speak for all the young ladies present when I say you are a snobbish little brat, with not an ounce of dear Daphne's—or even Amelia's—gentility! And if you are, indeed, Lord Dalmont's daughter—though who can ever be sure of such things?—you do not do him any credit at all! You do not dress with any degree of superiority and you are generally held to have your nose in a book. I am sure Lord Dalmont could not have wished for a bluestocking daughter. And don't look so regal, miss! If Dalmont's family had even *recognized* you, things might be different! *Then* we might consider you worthy of our notice!"

Amy paid no attention, though her eyes flashed at Honoria Murgatroyd's vulgar aspersions on her ancestry. Still, they were not worth defending to these people. So she gently took the ripped gown from Betsy's shaking fingers, bestowed a kiss upon her forehead, and bade her return to the kitchens.

Miss Fletcherson was tittering. "He was only a second son. Mama says that is nothing to give yourselves airs about!"

"Indeed!" Mrs. Corey bestowed a plump, rather stately smile upon Miss Fletcherson. She approved of simpering girls who echoed her own, jealous opinions. Then her eyes narrowed as Amy made some small movement.

"Where are you going, girl?"

"I am going to fetch my purse to reimburse you for your precious frock, Hyacinth. I don't trust you not to demand recompense from that poor little wretch."

"Poor little wretch? She was careless and should be made to pay for her faults."

"Just as I thought. I will fetch my purse, so you need harangue her no further. Then I am going to bed." Amy could hardly keep the contempt from her tone. Only the thought of Mr. Hartford, steadying, true, fascinating and undeniably attractive, made her remain a moment longer with these harridans. Given a choice, she would rather have braved the snows.

Mrs. Corey was looking at her, aghast.

"Not *here?*"

"Not here what?"

"You are not actually planning on *sleeping* in this place?"

"Mrs. Corey, I would very much prefer the comfort of my bed in London. Unfortunately, you have taken great and unscrupulous pains to prevent me from that particular pleasure, so, yes, I am going to sleep here. Where else?"

"Well, gracious, in this entire castle there must be more suitable lodgings! I have never been so insulted in my life! I am certain the duke would be aghast at such impertinence! And after all the exorbitant sums we have spent, you would think he would have been considerate enough to welcome us himself. . . ."

Miss Mayhew took a breath and contemplated her long, elegant fingernails. She did *not* see the butler hovering at the door entrance and nodding to Betsy. What she *did* see was a parcel of vulgar young chits, all pouting dissatisfiedly. None of them seemed to remember the splendid day they had just spent, traversing ancient halls, being privy to private collections of immeasurable importance, being hosted personally by a peeress of the realm, sampling the delicate cuisine and pillaging the ancient cellars.

She cleared her throat. Then, with a sudden imp of devilry, she remembered Mr. Hartford's teasing raillery. Assuming a *marvelously* gushing tone—not unlike to Miss Kirby's, or Miss Oliver's, or even Amelia Corey's—and explained.

"You see, ladies, I believe we are now operating on tick. We have undoubtedly already *had* our ten thousand pounds worth today. *Dear* Lady Caroline did us proud, too. Such *sumptuous* meals and such *elegant* displays! I think I particularly enjoyed the ancestral galleries and the turrets. No . . . no . . . the topiary gardens were better, though of course, to actually venture onto the castle battlements! Oh! It quite made me swoon! So romantic! So dignified. . . . Oh, just *think*, ladies! We have actually set foot on a ducal estate! We have truly taken tea with the sister of a duke. Indeed, I believe we have offered her all manner of advice, too.

That must count for hundreds of guineas, for not one of us received the cut direct! Dear Honoria, I think we can safely dine out on the memory for years. As for His Grace . . . well, it is *inconvenient* of him to have betrothed himself so out of hand, but I suppose it would be uncharitable to actually *blame* him for such a gross lack of conduct! No, all in all, we have certainly had our ten thousand pounds worth. Probably a bargain at that, for you would have to search far and wide to find *another* noble duke ready to suffer such an indignity. They are a rare breed, I believe. But as for these sleeping arrangements . . . how *kind* of Lady Caroline to throw in this little extra! Of course, she was not given much choice, but then, Mrs. Corey, you are adept at forcing people's hands, are you not?"

She appeared satisfied with her scrutiny of her fingers, for she now dropped them to the sides of her soft, green merino. It looked as if Miss Oliver and Miss Kirby were about to say something, though, so she held them up, once more, to prevent that noxious occurrence. She was strangely serene.

She dropped her garish tone and continued on in her own, delightful, well-modulated voice. "For my part," she continued, "I hope the beds are all that they look to be: lumpy, damp and uncomfortable. It is most certainly all we deserve, for if you, ladies, had not been so diligent in getting us snowbound, we should be halfway home to London by now."

The butler's lips quirked. He had been about to make a similar speech himself. Now, he shut the door gently behind. Amy had managed more adeptly than he. He only hoped that she was wrong. That *one* bed, at least, would be neither lumpy nor damp. He did not fancy the chances. When Amy was duchess, he would make it up to her. Which reminded him. He had an important letter to pen.

He avoided Caroline and made for his study. There, amid the leather-bound books, still smelling cozy despite the blankness of the walls, he began an extremely difficult task. Several times he stopped, screwing elegant, watermarked wafers into small balls. They caused the fire to spark playfully.

It was not easy, he found, to act the jilt. Though he and Lady Fortesque-Benton were not formally betrothed—for which he was heartily thankful—he still felt honor-bound. Only the certainty that the lovely Lady Raquel could take up with the marquis of Somerford at the snap of her jeweled fingers made him continue on with his task. The money, somehow, no longer mattered.

Eighteen

The night had not been nearly so unpleasant as Amy had feared. Though the others tossed and turned, bickered over beds—each young lady thought the other had a more comfortable resting place—moaned over ablutions, was scandalized by this and by that—she had selected for herself one of the low pallets and gone to sleep. This was just as well, for she found herself universally loathed. Not one of the merchant daughters was speaking to her, and it looked unlikely that she would ever be permitted to patronize the illustrious firm of Murgatroyd, Murgatroyd and Parsons again, despite the prodigious extent of her fortune.

Miss Mayhew, happily, did not lose any slumber over this sad state of affairs, despite Honoria's most eloquent and spiteful attempts. After a long, dreadful, wonderful, heart-wrenchingly fascinating day, she had merely curled up in her dove-gray undergarments and gone to sleep.

The others were naturally scandalized, for *they'd* had the foresight to pack nightrail, tooth powder, curling pins and all manner of accoutrements necessary to young ladies aspiring to elegance and fashion. Amy, being naive enough to believe in the myth of the day trip, had brought nothing save a dinner gown, a brush and a spray of pearls. Thus it was, that in the morning, whilst all the ladies—if such they could be described—

were still asleep, she was forced to don this unlikely attire, for her green merino was now irreparably crushed and travel worn.

The gown was beautiful, made of soft, understated silver, with tiny seed pearls stitched at the borders of the hem and scalloped sleeves. It was modestly cut for evening wear, but low in the extreme for such an unlikely time as the morning. Amy's only consolation was that her companions would be donning much more outrageous creations. They were inveterate creatures of fashion, but had no notions of restraint or the finer points of taste. Even now, the dressers were pressing hideous scarlet crepes with endless rosettes and plunging necklines that left precious little to the imagination. She decided not to dwell on the imperfections of her companions—it was too lowering, and the day, though cold, too fine. Stretching, she had a sudden impulse to get outside and embrace the day.

She wanted air upon her cheeks and exhilarating frost beneath her feet. Though there was a sun-faded carpet along the corridors, the south wing's walls and floors were of stone. They chilled to the marrow whilst the smoking, coal-coughing fires and the snores of buxom, recumbent heiresses gave an unhealthy impression of stifling heat. A strange combination.

Amy had never wanted to escape so much in her life. She wondered where Mr. Hartford was, and what he was doing. Not the *first* time she had thought of him that morning! Useless to pretend she didn't want to bump into him, to have one last, private, romantically intimate conversation with him before she left Darris forever. She blushed at her unmaidenly eagerness.

Mr. Hartford affected her very differently from the other gentlemen she'd had occasion to meet. That was not to mention all the fortune hunters, merchants, sons of merchants, bankers and even doctors who had tried to solicit her attention. Or her purse. She could not keep this wry reflection from creeping into her thoughts.

Her purse was large, but she did not think Mr. Hartford cared much for this fact. Certainly, his commanding presence and self-assurance did not speak of parsimony or untoward inclinations for wealth. She suspected that he was being whimsical in describing himself as impoverished. Very likely, set against his noble relations, he was. But penniless? He did not appear so. Neither, Amy reflected, did she particularly care. Not when he looked at her in that teasing manner, which made her heart melt and her knees threaten to revolt beneath her skirts, so that she might tumble at any moment in a lightheaded swoon—or at the very least, into his strong arms. . . .

Well, there she was, dreaming moonshine again . . . though his arms *were* strong, she knew that firsthand. . . . Definitely, she decided, a walk was required. Who would have ever thought she could behave like such a missish humbug! Scolding herself crossly, she found herself still hoping, as she crept belowstairs, past a young chambermaid with bright curls tumbling from a crooked mobcap, that she would somehow catch a last, precious glimpse of Mr. Hartford. She wondered whether he would keep his promise and call on her in London. She doubted it. Darris was far north. Too far, she thought, for making calls on ladies who mixed in quite different circles. A fact. A sad, unpalatable fact, though she believed Mr. Hartford to be sincere in his current intentions. At least, she hoped he was.

It was freezing outside, and an absolute lunacy, for her shoes, though practical and modish, were still wet from the previous day. Nevertheless, Amy ignored this particular obstacle and was just gingerly testing the depth of the snow—the winds had stopped and the flurries had halted as suddenly as they had come—when Mr. Hartford himself came striding toward her.

Amy could not know that he had been wondering for several hours how to detach her from her party, or that he had done nothing since leaving her to the tender mercies of the merchant maidens but scheme and connive to see her again. He had banished Caro, who had come to tease, and Miss Bancroft, who had doubtless come to fuss, and buried himself in his tomes of books. Naturally, he had not read a thing, which was just as well, for they were written in ancient Greek and were thoroughly hard going even for an avid scholar. But Caroline, giggling a little, had for once taken up the hint and shut the library door without haranguing him overmuch. Miss Bancroft had placed a bottle of the remaining Madeira alongside an empty glass and a napkin of coconut macaroons. Then she, too, had left him to his thoughts.

Now the object of those thoughts was gazing at him with splendid silvery eyes. They sparkled, Demian noticed with interest. And she blushed. And she looked adorable, trailing tiny pearls in the snow. Without a word, he lifted her off her feet and cradled her in his arms, grinning wolfishly at her ball gown cum day dress, and carrying her toward the stables without a solitary word.

Amy herself was bereft of speech. Her pounding heart was soaring, her pulse was beating madly and her lips were curved traitorously into laughter. She wanted to scream, for his actions were surely infamous, but she couldn't. How could she, when the wretched man was doing precisely as she had hoped?

Well, more, to be precise, but, then, her imagination had never been wild and scandalous, as this man's obviously was. He did not even avert his gaze chivalrously at the sight of her daring bodice. And who was to say the stables were empty? There would be grooms in and out all morning, and he setting her down in some straw as though she were a common maid and he about to . . . but no, surely he would not kiss her here, without words between them, without . . . but Amy stopped speculating. She was, she found, quite wrong. Mr. Hartford evidently could, would and did.

Far from being outraged, Miss Mayhew forgot about hostlers and grooms, and wrapped her slender arms about Mr. Hartford's wonderful, warm, deliciously masculine neck. She could feel his silky dark hair, but more particularly noticed his lips pressed against her own, a small smile dancing teasingly in his eyes, alongside some other, less easily definable spark. Miss Mayhew forgot all her ladylike principles and neglected to even try to define that other emotion. She only wanted to taste another of those highly improper kisses.

Mr. Hartford laughed, and unwrapped her arms from around his neck. "When we are married, you shall have more."

"Are we to be married?" Amy could not believe her audacity as she pulled Mr. Hartford into the straw, so that his cravat was askew and his extraordinary grin widened. Amy's heart beat all the faster, for there was something about the set of his jaw that told her such courage was to be rewarded. It was. Amy had never before felt such unutterable joy. Neither, to Demian's acute surprise, had he. As His Grace, the duke of Darris, he had never been short of kisses from the tenderer sex. More than kisses, in most instances. But never before had they been accompanied by this joy. He tested the matter again. Yes, undoubtedly Miss Mayhew had some special secret. He would need to investigate most thoroughly. But his investigations left Amy breathless, speechless, flushed and smiling.

"You are a rogue, sir!"

"Only under extreme provocation."

"I did not provoke you. . . ."

"Strolling outside in broad daylight in a gown that offsets your charms as bounteously as this one *is* provocation."

"Nonsense! If you have moved in the first circles, and I believe you have, you will know that the gown is coy and modest and—"

"Perfectly beguiling. But then so is a shabby green merino, so I am led to admit, Miss Amy, that you are right. It is not the gown."

Amy smiled, her lips parting in the most breathtakingly sweet way imaginable. Demian was inclined to kiss them again, but she ducked at precisely the right moment and frowned severely. Her eyes, however, twinkled lightheartedly, and she played with his sleeve, so His Grace was not alarmed. Merely intrigued.

"My merino is not shabby! It is stitched quite exquisitely and took hours—positively hours—to fit."

"Ah, I stand corrected. Allow me to examine it more closely, my dear."

"You rogue! I warrant you mean when I am in it!"

"When you are out of it will do, too."

The words were so silky soft that despite their gross impudence, Amy shivered and could not keep her eyes on his face. Her gaze fell to the floor so that he laughed.

"You are right. I am a most terrible rogue. But you bring it upon yourself, you know, and I have had to keep silent and all the while wait upon a group of harpies. . . ."

"Doubtless such self-restraint will do you good. You look, my good man, far too arrogant. It is a wonder the duke permits it."

"Oh, the duke thinks the world of me. You will find he is tolerant quite beyond bearing."

"I should like to meet this duke, then, who allows his impoverished relatives to rule the roost."

"Oh, you shall. He is a handsome devil. Perhaps I shall not, after all, allow it."

"More handsome than you? I think I should *definitely* like to meet him."

Amy regarded him demurely and positively invited another kiss.

"Baggage!" His Grace gazed at her for a heart-trembling instant before most happily obliging.

Miss Mayhew then forgot about meeting handsome dukes. Mr. Hartford, she knew, lied. None could be more personable, delightful, debonair or charming than he himself. As she shyly explored the masculine thrust of his dark, clean-shaven chin, she thought she just might possibly die from an excess of happiness.

His Grace possibly thought the same, but refrained from saying so, merely murmuring endearments here and there to Amy's immense delight. She wondered what her Aunt Ermentrude would say to see her thus and almost—almost—withdrew from the captivating circle of Mr. Hartford's arms.

But they were strong and relentless, and seemed to have a will of their own. Most happily, he did not seem at all keen to release her from their bonds, no matter how many times she muttered "Aunt Ermentrude" or berated herself for wicked, wanton behavior.

Mr. Hartford appeared to think such shocking want of conduct more than acceptable, for she kept feeling soft kisses fall about her forehead, and wherever he happened to escape the constraints of her bonnet.

She gave up worrying about Aunt Ermentrude, who would doubtless have preferred her to snare the duke. *This* was the man, she knew, who was destined to share her life. And because he was impoverished, and merely a relative of some noble scion, the gap between them did not seem horribly insurmountable. Amy knew her bloodlines, through Lord Dalmont, were more than acceptable.

True, she had never been reared in the first circles, and, indeed, had been brought up in a quite different class from the one she was born to. But equally, Mr. Hartford had always moved on the fringes of the haute ton, somewhere between the dowagers and the potted palms, she gleefully recalled. They were suited. Her fortune made it quite possible for her to wed where she pleased. Looking into Mr. Hartford's brazenly admiring eyes, she believed she knew, at last, where it was that she pleased.

"Was the bed hard?"

She was startled by the question. Then she smiled. "Oh, that! I slept like a baby on one of the pallets. Mrs. Corey snored all night and Honoria Murgatroyd kept lighting candles so she could make notes to the duke. I suspect she feared she might have forgotten the full extent of her discomfort with the dawn."

"Poor girl!"

"Not at all. I truly did sleep like baby. I only know of all this because the others were complaining among themselves as day broke. I waited for them all to drift back to sleep before escaping."

"I am glad you did. I nearly braved the ivory tower to fetch you down myself."

"How dramatic. I almost wish you had." But Amy wished nothing of the kind. Nothing could be so perfect, she felt, as being swept off one's feet into a warm, winter's stable. Hay mingled with little patches of snow. She removed just such a patch from Demian's shoulder and smiled luxuriously.

The answering gleam in his eye was unmistakable. Dark, shining strands of hair were soon being brushed tenderly from her face. There were movements in front of her, but she hardly paid much heed. Hard to be attentive when one is in imminent danger of losing all sense of decorum. Certainly, she was already worlds away from the proper . . .

The movements became less subtle. Amy peeked out from Mr. Hartford's grasp and gasped. She could swear she could see the face of Hitchins, Mrs. Murgatroyd's groom, peering at her over a bale of hay. Yes, there it was, a definite snicker, and the pointy nose was unmistakable. Her sense of well-being evaporated as nose and cap disappeared out into the snow. If she could strain her ears enough, she would have heard low voices and shocked tones and much talk of butlers and ladies "wot don't know their station." Amy could not hear a thing, but she was not such a scatter-wit as to not make the obvious inferences.

"Good Lord, now we are in the suds! The news will be floating about the castle in five minutes!"

The gentleman did not seem to mind. He fiddled with the bow of her bonnet. "Good. No one can then complain about the entertainment."

"Very flippant, Mr. Hartford! It is *I* who will have to explain just how the butler came to be kissing me."

"He came to be kissing you because he is terribly discerning and you are undoubtedly the prettiest maiden available to him."

"Nonsense! Amelia Corey—"

"—is an antidote."

"You are funning when you should be serious!"

"Nonsense! I am merely trying to recall . . . how *did* the butler come to be kissing the delightful Miss Mayhew?"

"By gross impertinence and outrageous levity." Despite the seriousness of her circumstance, Amy could not help responding with a tart reply. Mr. Hartford's lips twitched in that delightful manner which she found so hopelessly irresistible.

"Shall I remind you of the circumstances? Just in case, you know, you have forgotten the exact details. . . ."

"Yes, immensely funny!" Amy replied, straightening out her gown, and conscious, once again, of the low-cut nature of the front.

"You shall set a new rage in morning gowns."

"You are obviously not an arbiter of feminine fashion, sir. The gown is hardly respectable. I had none other with me, however."

"A fortunate circumstance, for you look positively delightful. When we are married—if you will marry someone as impoverished as I—I shall insist on such attire."

"Bully! You give me second thoughts."

"Then you admit to having first thoughts?"

"How could I not, when you look so . . . ravishing with your cravat askew and your hair tousled. You have lost your hat, by the way."

"A pox on my hat! We need to talk. I have something to tell you." Demian looked suddenly serious.

Amy, her eyes on the stable door, shook her head. "Not now! Not here! Mrs. Murgatroyd will be creaking into her corsets, desperate to catch a whiff of scandal."

"What a wretched woman! How came you to be in her company?"

"Aunt Ermentrude, remember?"

"Ah, yes. The plot to throw you in the way of the duke."

"Yes, and I was to rob his heart and ride away forever on his steed."

The duke regarded her speculatively for a moment. She seemed quite unconscious of her charm, or of the fatal truth her words had for him. She had certainly robbed his heart. Now it was simply a matter of his steed. . . . He grinned.

"Not a bad notion. Can you ride, Miss Mayhew?"

"Ride?" She looked at him blankly.

"Ah, but I forget. You can, of course. Come. I will show you my pride and joy. Then we shall escape our various servants and chaperons and take a mild trot over the snowy downs."

Before Amy could say anything, her hand was tucked firmly into Mr. Hartford's confident grip. The kid gloves were thin, so she could feel the warmth of his hands through them. Amy tried to keep the flush from her face. His hat was evidently not all that had gone astray in the straw.

"Your gloves . . ."

"I have another pair. Come."

So Amy obeyed the imperious tone instinctively. Again, she had that startling sensation that despite his claims, Mr. Hartford was a man of consequence. She peeked at him, but he was striding quickly, and apart from murmuring to her that the floors were damp and to have a care, he did not glance back.

Nineteen

It was several moments before they stopped at a remote stall. Mr. Hartford released her hand and unlatched the door. Amy gasped. Staring at her was the most magnificent beast of an animal she had ever seen. It was pitch black, gleaming with health and radiating energy.

"An Arabian."

The duke nodded. "A beauty. He rode like the wind all day yesterday, but see how he strains to be let out again? Yes, and so you shall, my friend."

Expertly, His Grace reached for the saddle and bridle hanging close by. The horse seemed pleased, for he pawed the ground and nuzzled Demian's capes.

"What is his name?"

Amy asked the question idly, for she was bathed in a haze of euphoria. She did not seem to care that doom, in the shape of bony Mrs. Murgatroyd, was shortly to befall her. All she cared for was the fact that in the most unlikeliest of places, she had finally met a man who touched at her heartstrings, a man whom she could esteem. He was neither rich, nor noble, but he was respectable, upright, well-connected and spirited. She could not ask for more, especially since he was liberally endowed with such impeccable good looks, and charm and grace. Even fussy Aunt Ermentrude would not complain.

How *could* she, when he would silence her with his address, his smile, his brazenly cozening humor and his wheedling wiles? Aunt Ermentrude, Amy thought, would be clay in his memorable hands. Like her. A smile hovered about dreamy lips.

Demian wondered if such a creature could possibly realize how infinitely kissable she looked. He would spend his days telling her—and his nights. But he must not dwell on the nights, lest Miss Amy think him entirely reprehensible. Which in truth, he was.

And how to tell her? How to tell her that he had been leading a double masquerade? She had uncovered the one, but he fancied she had not the other. Perhaps he would say nothing until his betrothal with Lady Fortesque-Benton was scotched by her own hand. He would find a way down to the sentry cottage today. He must.

Matters were untenable to him. They must be a hundredfold to the Lady Raquel, isolated with no one but Thomas for company. But then, Thomas could be such *good* company. . . . Demian smiled. He wondered if there was any truth in naughty Caro's wild imaginings. Perhaps she had interpreted Thomas's interest wrongly. But then, knowing Thomas, she had not. And Thomas had sent that cryptic message to him. He only hoped that Mr. Thomas Tyrone Endicott was acting with his traditional languid good sense. If he was not, he would naturally have to run him through with a sword. Oh, how complicated life could get!

But His Grace had no notion of how much *more* complicated it was about to get. Still reeling from Miss Amy's unwitting assault upon his masculine senses—it should be illegal for a young lady to have such delectable eyelashes, or to reveal quite such a delicious cleavage in the presence of susceptible noblemen—he stroked his horse's nose. Then he answered her question.

"His name, Miss Mayhew, is Season's Glory. Season's Glory, meet Miss Amy Mayhew. She, you will perceive, is *my* season's glory."

But Amy did not notice this elegant tribute to herself. Instead, she rather foolishly said, "Oh!" and looked from the horse to its master.

Both were dark, tall and impossibly handsome. But the man's possessive poise seemed suddenly the more marked. The horse nuzzled into his hands with a familiarity that confirmed Amy's suspicions. Mr. Hartford, far from being the eligible young man that she had taken him for, was the duke himself. How stupid of her not to have puzzled it out before!

There was a marked resemblance between himself and Lady Caroline. His attire was elegant far out of the ordinary way and his carriage, though not in the least stiff, was nonetheless regal. Oh, Amy could think of a hundred things. . . .

She felt tears sting at her eyes. Season's Glory was the duke's exclusive mount. There could be no mistake. What a jest he must think it, contriving to conceal his identity even in the face of her first suspicions. He had fobbed her off with the distant relative explanation and she had believed him implicitly. Worse, she had actually abetted him in this deception. It was really quite unbearable. Amy's thoughts wandered to further unbearable matters that had transpired between them. She grew crimson in the process. Her eyes, glittering like stars, became suddenly stony. It was an acute transformation from the melting of moments before.

If he had confided in her, she would have kept his secret. There had been no need to take such elaborate pains to deceive her. Worse, it had gone far worse than deception. Amy's horror was now quite palpable. She stood rigid with shock, staring at the stallion. She could look no longer at the man who had called himself Mr. Hartford.

Demian, puzzled at this sudden change of mood, stepped forward and took her hand. She dodged his grasp, though his warmth still seared at her skin.

"How could you, Your Grace?" Amy half spat the words at him. Demian realized that Miss Mayhew had finally uncovered that which he had been about to confide. What he could *not* understand was her distress.

"I am sorry. I had meant you to discover the matter quietly—"

"Quietly? What would it matter, the manner in which I discovered such a gross deception? Would it break my heart less, or make me feel a smidgen less foolish if you *whispered* the matter in my ear? Or were you rather hoping I would be so utterly compromised by the time I made the connection—the *scandalous* connection—that it is *I* who would be quiet? Yes, I would surely never dare to whisper to my circle that it was His Grace himself who served at table or who masqueraded as a common house servant. Think how such a knowledge would be interpreted! Very clever, but quite unnecessary for all that. I may be a dullard, I may even be too free with my kisses, but I am *not* a tattle bearer! Your betrothed—the Lady Raquel Fortesque-Benton—shall hear nothing from me. So much tedious effort for nothing."

Demian would have seized her in his arms and told her what fustian she was talking, but his guilt at the mention of Lady Raquel's name cut him to the quick. Still, he might still have said something had Season's Glory not pawed the ground restively. He was afraid the animal might bolt. Simultaneously—and he wiped his brow with frustration—the shrill voice of Mrs. Murgatroyd could be heard calling in ferocious tones.

"I shall excuse you your dalliance, my lord. No doubt you considered me in the same category as Miss Amelia Corey. I take leave to tell you, however, that you were mistaken. I should also, strictly speaking, slap your wickedly wonderful countenance. But that, I find, I cannot undertake."

"Amy—"

"Miss Mayhew, though I ask you not to address me again. As I have always maintained, I should never have come. Now I shall leave you to the tender mercies of Honoria Murgatroyd. If she still thinks you are the butler, she will doubtless rip you to shreds. Good-bye. You shall not be troubled by me again."

With that, proud Amy turned on her heel and pushed past the contingent making their interested way into the stables. They would have stopped her, but she veered to the left, behind a trap laden with firewood. Beside it, a donkey ate contentedly.

Amy pushed past a half-eaten bale of hay, patted the friendly creature and watched as the contingent moved onward. His Grace looked positively trapped. And unbearably handsome. Amy schooled herself not to linger over his familiar, dear features, or wonder why he looked round after her, rather than making good his escape. The spectacle of the butler must have been infinitely intriguing, for five ladies at least were advancing toward him. Mrs. Murgatroyd's lips began speaking long before she reached him. Whatever she said, Amy could not hear.

It would not be long, Lady Raquel thought, before His Grace came to fetch her. And what a spectacle she would make, in her borrowed petticoats, with hair tumbling from her shoulders to her waist. If he examined her closely, he would see hands reddened from labor and dark smudges under her eyes, for she had not slept. No one, she decided, needed to know she had tended Thomas when she might have slumbered herself. Certainly, all her manual efforts would have indicated that a reviving sleep was necessary.

She dreaded the knock that would indicate that this curious state of limbo was at an end.

She was currently the recipient of two offers. She should be humming tunes and frowning over fashion plates and playing one suitor against the other. But, oh! How ridiculous was her curious sense of honor, that she would now accept neither. Not Demian, because she was ruined—hardly the bargain she had always prided herself on being. Nor Thomas, because he had ruined her. No, she would care not a fig for that if he would declare he loved her. How the proud had fallen! But Thomas did *not* love her. One did not enter into a marriage contract without that key ingredient.

How foolish that she had not realized this before, when she'd had the whole of London at her feet and been swathed in honor, rather than ruined. She would not have agreed to become the duchess of Darris, she would not have undertaken this fateful trip; and she would not have explored Thomas's complexities. This last gave her pause, for truly a life without the rogue now seemed sterile and pointless.

The duke was out of the question. The marquis of Somerford and his precious rank could go hang. She would not do it. She would never sell her soul for some precedence at table or crest on a carriage door. Thomas had shown her that. Thomas had shown her many things she had never known about herself. She pitied that whey-faced creature who had recounted endless points to His Grace of Darris and expected him to be grateful. *That* was not who she was.

She was the creature who trembled in Thomas's

arms, and yearned most humbly for his kisses. She was the person who needed no maid to light a fire, or nurse a fever, or even undress ninety-nine shining buttons. Only Thomas . . . she needed Thomas. Damnation! She needed him, but though he lusted after her, he did not love her. How could he, when she had shown him nothing but arrogance and spoiled pettishness? But that could change. . . . Slowly, a smile crept onto those beautiful bow-shaped lips.

She set down the mug of cocoa she had prepared over the fire. Then, with immense fortitude, she opened the door between them.

"You are not sleeping."

"No. I am watching my back. Have you come to murder me, yet? I must warn you that I believe I have recovered more than half my strength."

"How fair of you! I take back my earlier words."

"About murdering me?"

"No, not those. I believe I shall suffer that as a recurring inclination."

Thomas was suddenly alert. He sat up in bed and Raquel tried to ignore his smooth, muscular and distinctly naked chest.

"Then you have reconsidered my offer? You will stay with me? You must mean that, if you are seriously going to suffer these recurring pangs."

" 'Must' is not a word that should be used lightly, Mr. Endicott. But since your fever seems to have abated and I am about to reject His Grace's kind offer, I have been thinking, yes."

"That you shall marry me."

"No, not that. Far too noble, Thomas. And you will be bored in a day."

"I begin to think not. Lady Raquel, you intrigue me."

"Excellent, for I propose to become your mistress."

"Now you shock me." But a definite gleam of amusement crept into those alert sapphire eyes.

"Good. I believe that is the role of mistresses."

"What in the name of heaven do you know about the role of mistresses?"

Raquel regarded Thomas steadily. She was beyond amazement at her own audacity. She actually felt light-headed with exhilaration. And of course, there was no going back. If she was not ruined before, the very *suggestion* was ruining her. There was no going back.

"What I don't know, you are going to teach me."

"And what if I won't?"

"You will, Thomas Tyrone Endicott. You owe me that at least."

"Very well. Climb up here for your first lesson. There is plenty of space."

Raquel flushed. "In the daylight?"

"Good Lord, woman! We are going to have to start, I see, right at the very beginning. Hop on in, the syllabus is enormous."

Raquel fingered the petticoat skirts.

"Perhaps I shall just kill you, after all."

"I preferred your second, rather novel, alternative. But feel free to try. Here, it is my neck you desired, was it not?"

Thomas made a sudden movement and lifted Raquel up onto the tattered petticoats-turned-sheets. He was warm, but she noted that the fever had abated, and the eyes, mocking and disastrously compelling, were clear. She also noticed that his lips were too close for comfort. The wretch knew it, too. Her heart beat wildly but she did not complain. This madness was of her own doing, after all. Thomas pulled her a little closer, wriggled from the horse blanket and obligingly lowered his head.

"You can suffocate me, but I fear I might struggle.

Strangle me, rather. If you use your petticoats it will be pleasant. They smell sweet. Like you."

"Don't be ridiculous. And you are mocking me. I had not expected that."

Raquel swung her legs from the bed. Thomas halted her with a lithe movement of his forearm.

"No? My foolish girl, I have mocked you the very first moment I laid eyes on you. Do you not remember?"

"Yes. But you had not then deflowered me."

There was a silence between them. Mr. Endicott loosened his grip but used his fingers to stroke her chin. Then her mouth. Raquel had to bite her tongue not to taste him. He would be salty and warm. . . . He was speaking.

"Nor have I now. Have the goodness to credit me with a little sense, if not decency. And before you swoon, I might add that when I *do* deflower you, I would prefer you to remember the occasion."

"Then . . ."

"Then you are still a perfidiously attractive maiden."

He dropped his arm and swung off the bed. He was naked to his waist, and Raquel could not help but stare. He threw the remains of Demian's shirt on his back and paced over to the window. There was a woman struggling through the deep pile of white. She looked cold. Crying. Mr. Endicott felt empathy.

"Marry your duke. There is no reason, I assure you, not to." Was Thomas's tone harder than usual? Difficult to tell, when he had stopped looking at her and was throwing on his hopeless cravat. It was crumpled, but he managed to achieve miracles with it in seconds. He looked debonair and aloof.

"None?" Raquel sounded hopelessly forlorn.

"None that must concern you." Again, the abrasive

tone. Raquel, restored to her status and rank as lady, felt ludicrously like weeping.

"I spent the night with you unchaperoned."

"Easily remedied. You spent the night as Lady Caroline's guest. I returned to London yesterday. My staff shall testify to that, though there is no reason for anyone to ever doubt it."

The room suddenly seemed dark and cold to Raquel. She climbed off the bed and wandered close to the window. Close to the motionless Mr. Endicott. Their arms almost touched. When she looked out, she realized it was *not* dark. The snow was bright with sunshine. She caught a glimpse of someone walking toward the cottage. Fleetingly, she noticed the approaching woman was beautiful. And well-dressed, with heavenly little pearls at her hems. Lady Caroline Darris? Perhaps. Time was running out. Raquel shivered.

"Why did you offer for me?"

"Madness. I forgot how you value long titles."

"I don't. Not anymore. And I *won't* marry Demian." Defiantly, she stamped her unslippered foot. The floor was relentlessly hard. She scowled in a *most* unladylike manner.

"Ow!"

Warmth crept back into Thomas's eyes.

"No?"

"No! And don't try to talk me into it, my mind is quite made up."

"Your father shall have an apoplexy."

"He would have, anyway."

"If you'd become my mistress, you mean?"

"Yes." Raquel met his eyes at last. They were twinkling. She could hardly think why.

"Don't look so glum. You can still be my mistress, if you wish." Some of the laughter was back in

Thomas's voice. She peeped at him from under her long, curling lashes.

"You will be well served if I do!"

"Is that a promise, Lady Raquel?" Thomas's arrogance seemed to be reemerging. The room brightened even as a rosy flush appeared on Raquel's cheeks.

"As much of a promise as the one you made two minutes ago."

Mr. Endicott searched his memory. "Ah, yes. It is, as I said, a long syllabus." Raquel caught her breath, for he was indeed beautiful when his face was animated.

"When we are married, we shall begin our second lesson instantly."

"We are not getting married."

"Don't argue with your teacher. Would you prefer banns or a special license?" Thomas took her in his arms and placed a kiss upon her tousled head. Sad to say, the lovely Lady Raquel Fortesque-Benton was looking like a dresser's worst nightmare. He continued, for Raquel was staring at him blankly.

"You will note, I am not entirely autocratic. Here and there I permit a modicum of choice. Personally, I would go with the special license, but far be it for me to influence your decision." Another kiss, this time on her brow.

"Why are you doing this?"

"Kissing? It is pleasant and imperative to my curriculum."

"No. You know what I mean! It is not necessary to wed me. You said yourself—"

"Good God, don't start quoting me! I say some hideously foolish things at times!"

"But marriage . . ."

"Yes, a severe but necessary step, I am afraid. I never

impart my . . . uh, *considerable* wisdom to unversed maidens. A foolish quirk of mine, but there it is."

"But you do not love me."

"Do I not?"

"No!"

"How remiss of me not to mention it, but that is the first lesson, you know."

"What is?"

"Mmm . . . a slow pupil, but we will progress." Now he was playing with her hair, wreaking more havoc than ever. It was nothing compared with the havoc of her racing heart. He seemed likely to kiss her.

"Lesson one. Both partners must love each other. Utterly essential, not an issue. I have loved you since you first turned your back on me at the ball. Heaven knows why, but heaven works in strange ways. *Now* I love you because you are kind, you are caring, you are capable, you are a diamond beyond compare and . . . you are mine. You cannot deny that, Raquel, can you?"

"No, I cannot." It was a tremulous whisper, but Thomas heard it. He lifted her chin and examined that beautiful, pink bow. It was begging for a kiss. He did not think he could be so heartless as to decline.

But just then, there was a timid knocking at the door.

Twenty

Miss Amy Mayhew regarded her surroundings with interest. The house was bare of almost all furniture, but clean. A small fire burned in the grate, but there hardly looked to be the wood to feed it. Behind her, a beautiful young woman busied herself above the boiling pot, stirring all the while so that steam rose into her face. She did not seem to mind, but poured water into the only cup that seemed to be available and stirred in cocoa from a very old jar. Her husband—Amy surmised him to be so, for the woman scolded at him for neglecting to clean the mug, and for not ushering her in immediately when she had stood in the doorway—seemed to find something spectacularly amusing, for a grin kept creeping onto his delightfully handsome face. Not godlike, like the duke's, of course, but rakish. She liked them, though they seemed rather odd, especially the woman. For some reason, she was dressed only in underclothes. She did not seem in the least conscious of this fact.

Truth to tell, Raquel had forgotten. In a whirl of unutterable bliss, she handed Amy her drink and smiled. "I am so sorry. We appear to be out of all refreshments."

"Not so!" Thomas pointed to the laden basket.

"Goodness, I am a scatter-wit today! Lady Caroline,

we must thank you most sincerely for this. I was famished, and the pies were excellent."

"Were they? I do not believe I sampled them. *I* was the recipient of some horrible gruel." Thomas glared at Raquel, who smothered a giggle. It had been years, she thought, since she had been so unladylike as to giggle.

The lady in the damp silver ball gown shook her dark head. "I am glad the pies were good, but they were not from me. Lady Caroline is still up at the castle. *I* am—"

But Thomas, who suddenly had a very good notion of who she was, hushed her.

"Miss Amy Mayhew? I believe I have heard of you."

The lady looked confused. "That is impossible, sir. No one knows me hereabouts!"

"Lady Caroline does. I spoke to her about you up at the castle. She seems to feel, you see, that her brother—"

"Oh, *pray* do not speak of him!" Amy surprised herself by trembling. Thomas fetched in the smoke-charred chair and bade her sit.

He wondered what Demian had done to cast the lady into such an agitation of nerves. She seemed, otherwise, quite sensible.

The lady with the glorious golden hair smiled.

"Drink your cocoa, Miss Mayhew, the sweetness shall revive you and you shall tell us what you are doing wading through all this snow. Not even *I* have been intrepid enough to try it, though Thomas nearly caught his death in doing so last night."

"It was foolish." Tears lent a sheen to Miss Mayhew's warm, direct eyes. She brushed them away with embarrassment. "I am not usually such a watering pot. You must excuse me."

"Oh, think nothing of it! I daresay I am worse!"

Lady Raquel answered sunnily. Whoever she was, she liked Miss Mayhew. Despite the fact that her entrance was rather inopportune—for she was certain Thomas had meant to kiss her at last—the lady was charming, friendly and obviously in distress. It behooved Raquel to help. Impulsively, she set her arms about the dark-haired lady.

"Oh, what a beautiful dress! And look at *me!* I should not be seen *dead* in these borrowed plumes. They are Lady Caro's shift and petticoats! What you must think! Thomas, see if my organdy has dried."

Thomas stifled a grin at Raquel's imperiousness. It was good to see her in spirits again. He quirked a lofty brow in her direction so that she blushed, then bowed mildly and did as he was bade. The dress was creased, but dry, so Raquel stepped into it and made a face. "Yours is much better, though I fancy it is damp, too."

"Yes, though I will take my chances! Your husband might not like me in my petticoats."

Raquel glanced at Thomas. He looked most unhelpful. Quite amused, in fact, so she tried to explain herself. "He is not my—"

"Hush, dear. We do not want to shock Miss Mayhew."

Amy looked puzzled. Then light dawned. "Oh!" She blushed crimson.

"You have never met us here, Miss Mayhew. We are merely a figment of your imagination. And the next time we meet, which we undoubtedly will, we shall certainly be man and wife."

"Oh! So that is the way of it!" Amy sounded a little wistful. "It is wonderful to see true love go so smoothly. I shall not breathe a word of the matter."

"Very kind of you. Now, tell us your story. We are agog."

"It is not mine to tell. I needed to get away and like

a scatter-wit I simply dashed off, thinking to get to the nearest inn, which I believe is some six miles back. In my haste, I hurried off without even my reticule, so my situation is now thoroughly hopeless. I shall have to go back, I suppose." Amy did not appear pleased at the prospect.

"Miss Mayhew, I did not have much conversation with Lady Caroline, but that which I did have led me to believe you were in good hands. Demian, though I would not puff of his consequence to tell him so, is truly the best of good people. It is not he, surely, who has put you in such a pelter?"

"I would rather not answer that." Amy sounded stiff, but Raquel could see the sparkle of silver tears threatening to drown her elfin face. She clasped one of Amy's hands.

"Come! Even *I,* who have the greatest reason to be in dread of the duke, cannot think ill of him. Are you sure you are not mistaken in his use of you? For though you are circumspectly quiet, your very silence speaks volumes."

"I am sorry for that. His Grace is undoubtedly charming."

"But you are not charmed?"

Amy blushed. "Oh, I was! It is foolish to deny it. He is . . . oh, he is everything a young lady dreams of."

Raquel shook her head and pointed saucily to Thomas. "Nonsense. *He* is everything a young lady dreams of."

"Spare my blushes, my lady!" But he did not look like he was blushing, only smirking, slightly, so that Raquel was inclined to throw one of Lady Caroline's peaches at him.

"He did not . . . oh, don't say he . . ."

"No, he was all that was gentlemanly. At least . . ." Amy hesitated and blushed.

"Yes?" Both listeners were captivated. They prompted Amy together, eager to hear the cause of her embarrassment. Her eyes, cast down in a tangle of lashes, revealed little, but her hands, playing convulsively with the ribbons of her gown, said much for her agitation.

"I believe I might possibly have encouraged him . . ."

Thomas laughed. "You are a beauty, Miss Mayhew. Demi is no saint. I still do not see the problem."

"I did not know who he was. I thought he was a glorified servant. Genteel, but impoverished."

"Well, two out of three is not a calamity!"

"It is to me. I am not a lady; we move in different circles, he and I."

"Not insurmountable. There are many countesses—even princesses—about these days that could claim the same."

"Possibly. You may not realize, however, that His Grace is betrothed to be married. Lady Caroline mentioned it only last night. Not common knowledge, but a fact, nonetheless."

"Oh, is *that* all? I wouldn't worry your head too much about that fact!"

"Sir, I may have had my head turned, I may even have acted . . . wantonly. I regret that, but I would never knowingly hurt another. Think of the lady for one moment. *She* didn't ask the duke to behave so unpardonably! I, had I but known, would not have countenanced his outrageous behavior whatever my private inclination. And, there! Now you know all, though I had meant to be silent. I trust you will be discreet with this confidence as I shall be with yours."

Mr. Endicott nodded.

"Perhaps the duke knew the lady's affections were not engaged?"

"How could he know that?"

Now it was Raquel's turn to blush. "Not hard, Miss Mayhew, for the lady has a shrewish disposition, treated the matter like an unflattering business proposition, behaved as cold as ice, froze his blood, and threatened to have lovers within wedlock."

"Impossible! I am told the lady is beautiful beyond compare."

Now it was Thomas's turn to join in the singular discussion. "She is, but shrewish, with a tongue like a whip—"

"Only when necessary."

Amy looked bemused. "You speak as if you know her."

"Not as intimately as I shall, but yes, I know her." Mr. Endicott's laughing eyes never left Raquel's face.

"You mean . . . oh, no! I must surely be dreaming! You cannot be . . ."

"The Lady Raquel Fortesque-Benton. I am, Miss Mayhew, and delighted to make your acquaintance. You seem nice."

"So do you, but—"

"Hush! Is that the door?"

It was. Thomas looked resigned.

"It is the duke. I know his knock. What do you want us to do?"

"Oh!" Amy could hardly think. He might have followed her footprints down, or else he might simply be wishing to visit his affianced. Either way, she was in no case to face him again.

"Oh, I couldn't, I . . ." She was trembling.

"Come, Miss Mayhew! Demian may be many things but he is not an ogre! Nevertheless, if you wish, we shall retire together to the bedchamber. I fancy Lady

Raquel has something to say to him, at all events." So saying, he held open the bedchamber door and gestured her to follow. Just as well he did, for His Grace was not a patient man.

He pushed open the door and beheld Raquel, in crumpled organdy and flowing hair.

"Good Lord! You look . . ." He had been about to say "human" but bit his tongue in time. Lady Raquel smiled.

"I do look like a dishrag, don't I? Come in, Your Grace. There is precious little warmth left in our fire. I hope you mean to rescue us."

"Us? Oh, you mean Thomas? Where is he, anyway?"

"He has tactfully left us to our own devices. Your Grace, I have something to say . . ."

"No, wait! It is *I* who must say something, though if you wish to cut my heart out, I shall not blame you in the least."

"This sounds serious. Care for a peach?" Raquel held out one of Lady Caroline's offerings.

"No. I don't know where to begin, really."

"At the beginning?"

"Hard to say where that is. Lady Raquel, when I offered for your hand, you begged me to wait. You wished me to speak to your father before announcing anything or posting the banns."

"Yes?"

"In that intervening time, something has made me wish to withdraw that offer. If you can find it in you to release me from my bond, I would be most grateful."

"And if I cannot?"

"I shall endeavor to live with the fact, but I cannot guarantee you a happy life. For myself, I believe it will be bleak."

"I am not such an antidote, Your Grace!" Her ladyship's eyes twinkled. Demian thought it from indignation, but in truth, Raquel could hardly stifle her laughter. She hoped Amy could hear everything from within.

Demian played with the folds of his cravat. "Indeed, no! You should get rid of your dresser. She does you no justice. Much better to have rumpled skirts and flowing locks."

"Indeed? Then I must release you from the betrothal at once, my lord, for you clearly have no sense of decorum or taste. Rumpled skirts indeed!"

His Grace looked so comically relieved, Raquel actually *did* chuckle.

"You are not sorry to lose my fortune?"

"No. I am richer by ten thousand pounds and a whole heart." Demian grinned lightheartedly. His hand was already on the handle of the sentry door.

"Tell Thomas I shall send a chaise down within the hour. I am so sorry, Lady Fortesque-Benton. I must leave you."

"Why such a hurry? Most unseemly, Demian." Mr. Endicott appeared seemingly from nowhere.

"I am sorry, Thomas. I have to go. There is a lady—"

"Ah, a lady." Thomas grinned and folded his arms across his broad chest.

"That is my shirt!"

"Indeed. It is a pity you are such a paltry fellow, Demian, for I can hardly get the buttons up; I must look like a pirate."

"You always look like a pirate. But come, I am in haste."

"Ah, yes. The lady. Is she worth such exertion? Have a drink of burgundy. Caroline, dear soul, tucked that in with the muffins. Naturally, she forgot a new gown for her ladyship, but then, one *must* have priorities." He slung his arm casually about Lady Raquel, leaving Demian in no doubt about his new circumstances.

The duke grinned. "Lord, Caro was in the right of it! She guessed there was something havey cavey going on down here. I wouldn't put it past her to have forgotten the gown on purpose. Just so long as I don't have to draw swords with you?"

"Close run thing, Demian. But no, her ladyship is still entirely virtuous thanks to that miserable promise you elicited from me!"

"Excellent. I would drink to your health, but I have a young lady to pursue."

"Where to?"

"To London. There to find an Aunt Ermentrude and beg her a thousand times for the felicity of her niece's hand. It shouldn't be difficult. From what I hear, if I travel in the ducal chaise she will swoon with ecstasy."

"And the young lady?"

"Has much to forgive. I shall have to grovel. She is worth it."

The door opened once again.

"Am I?" Amy stood shyly in the doorway between the two rooms. Demian looked from her to Raquel to Thomas.

"You knew all along!" His tone was accusatory, but he could not take his extraordinary gaze off Miss Mayhew's eyes. They were shining silver, matching her ribbons and her sparkling gown.

"Knew what?" came Thomas's innocent remark.

"That I am in love with that witch over there. How could you rush off like that, leaving me at the mercy of those vixens? You cannot be fond of me at all."

"Oh, but I am, Your Grace. I am."

Amy sailed forward, all doubts banished in that single revealing moment. She was not given a chance to escape again, for the duke forgot his unpropitious surroundings, and that two other human beings scrutinized his lordly technique. Thomas, however, was always one for seizing opportunities.

"Lesson, two, Raquel . . . see how he masterfully sweeps her off her feet and kisses her till her eyes close and she appears quite faint? Excellent technique, but the appropriate response would be, I think, this." At which, Mr. Endicott's demonstration became more practical in nature, much to the Lady Raquel's complete satisfaction.

Outside, three carriages were rumbling home. For once, both Mrs. Corey and Mrs. Murgatroyd were equally crushed. The butler, it seemed, had provided them with the thorough scolding that they deserved.

Only, he was not the butler, he was the duke, and horrible Miss Mayhew was going to be a duchess. Amelia Corey wailed into her handkerchief and for once was not admonished. Miss Oliver and Miss Fletcherson sulked, but Daphne Murgatroyd was already talking, in high-pitched accents, of her bosom friend Amy. It was "Amy this" and "Amy that" for as long as seven tired travelers could stand it. She was silenced, at last, by the vicious flight of a carriage squab. It caught at her bonnet and played havoc with her ribbons. Miss Mayhew, had she been present, would certainly have approved.